The House of
Gentle Men

THE HOUSE OF GENTLE MEN

KATHY

HEPINSTALL

Perennial

An Imprint of HarperCollins*Publishers*

A hardcover edition of this book was published in 2000 by Avon Books, Inc., an imprint of HarperCollins Publishers.

THE HOUSE OF GENTLE MEN. Copyright © 2000 by Kathy Hepinstall. All rights reserved. Printed in the United States of America. No part of this book may be used or reproduced in any manner whatsoever without written permission except in the case of brief quotations embodied in critical articles and reviews. For information address HarperCollins Publishers Inc., 10 East 53rd Street, New York, NY 10022.

HarperCollins books may be purchased for educational, business, or sales promotional use. For information please write: Special Markets Department, HarperCollins Publishers Inc., 10 East 53rd Street, New York, NY 10022.

First Perennial edition published 2001.

Designed by Kellan Peck

The Library of Congress has catalogued the hardcover edition as follows:
Hepinstall, Kathy.
The house of gentle men / Kathy Hepinstall. —1st ed.
p.   cm.
ISBN: 0-380-97809-1
"An Avon book."
I. Title.
PS3558.E577H68   2000   99-36278
813'.54—dc21   CIP

ISBN 0-380-80936-2 (pbk.)

01 02 03 04 05 JT/RRD 10 9 8 7 6 5 4 3 2 1

To my mother, beautiful friend and fishing partner,
Polly Hepinstall
In memory of her mother, beautiful friend and fishing partner,
Rozella Havens Peddy

ACKNOWLEDGMENTS

Thank you, Simon, for the tears.

Thank you, Henry Dunow, builder of tree houses and shelves for new books.

Thank you, Patricia Lande Grader, for your courage and your commitment. Thank you Sarah Durand, Elaine Brosnan, Sharyn Rosenblum, Kate Weaver, Gilly Hailparn, Heather Garvin, Mike Spradlin, and Dale Schmidt.

Thank you Terry McMillan, Elizabeth Forsythe Hailey, and Gail Godwin, for your wisdom and for all the things you did out of your reckless generosity. Thank you Grace Cooley. Without you there would not be the Louisiana we know. Thank you Leon Swain. Thank you David Bingham at Fort Polk; John and Bonnie McMillian at Bonny Plants; Mary Cleveland at the Museum of West Louisiana; Gussie Townsley, Velmer Smith, and The Merryville Historical Society, especially the Keitha Donnelly mother and daughter team. Thank you Madge Noble, for your many efforts on my behalf. And thank you Catherine "Granny Cat" Stark, magical friend, for letting me discover you.

Thank you Lynn Branecky, Charlie Scott, Sandy Jordan, and Sherman Judice for the early faith. Thank you Wayne Day, whom I've admired for twenty years. Thank you Marc Olmsted, for your loyalty and friendship.

Thank you brother and sisters: Randy Hepinstall, Becky Hepinstall, and Margaret Plsek. Thank you Shari Peddy, Shonie Cooley Warden, June and John Grahams, Catherine Hamilton, Laura Landry, and every one of my relatives, especially my father, Jack Hepinstall, and his gift of storytelling. Thank you to those who gave suggestions about this mythical house, and to my research assistants, B. J. Terrell and Lee Burge. Thank you Adrienne Brodeur, Kitty O'Keefe, Ray Lazenby, Matthew Snyder, Jerry Sussman, Arne Glimcher, Matthias Weiner, and all the Blancaneaux punta dancers. Thank you Dawn Dekeyser, Tim Barrett, Abby Henry, Melinda Haynes, Amy Krouse Rosenthal, Beth Anderson, Chris Blum, Court Crandall, Kirk Souder, Marie Smith, Lorraine Alper-Kramer, Rohitash Rao and Stefanie Zelmer-Rao, Scott Gilbert, Melinda Kanipe, Jean Robaire, Sally Hogshead, John Stein, Ann Young, Terry Balagia, Jeff Weakly, Laura DellaPenna, Valerie Jerome, Nancy Sundquist, Liz Foster, Thad Russell, Elizabeth Wika, Shari Long, Dan and Deborah Morrison, Deb Hagan, Woody Kay, Ed Godwin, Matt McDonald, Joan Lyons, Dan Wieden, Susan Hoffman, Todd Waterbury, Peter Wegner, Mike Woolf, Juan and Judy Perez, Karen Evans, Thelma Shoemate, Delores Hargett, Mary Gay Shipley, Nancy Nelms, Jeremy Ellis, Sharon Miller, Susan Nicholas-Graves, Chris Graves, Elizabeth Wika, Edna Johnson, Janet Murphy, and Jane King.

Thank you, Eric Silver, for the laughter.

THE HOUSE OF GENTLE MEN

1

From the beginning, the child growing inside her seemed aware of the need for secrecy. It took her monthly flow quietly, swelled her fingers quietly, introduced quietly a craving for mayhaw jelly and Karo syrup straight from the bottle. And the girl—Charlotte—told no one, and no one suspected. For in that fall of 1941, the people of the town could not look at her and see a growing baby. They saw only Charlotte's mother, ambushed by sudden and merciless flames.

The outrageousness of Charlotte's condition furnished more protection. How could a barely kissed Baptist girl—newly sixteen—have conceived anything two weeks after her mother was killed? For in the grief that follows horror there is no room for any Events, only the slow opening of doors and pickle jars, the refusal of a pet to leave the site of a grave, the sudden tears called forward by the sound of Bible passages and the faint aroma of bacon in the black-eyed peas. Tragedy cannot follow so closely on the heels of Tragedy; the Bundt cakes the neighbors bring over must first have time to cool.

Her father and her little brother Milo knew nothing about monthly blood and its comings and goings, nor of morning sickness. Like men, they were busy basking in their sorrows. In the corner of the backyard, not far from the edge of the woods, Milo built a shrine to his mother: loose buttons he'd found in her drawer, her garden gloves, a set of silver teaspoons, her lavender hand cream and the laces of her Sunday shoes. He worked on it every morning before school, adding little trinkets, straightening the border of magnolia leaves, mumbling to himself, while Charlotte held her long black hair away from her face and threw up in the pink impatiens.

"Are you sick?" Milo asked.

She shook her head.

"Charlotte, don't be sick. You can't die."

Charlotte had stopped speaking on the day the soldiers had held her down, and so she went inside the house for her tablet and wrote: I'M NOT GOING TO DIE.

"You better not," said Milo when he read her message.

No, she thought, she was not the one whose death was deserved.

She had heard of treatments. Folklore. Things other girls had tried. She found a bottle of apple cider vinegar in the cabinet and drank as much as she could, tears running from her eyes at the taste of it.

It didn't matter. Deep in her womb, that trembling inch continued to flourish.

Salt had worked for a girl in Baton Rouge. So Charlotte had heard one night at a slumber party, years before, when the girls were gathered in her friend Belinda's room. One Saturday morning Charlotte poured a large handful of salt into a glass and forced herself to swallow all of it. She sat on the back porch afterward, looking into the woods.

By noon her head was swimming, and she was seized by a ravenous thirst. Belinda was having a garden party at one o'clock, despite the chill in the air. She had advised Charlotte to attend. "All the girls are turning against you, Charlotte," she had whispered urgently. "They understand about your mother, but they think you're being stupid. You won't say a word and you don't want visitors." Belinda was Charlotte's best friend, but enough of an enemy that Charlotte could not confide in her. And so Charlotte drank three glasses of water and went to the party. The girls were sitting outside on filigreed lawn furniture, sipping strawberry punch. Belinda greeted her in a wool dress, her eyes red. She had been grieving ever since her boyfriend, Richard Stanley, had been called to an air base in Virginia in preparation for the new war.

"My soldier of the sky," she whispered. "Sometimes

I wish I'd never fallen in love with him. What if he's killed?"

"Don't think like that, Belinda," the other girls said soothingly. Charlotte started to write something on her tablet, then thought better of it. Instead she drank another glass of punch. And another.

Belinda was telling the story of how she'd met her perfect boyfriend, although everyone had heard it before. *She was standing in a green field, in a dress once worn by her grandmother . . .*

Charlotte drank another glass.

And the sky was so blue . . .

Charlotte drank another glass. Her head was filled with patterned light. Her breath fast. Thirst like a seizure.

And his plane came out of the clouds as if in a dream . . .

Charlotte leaped to her feet and staggered behind the house. She was drinking from the hose when Belinda found her.

"Charlotte," she said severely, "what are you doing? Why did you interrupt my story?"

Charlotte didn't answer.

"Listen to me. None of the girls really likes you anymore. You won't talk. You do strange things. And now you're drinking from the hose like a dog. I'm sorry about your mother, Charlotte, but there are other people suffering too. My boyfriend's *gone*. And he may not come back."

But Charlotte hated soldiers, even soldiers of the sky, and could not feel grief at the thought of one dying.

Steeped in salt and vinegar, the baby grew. She felt it within her, and yet when she stood naked before the mirror the curve in her figure was slight. She didn't have to guess at whether it was a boy or a girl. She knew it would be a boy, although he was girlishly quiet in the womb. The deed had been unforgivingly male. Would not the product of that deed be male as well? She tried not to think about it. Instead she busied herself. Chores had to be done around the house, for grieving men still stain their clothes, wait for dinner, track mud in the kitchen.

Her father did not ask about the look in her eyes, or her suddenly missing voice, or her new habit of writing down her words on paper. His wife was dead and his faith in God had left him, for nothing in the Bible had told him what to do when flames fill up a cotton dress. And so he drank whiskey in prodigious amounts, from a small blue glass through which the liquor had turned the color of skin exposed to creosote. He drank in gulps, laughed at the fire it made in him.

Charlotte wrote him notes:

WHAT WOULD YOU LIKE FOR DINNER?

I IRONED YOUR SHIRT.

DOES YOUR BACK HURT?

These were Charlotte's words of love, delivered to her father in fragments. Most of the time he didn't answer her.

Charlotte's family lived less than two miles from the new air base, and in March of the new year her brother was caught trying to burn down one of the outbuildings there. Milo was taken to jail for a night and then released into the custody of his father and his silent sister. And the parish felt a new and deeper scorn for this crazy boy who had burned up his own mother and now was trying to set the war effort aflame.

Milo at twelve became a traitor to the cause of freedom. Banished. Avoided by the other boys, who used to be his friends. Only Charlotte knew the reason why her brother had gone to the air base with his father's old Zippo lighter in his hand. She found him sitting cross-legged on the propane tank behind the house, crying. Went to him and touched his face.

He looked at her, his eyes red, his hair grown wild. "I hate them, Charlotte. Those pilots."

She stroked his black hair.

As the dogwoods bloomed she turned inward, avoiding the other girls, let the spring fill her dress with wind, wore brightly colored scarves and a haunted look to distract the gaze of others. In her eighth month she went to the parish library just before it closed, checking out as many books as she could on the subject in question. Once home, she spread the books out on her bed and pored through them. Some girls, she discovered, swelled up like watermelons, and some like herself didn't show a pregnancy nearly as much. She saw illustrations of babies in the womb in various stages of growth. The brain forming. Eyes opening. Fingers separating. She shook her head. Her baby was not a human, not a creature even, but a demon. A condemnation from God, an atrocity nurtured by the trimesters until it took form and weight.

This boy of three fathers.

She turned the pages. Twine was needed. The scissors or knife should be clean and sharp. When the time came she would feel a sudden cramp or the rush of warm fluid. The pain would be intense, an unmanageable pain that women had been given throughout history and then told to forget.

In June of 1942, the season of zinnias, she went out into the woods by herself, walking very deliberately, her face red and her legs shaky. The baby moving inside her. She wore a waistcoat dress and carried a cotton feed sack. Inside the sack was a spool of twine, a sugarcane knife to sever the umbilical cord and a garden spade to bury the creature once all was said and done.

2

M en who have demons walk stiffly. They sleep without snoring. They drink without sound. Their voices are low, as if newly shaken out of a prayer or a gasp. Certain senses are lost to them, and others overpower. The back of their tongues, which owns the taste named "bitter," must now share that taste with their mouths, throats, stomachs. They will wear duffle coats in the summer and the lightest gabardine in the winter, for guilt has played havoc with the temperature of their bodies. They eat very little, but are haunted by sudden and intense cravings, like those for Old Gold cigarettes. Once they are healed, Louise noticed, they switch to Camels.

Louise had been studying the new arrivals to The House of Gentle Men for eight years now, enough time to grow bored by those who crept in at nightfall and stood penitent under the hot porch light, hands in their pockets, top lip trembling. "Is it true?" these men would whisper to her. Cautiously, because they were half convinced it was a joke, a rumor, and that they had come all this way for nothing.

"Is what true?" Louise would answer, playing with them.

"What men do here."

"I don't know. You'll have to ask my daddy."

Louise would gaze at the badness still on their faces and sigh inwardly, for she knew that the demons would soon be banished by the work the men did in the house, and leave nothing but martyrs behind. Men who smiled too much. Crippled with manners. Contented men whose faces showed relief. And so Louise had learned not to get too attached to badness, for it was fleeting in this house, at first a black and solid thing, then declining kiss by kiss to the palest of shadows, vanishing at the smallest movement in the air—the draft produced, for instance, when a woman's dress is complimented.

On this night, her knees pressing into the wet porch as she moved the suds around with a nylon brush, Louise sized up another new man. He moved up the walkway, stiff-legged, his back hopelessly straight. Past the crape myrtle, whose sassiness was tamed by darkness. Past the pistachio tree, into the glow of the floodlight.

He slowed and then stood still, and she looked him over more carefully, her brush slowing and the bubbles slithering down through the cracks in the porch. He set down his suitcase so that he could battle with both hands the lovebugs that swirled around his face and settled on his jacket, their insistent coupling obscene. Louise found it fitting that lovebugs swarmed around this particular porch, although unlike the bugs, the men inside the house were not allowed to form double bodies with anyone.

This man was tall, and his face was handsome and yet set in a vague half-wince, as though he'd been stung by some comfort he didn't feel he deserved. She could tell he had been a soldier by his straight back and his demob suit. Even three years after the war, soldiers wore these suits because they couldn't afford another.

A demob suit in September heat. Demons.

Louise rose to her feet, brushing her wavy brown hair out of her eyes and leaving a froth of soap scum across her cheek. Warm water ran from her knees down her shins, onto virgin pine. Crickets suddenly made themselves heard, as they always did just before an introduction, or after the howling of a dog. Her clean feet shifted on the clean planks.

He stared at the front door, where the address was painted in black: 1134 Burgess Street. A joke, because there was no Burgess Street, no street at all.

Louise liked the darkness on his face where the guilt of a hard war was kept. His unhappiness was coming off his body with such a force that it practically lifted the wings of the lovebugs clinging to him, and to Louise this sad mood was welcome in a house where most of the occupants could not stop grinning. 1134 Burgess Street. Where the men served the women. Where the past served the future. A house set off at the end of a dirt road, so far back that creatures from the forest were startled by the wet shirts that flapped on the clothesline.

The soldier's lips moved as he read the address again.

"You here for a job?" Louise asked.

His were the gray eyes of a marksman. They shifted over to her, moved down to her wet knees, looked up again. Almost steadied on the delicate features of her face, and then moved away, back to the house number. His fingertips searched through the crop of his black hair, came out with a struggling lovebug.

"Yes," he said. "I need a job. I'm handy with a hammer or an ax—"

Louise burst out laughing. "That's not the kind of work the men do here. Haven't you heard?"

He paused. "I don't know."

Louise had lived long enough—seventeen years—to know that sometimes the only way a man can express his guilt is through confusion. A sort of early senility that shelters something old and indecent. It sent a thrill through her even as she noticed a patch of the porch that was still dry, next to the bromeliad.

"You a soldier?" Louise asked him, although she knew.

"Used to be. I trained here before the war."

"But you're not from Louisiana. I can tell by the way you talk."

"I'm from Ohio."

"You ever kill anyone?"

He blinked, then picked up his suitcase. "Can I come in or not?"

"Sure. You'll need to talk to my daddy. He runs this house. But take off your shoes. They're dirty."

The soldier did not protest, but reached down and unlaced his shoes and pulled them off. He stepped onto the porch in his white socks.

"Wait," Louise said. "Your socks are dirty too."

"No, they're not."

"Your socks have been down inside your shoes, right? And how clean can the inside of your shoes be? Who knows what you've got into?"

He sighed and took his socks off.

"Now let me wash your feet."

"Don't tell me my feet aren't clean."

"Give them here." Louise got down on her knees and pulled the bucket full of soap suds over to her. The soldier offered up his right foot, reluctantly, the intolerant look on his face she'd come to expect from a man unbalanced. She scrubbed the top of his foot with the brush, then the toes, then the heel, moving methodically as the unseen dirt dissolved.

Holding a warm foot always reminded her of tending to her grandmother, who had a stroke and lay in bed for eight months with her eyes closed. Her body was dying, her soul steeping in the breath of the impatient angels, and yet her feet had stayed pink and warm. Her feet had wanted to live.

"You have nice feet," Louise said finally, restoring his balance. "Go on in through the foyer. It's late and all the women who wait in there should be gone by now. But if they're not, don't look at them. Privacy equals dignity, that's what Daddy says. And he's an educated man.

"Knock on the first door on your left. That's Daddy's office. He can tell you if we're hiring. And if he starts talking about lost love, change the subject. Otherwise you'll be there all night."

The soldier grabbed the porch rail to keep his balance while he reached down to pick up his wicker suitcase. He opened the screen door and let it close softly behind him.

Louise returned to scrubbing and listening to the crickets, to their single agreed-upon note. Heat came up from the bucket and blew in from the forest. She looked at the prints the man's bare feet had left on the slick porch, and breathed in the just-baptized odor of cleanliness. This was her favorite time. The hour, the minute, the second that made up purity. All the germs dying in each other's Jezebel arms.

Louise paused to smooth her hair back over her ear, and winced. She ran her fingertip over the sore part of her scalp.

Charlotte the Mute had appeared out of nowhere that morning in the forest, and pushed Louise down for no reason at all, preventing her from putting the final touches on a giant oak stump she'd been washing.

Each week, it had been Louise's habit to run into the woods with a brush and scrub down one lucky tree, from the roots all the way up, as far as she could reach or climb, for she believed that every tree deserved a few hours of cleanliness, a temporary banishment of bugs and dust and dirt and squirrels and Spanish moss. For if spiders can keep their tight webs clean, so clean that sunlight slips down their silver threads like bare feet on waxed floors, couldn't the rest of the forest follow the spiders' lead? And though the men in the house teased her, she continued to liberate the filthy world tree by tree: black gum, dogwood, birch, oak, weeping willow, magnolia, cedar.

This morning she'd had a sudden inspiration. Why not go deep into the woods, to the intersection of the two main paths—one that led to Lake Swane and one that led from the Burgess property—and wash down the giant oak stump that had given her so much, all those years before?

By the time she reached it, her bucket of water was cool. She went to work, scrubbing down the bark on the sides, then working on the smooth top surface, ring by ring, as sap splintered and pollen clogged the bristles. Louise had just begun to whistle when Charlotte materialized, plowing into her and sending her sprawling. Louise felt her head strike something made of wood, and heard the sound of Charlotte's clogs stomping away. She opened her eyes. Two birds circled over her head, the orange ends of rainbows trailing out of their tail feathers. She blinked and the birds vanished. Slowly she stood up, too stunned to shriek at her dirtiness but clearheaded enough to note, with satisfaction, that the stump was shiny clean.

And now her head still hurt. Louise smoothed over the prints the soldier's bare feet had made on the wet porch and wondered if Charlotte the Mute was growing even crazier. She scrubbed harder as she thought about the strange woman, until the utter cleanliness of the porch soothed her memories of the morning. She breathed deeply, closed her eyes.

Stomp stomp stomp. Louise's eyes flew open. As she swung around she elbowed her bucket, sending yellow suds rushing down the porch.

Her younger brother grinned at her and kept stomping, his boots leaving smears of mud and bits of grass and leaves.

"Benjamin! Stop it, stop it!"

Her brother kept up his march. "The porch is dirty, the porch is dirty!" he sang.

"Get out of here!"

"Deadly dirt and greasy grass and messy mud!"

Louise lunged at him with her hands outstretched, and felt the bulge his slingshot made in the bib of his second-hand Crown overalls as she pushed him off the porch. He fell backward in a heap. Laughing. His legs flailing. The soles of his boots crusted with mud and a few sprigs of dead grass and broken pine straw, all available under the hot porch light.

Louise threw her scrub brush at him. "That's not funny, Benjamin! Everything was clean!"

Benjamin sat up and dusted himself off. "Everything's not clean. No matter how hard you try. In a couple of hours, a bug will come and shit right where you scrubbed."

"You're not supposed to say 'shit.' "

"Shit," said her brother. "Shit. Shit. Shit."

The soldier, Justin, had moved through the dark foyer, had passed the grandfather clock, whose pendulum was motionless, and the hall tree with its myriad hooks that held not a single coat. He stood before Mr. Olen's office, his knuckles poised to tap on the door. His naked feet shamed him, as did the ammonia smell of the walls and the curtains, and the shadows which were darkest near the windows, and the deep, sweet odor of pine, and the murmuring that seemed to come from the ceiling above his head.

Justin had heard about this house from a drunken woman in a bar who was talking so loudly that other people were looking away from her, at walls and windows and coasters and half-empty glasses.

"The owner leads you up to a warm room and you meet your man," she said. "The ammonia in the air made my eyes water, but such peace! And the man I chose was so happy. It made me feel like a girl, to touch such a contented man."

"Annette, be quiet!" the woman's friend had hissed. "You don't know what you're saying."

Justin's knock sounded too loud, and he withdrew his hand quickly, afraid that he had interrupted some whispery balanced system in the house, as skipping a rock across a lake upsets the fish, as stepping on an ant dooms the other workers to hoisting heavier seeds.

The man who answered was impossibly tall, and the look on his face, wistful and yet full of hope, told Justin he was expecting someone else.

"You must be here about a job."

"I think so."

"It's all right to be tentative. The sober men who come here are very hesitant. The drunks are fervid."

"I'm not drunk."

"Then your reaction makes sense. My name's Leon Olen, but everyone calls me Mr. Olen. Leave your suitcase there. No one's going to bother it." He looked down at Justin's feet and nodded. "I see you've been bathed by my daughter. You must excuse her. She's a dramatic girl and she's cast herself as dirt's antagonist." He motioned for Justin to come into the room and pointed at a channel-back chair for him to sit in. Mr. Olen himself sat down behind an oaken desk.

"What's your name?"

"Justin."

The tall man swung his feet up and rested them on the desk. Two dime-sized holes in one shoe.

Justin looked around. Papers and books were scattered here and there. Four framed pictures sat on the sideboard and faced the wall.

Mr. Olen opened a drawer and pulled out a pouch of tobacco, then unfolded a pocketknife. "You chew, Justin?"

Justin shook his head.

Mr. Olen cut off an inch's worth and put it in his mouth. "Louise finds it abhorrent, as did my wife, back when I had a wife. She said an educated man should only chew on the end of cigars, and she absolutely hated it when, on occasion, I'd spit in her Fiesta cups. A woman's habits never mix with a man's. Except here in this house. Know what I mean?"

"No."

"You'll see. You a soldier?"

"Was."

Mr. Olen spit into an old tin can. "Lost a lot of men at this house to the draft, that's for sure, just a few years after we started up. Some of them came back after the war, but it wasn't the same. The women complained. Bad for business, that war. It took the spontaneity out of the kiss. Made it a grim task, like liberating Dachau."

Justin looked at his lap.

"Can I ask you something, Justin? Why are you here?"

Justin shifted slightly in his chair and his shadow

hunched down on the wall. "I told you," he said at last. "Maybe for a job."

"There's only one kind of man who comes here looking for a job. A man who's done something he can't live with. Robbing a church. Cutting another man's throat. Breaking a woman's arm. Or doing something in war, maybe. Anything sound familiar, Justin?"

Justin didn't answer. He reached into his pocket and drew out a cigarette.

"Old Gold?" said Mr. Olen.

"Yes."

"Figured. But sorry. No smoking inside the house. Only out back. That's a cardinal rule."

Justin returned the cigarette to his pocket, irritated that he couldn't smoke, that his feet were bare, that he hadn't found the peace promised by the drunk woman in the smoky bar.

"This house is made of virgin longleaf pine. A stray spark can bring this whole house down, and a conflagration of happy men and satisfied women is still a conflagration."

"Are you saying that every man in this house is happy?"

Mr. Olen cut another hunk of tobacco. "Just about, with an exception or two." He looked away as he said this, and Justin knew that by this gesture he was pointing to himself, to his own life. And now the strange girl who had bathed his feet came back to him. *Don't get him talking about lost love. Otherwise you'll be there all night.*

"You know," said Mr. Olen, "happiness is a quality that women don't necessarily look for in a man. They'd rather have the broad shoulders or the Roman nose. But these men do have a good time. Of course, a lot of 'em are a mess when they first walk through the door. They all feel better, sooner or later."

"Really? Every one?"

"By and by. You see, there's something about the work we do that soothes the conscience."

Justin leaned forward in his chair. "I want you to hire me," he said urgently.

"Whoa. Hold on. Let me tell you how it works. A strict process must be followed, for the sake of the women and our own healing souls. Tonight, you sleep. Tomorrow, you and me sit down and we have our first interview. That's when you tell me exactly what's haunting you."

Immediately Justin rose from his seat, crossed the room and seized the doorknob.

"Wait." Mr. Olen came around the desk and touched Justin's arm. "Please, son. Many men have your reaction."

"I'm not telling you anything."

"Just hear me out. All right?" Mr. Olen gently pulled on Justin's arm until he released the door, then gently got him back down in the channel-back chair.

"No one ever sees these notes," said Mr. Olen. "I keep them locked in a safe in the cellar. I'm the only one that knows the combination. Even Louise has never looked in that safe, although God knows she wants to."

Justin said nothing.

"In a way, whatever you've done is none of my business. But I have to know what's in a man's heart before I can let him serve a woman. You see, this is a place of redemption. All redemption begins with a secret spilled."

Mr. Olen went behind his desk again and sat down, completing the motion by spitting into the can. "Anyway, suppose the interview goes well. The other men will show you all their little tricks. For example, did you know that women like to be touched right here with the fingertips?" Mr. Olen indicated a place under the line of his jaw. "You have to know these things before you service your first woman."

Justin drummed his fingers on his knees.

"I can see you're not sure about all this," said Mr. Olen. "And some men find this house is not for them. One man told me on his way out: 'I'd rather keep my demons than have to take all these damn showers.' You might find you feel the same." Mr. Olen paused. "You think you could spend all night with someone, just kissing? Touching? Whispering sweet nothings? Maybe a little waltzing?"

"Waltzing?"

"Women love to watch a man move without an erection." Mr. Olen crossed his arms. "I don't mean to be indelicate, but, like cigarettes, intercourse is strictly prohibited. Both of them create an incendiary environment." He looked over at the backs of the picture frames, then back at Justin. "You think you could refrain from that? Intercourse, I mean."

"I don't want to do that anyway."

"Why? You wounded there?"

"No."

"Then why? Hold on, don't answer. You can explain during the interview tomorrow." Mr. Olen stood up and stretched. "Tonight, you sleep. For now, you can use the empty room on the third floor. There's a cot in there, but we've been using it as a place to keep tools and such. Hammers and saws. Rope. There's a ceiling fan but no overhead light. Louise will set you up with a kerosene lamp. I don't like using them in the house because of the danger of fire, but we've got no choice. The electricity in this house goes out when a dog barks in New York City."

"That would be fine. The cot, the lamp. Fine." Justin said the words with an undercurrent of hostility, as if he held a grudge against comfort and yellow light.

"All right, then. Let me call my daughter. She'll show you to your room."

Louise's annoyance at her brother and his stomping feet had been soothed by her scrubbing not just the porch but the front door as well, and the good mood of a hostess had returned to her. She pointed out features of the house as she climbed the steps, one hand petting the handrail with an endless stroke and the other pausing to rub her aching scalp.

"All the baseboards and the windowsills are curly pine," she explained. "Daddy accidentally stained it too dark, so you can't see the swirls."

As she spoke Louise imagined the goings-on in the rooms around her, endearments and kisses and sliding waltzes and skin charmed into a glisten or a blush but not into an outlawed sweat. The silence of the soldier behind her pulled like static at the back of her dress. He moved slowly, so that quite often she had to stop and wait for him and his bulging suitcase to catch up with her. And when she occasionally turned around to mark his progress, she could see the same expression on his face as that of someone very old and frail, someone who dreads the effort of leaving the ground floor.

Louise fell silent as they reached the third landing, picturing guilt frothing in the soldier's stomach like the meringue on a lemon pie. Fluffy and yet filling. She was sorry to know that if he was like the others, the guilt would soon be gone.

"Here we are," said Louise. "Room twenty-one." She turned the key and opened the door. "It's a little warm in here. And it's musty. There's no overhead light. I'll fix the lamp."

Justin moved past her into the room. He dropped his suitcase on the floor and sat down on the cot while Louise removed the glass chimney, turned the wick up and struck the match.

"Sorry about the tools. Daddy won't let me clean in here. He says every man deserves one dirty room in the house."

The lamplight glowed on his face, slid around it and filled one corner of the room. Ancient tools littered the floor, and their shadows decorated the walls down near the baseboards.

"This used to be Daniel's room when he was a baby. He's my little boy."

"You have a son?"

"He's not my son. He's a gift from God. An angel."

"Boys grow up to be men," he said with bitterness. "And men are not angelic."

"They are when they really, really try."

Justin fell silent for a few moments. Then he said: "I'm not telling your father anything."

"I don't care. You do or you don't."

He stared at her for a moment. And then burst into tears. She watched him weep, a little stunned. Men had entered the house crying before, but none so previously reserved as this one. She stood there awkwardly and then said: "You make yourself at home. And be careful where you step. Daddy's going to have to let me clean this floor, since there's someone staying here now."

He did not remove his hands from his face. She wanted to kiss his forehead. Her impulse surprised her.

⋆ ⋆ ⋆

It was past midnight. Louise ran the water in the tub and used the bar of Octagon soap to wash both feet, which had begun to feel unbearably dirty from walking in the toolroom. As she washed her feet she imagined scrubbing the toolroom the same way she'd imagined kissing the soldier's forehead: up and down, then side to side, never missing a patch. How strange. She never desired the new men, never wanted to kiss them, for she had seen them all turn into sissies within just a few days. Perhaps this man was different.

The water streamed down on her foot, cold and clear. And yet if she put her tongue to the water she would taste the ghosts of metal elements, the bitterness of rust. A little salt, perhaps. Or sand. Even water had its demons.

Louise dried her feet and went next door to her father's office. He was sleeping with his feet up on the desk, his pouch of tobacco left opened. The light was so dim that she could barely make out the edges of the picture frames arranged along the sideboard. In each turned-around picture was the same woman in a different dress and with short hair, long hair, curly hair. Sometimes with her hand on her chin, sometimes gazing off to the right or the left.

The poses that make up a marriage.

Louise kissed her father good night and was rewarded by a twitch in his left eye and a softly mumbled "Janey?" His hair was wet when she smoothed it from his face.

When Louise crawled into her bed, she was still thinking about wanting to kiss the soldier. Her own first kiss had been with Milo Gravin, outcast and fire starter and brother to Charlotte. Milo's mother had burned up during the Louisiana Maneuvers of 1941, when Milo was still a boy, but he wouldn't speak a word of it. That had been the origin of the kiss. Louise had asked him, as they sat at their favorite place at Lake Swane with their feet in the water on a summer day, how exactly his mother had died. First the fabric, then the flesh, Louise had heard. The hair and then the eyelashes. Then bones and teeth and a pair of wire-rimmed spectacles. Shoelaces and buttons. The pearls of her necklace. All turned to cinder.

"That's bullshit," Milo had said. "She didn't even wear pearls."

"I heard you killed her, Milo. Is that true?"

Milo had leaned over and kissed her—just to distract talk of his mother's burning body with his own temperate lips—but nevertheless, that kiss was as grand as she'd ever imagined. Milo was said to be crazy but there was sanity in his lips, and a respect for limitations, and a sadness that Louise couldn't place as she closed her eyes and pressed her nose to an old scar on Milo's cheek.

His scar felt softer than she'd imagined. The gentle side of a bad man.

A few weeks later she had kissed Milo again, then let him take off her dress and touch her breasts. She and Milo had lain down together and had almost become one before

Louise decided that one was more germy than two. And then they went back to just being friends, although Milo's badness did make his face handsome and his smile perfect.

Now Louise stared at the ceiling and considered the things that had made up the night. The new arrival. The clean porch. Her brother's stomping feet. The dirty room. The eyes of the soldier in the unambitious light of a kerosene lamp.

It had been a long time—several months—since a new man had crossed the porch, antsy with untold secrets and dying for the cure.

Women have no demons, thought Louise. Just hurts and regrets. Women don't howl with the things they've done, but keep their heads low from the things done to them. Or at least that was what it seemed to Louise, after watching so many of them enter The House of Gentle Men under cover of darkness.

Louise opened her eyes suddenly. She hadn't left the soldier any soap and towels. And this dedication to her duty and the curiosity that she felt in his presence made her decide to leave her bed, ascend the stairs and knock on his door once again, a towel under one arm and a bar of soap in her hand.

No answer.

"Hello," she called.

She turned the knob and pushed the door open.

She gasped.

His dangling feet.

3

Charlotte pulled her line out of the water and saw that her fishing hook was bare. Some little bait-stealer had made off with her minnow. She reached in the bucket and chased down another minnow, looking up again in time to catch sight of Louise Olen approaching Milo, who sat fishing a little farther down the bank. Milo watched her walk up to him with a look of open admiration on his face, which Charlotte noticed but pretended not to. Instead she baited her hook and threw it back into the water. She had never liked Louise Olen, with her smug glances and her uppity way of scrubbing down the world, and when Charlotte had come upon this girl the day before, washing the giant oak stump, she had wanted to smash into her and so she had. But here she was again, barging in on a quiet afternoon at Lake Swane to flirt with her brother and ruin the simple peace of fishing.

And yet Charlotte did not edge farther down the bank away from them, for she knew that from time to time

Louise told Milo things that went on in that house, things that Charlotte could learn simply by holding her breath and listening very intently, as she did now.

Outside of what Louise Olen said, there was no separating fact from fiction: That the rooms were lit by candles. That the kisses were paid for nickel by nickel. That the floors were impossibly clean. That the men had been castrated. That the owner had poisoned his wife long ago, with strychnine. It was all rumor, for only those who had been there really knew, and they remained silent. But it was the name itself that most fascinated Charlotte.

The House of Gentle Men.

She imagined them in creamy linen suits, moving to waltzes that rose up from the turntables, the soles of their shoes sliding on the polished floors. Men made ghostly by their gentleness. Looking into her eyes. Kissing her neck. Their voices a whisper. Their fingers soft as a fable, moving along the length of her collarbone. No thrust in their swirling waltz. All the violence gone from their bodies, replaced by a moonlit grace.

Once, she had traveled through the woods and peered through dogwood branches to see the house for herself. There it was. Ordinary-looking, with hounds wandering around outside and laundry on the line. No men were outside, although the table and the hammocks spoke of their existence. Charlotte squinted. Lights were on inside the house, and she could see indistinct forms moving from room to room. The haziness of their bodies gentle in itself.

She had not been brave enough to knock on the door. To ask, "Are you real?" or, "How much for the night?" Because she could not speak, she would have to write the words down on a pad and hold them to the light, which to Charlotte felt as naked as baring her heavy breasts. And so, red-faced, she had retreated, back down through the woods and out a side road where she walked along slowly, her head down. People staring as they passed her. Charlotte the Mute, who had given up her voice all those years ago, along with her friends.

Louise threw her quilt down next to Milo. She had seen him look at her as she approached and then look quickly back to his bobber. He was nearly nineteen, but still flirted shyly and unevenly, like a boy.

Fire season was approaching and Louise wondered if Milo's fingers were itching. For the past four years he had been the prime suspect in a series of mysterious fires, and had almost gone to jail in late August, after a sudden blaze took down Sid Havens's miraculous ribbon cane patch. The only thing that had kept him out of trouble was the fact that the sheriff hated Sid Havens and had looked the other way.

Louise found Milo's love affair with fire intriguing, not just because it made him Bad, but because fire was the cleanest element she could think of. Cleaner than detergent. Cleaner than rubbing alcohol. Cleaner than Dr. Tichenor's Antiseptic. A fire eats germs along with pets and sheet music. It is pure and yet full of sin. Righteous but evil.

"Don't knock over my fishing machine," Milo warned her. She looked over by his knee. A Coke bottle was turned upside down in a bowl of water. Milo believed that when the water moved up into the Coke bottle, fishing was good. Louise squinted at the bottle and saw that it was dry.

"Why are you even trying?" asked Louise. "Your machine says don't bother."

"Hell, that thing ain't right," said Milo. "Charlotte caught a blue cat this morning on a piece of Spam." He raised his voice. "Hey, Charlotte. Show Louise your fish."

Charlotte retrieved her stringer and held up the catfish for them to see.

"Five pounds, I'd say," said Milo.

Louise sat down gingerly on her quilt. She cast a quick glance over at Charlotte and rubbed her head ruefully.

"Where you been?" Milo asked Louise. "I've been bored and there's been no one to talk to. Except Charlotte. And she's tired of listening to me." Talking was Milo's greatest pleasure. To anyone and anything. Even the trees that he punched when his temper flared. He would come back later and speak to the trees soothingly, apologetically.

The way Southern men treated Southern women.

Milo put down his fishing pole, stood up and reached into his pocket. "I've got something to show you."

The object was so big that Milo had to stand up and pry it out of his pants. He handed it to Louise, carefully turning his back to Charlotte as he did so.

She turned it over in her hands. "What is it?"

"It's a cypress lamb," Milo whispered. "I whittled it for Charlotte's birthday. She'll be twenty-three years old on Friday."

"Why does the lamb have horns?"

"To make it different. Do you think Charlotte will like it?"

"Sure."

"Good. She's always sad this time of year."

Louise looked at Charlotte again. Same tangled hair, same thick body and the dress she'd worn the day before.

"Milo," she said in a low voice. "Guess what your sister did to me yesterday."

"What?"

Louise took his hand, intending to press it against her head so he could feel the swelling, but noticed that his fingers were dirty and let him go. Instead she parted the hair in her scalp and bent toward him.

"See? She pushed me down. In the woods, where the paths cross."

"What for?"

"Nothing. I was just bathing the tree stump."

"Bathing the—?" He laughed. "I almost forgot you wash trees."

"It's not so funny, Milo. She attacked me out of nowhere. I could have split my head open."

"What problem could my sister have with you? You two don't even know each other. She's never said a word to you."

"How can she say a word when she can't talk? She's looked at me funny ever since I've been friends with you."

"Aw . . ." Milo noticed a little blood from where the hook had entered his finger, and sucked on the hurt place. "Charlotte's real sweet and quiet. She'd never pick on some little girl like you. She must have run into you by accident." He threaded a worm on the hook and flipped it back into the water.

"That was no accident. She did it on purpose."

"You calling my sister mean, Louise?"

"No. You're mean. She's crazy."

His face turned red, and Louise knew that she had gone too far. He seized her head, forced her ear to his mouth and whispered: "Louise, if you ever say that about my sister again, I'm gonna hold you down and pour these slimy night crawlers down your throat. And you know I'll do it."

She pulled away from him.

"You're a bully, Milo."

She watched his cork bob in the current.

"How about a kiss?" he asked.

"No. I'm not going to kiss you and I'm not going to tell you the big news."

"What news?"

She hesitated, letting him suffer. Finally she said, "Someone hanged himself last night at the house. A soldier."

"Really?" Milo's eyes were wide. "Who found him?"

"I did."

"Was his face all swelled up? Was his tongue blue and sticking out?"

"No."

"Oh." He seemed disappointed.

"Because he wasn't dead. He had just done it when I found him. Two men cut him down. The doctor worked on him a while and he came around, but he's real quiet and lies real still. I tried to bathe his face this morning and Daddy told me to go swimming."

Milo sat down again and went back to staring out at his cork. Louise could tell he was losing interest now that death had been cut out of the story. So she said: "The soldier must have a real bad secret to do that to himself. Daddy's going to talk to him about it when he feels better. He'll find out the secret and he'll lock it in the safe with the others."

Milo lifted the tip of his pole to check on his bait. "You have to find out the secret. Open the safe."

"Daddy's got the combination."

"Figure it out."

"I've tried. But Daddy's an educated man. He's using numbers I wouldn't even think of."

Milo shook his head. "Those men over at that house are all sissies. I done some bad things but I ain't no sissy. I'm man enough to live with what a guilty thing does to you."

"Like what you did to your mama? Is that a guilty thing?"

"Shut up, Louise."

"You can tell me. I'm not one to judge."

He leaned in close again. "Come on, Louise, kiss me. I've seen you mostly naked."

"So?"

"So that means we're bound together. And not just 'cause of that. We're bound together because both our mothers *are dead*. Kiss me to honor our dead mothers."

Louise's eyes opened wide. "My mother is not dead!"

"Might as well be," Milo said softly. "You know what I mean?"

Louise punched him in the side of the head. "Don't you ever say that again!"

He laughed. "You punch like a girl."

"I hate you."

"You do not."

"Go burn down the forest."

"Go wash a tree."

Milo looked back at his cork as it jerked suddenly under the water. Louise watched his back straighten and his hands grip the pole. The cork bobbed once, twice, then disappeared entirely. Milo reared back.

From her place by the bank, Charlotte watched her brother struggle with his fish as Louise shouted her instructions: "Don't jerk on it. The line will break. You're getting too close to the edge. You're going to fall in. Milo. Milo."

Milo had fallen silent for once, caught up in the fight to land the fish. Charlotte's brother loved to talk—endlessly—about fishing, hunting, the old war, shotguns, women, dogs, weather, planes, slot machines, heaven, hell, panthers, snakes, money, graveyards, trains, whiskey and (almost shyly) about fire. About the wife he had married the spring before, almost killed in a fit of rage, and divorced two months later. Charlotte felt outnumbered by words in his presence. Drowning in a sea of them.

As usual, Charlotte had heard only snatches of the conversation of Milo and Louise. Phrases lost in the summer air, covered by the sound of lake water against the muddy bank. Louise had murmured something about a soldier. Something about a secret. Two words that hurt Charlotte when used in the same sentence. She had gone back to fishing and tried not to listen any further.

But because Milo's whispers had a shrill note that announced themselves, Charlotte then clearly heard Milo asking Louise for a kiss. Just a little one. Just a secret one. A tiny peck to be accomplished between blinks. Charlotte had looked at them then, dead on, to see if Louise would agree. The girl in this afternoon light reminded Charlotte of herself at that age. Ready and willing to bloom—bursting in fact from that hidden bloom, like a crape myrtle pining for high summer.

The catfish Milo had been struggling with now lay on the bank. But what was caught did not quite undo what was not. For Charlotte knew the value of a kiss.

Her thoughts drifted back to her own first kiss, when she was not quite fifteen and still a silly girl, given to laughing and curling her hair with tin cans heated over a kerosene lamp. The cans would burn her fingers when the oilcloth slipped. Fire and curls. Blisters and beauty.

The boy's name was Kane. A serious boy she'd met in the darkness of a brush arbor during a revival meeting. She and the boy had stolen away for a walk in a meadow, through tall grasses and wild asters and among butterflies forsaking purple blooms for yellow. He had let go of her hand to pick up a stick and poke the high grass in front of them, worried about the angry snakes of late summer that might be hidden within.

"My dog got bit by a snake once," Kane said. "His head swelled up but he lived."

"Really?" said Charlotte, who could speak then.

"Uh-huh. He ended up killing the snake, but he would never go near the woodpiles again."

Charlotte nodded. She knew that boys started off telling stories about snakes and dogs, then about other people, then about themselves, then about their mothers, who were closest to their hearts.

No kiss then. Just the rhythm of footsteps and breathing and the whoosh of beaten grass. The imagined hissing of serpents panicked by the stick and the talk of dogs.

The kiss came later, after four or five more secret meetings away from the eyes of her parents.

Milo caught her slipping away through the backyard. He was a boy then. Clear-eyed and innocent. A pet frog and a slingshot and a folding knife for mumblety-peg, not to carve kindling for a slow match when a breezy day called for arson.

"Where you going, Charlotte?"

"Nowhere. Shhhhhh."

They lay together under old Minnie Neilor's grape arbor. The kiss had started long ago. Through its duration Charlotte's eyes had opened and closed. Her mother had forbidden her to wear pants, believing, like many backwoods Baptists, that long skirts made kneeling before God more graceful and true. Charlotte, though, was more concerned with Kane than with God, and had changed into the forbidden pants behind the skinny cover of a dogwood tree. And because Kane had a thready streak of rebellion as well, he was wearing his father's Borsalina hat, which had not yet slipped off Kane's head despite his acrobatics. Certain bees made a home of the brim of it as Kane and Charlotte kissed.

And so they lingered under the crossed vines and the chill of gathered leaves, under the muscadines and the threat of sudden stings from the gently agitated bees. The chill of that protected space.

Old Minnie Neilor was two years away from a sudden death in an overstuffed recliner, but her senses were still sharp. She could detect a coyote's presence in the watermelon patch, or a deer in the cornfield, and was certainly capable of sniffing out a small sin among the ripened grapes and the droning bees. Thus Kane and Charlotte kissed in the late-summer air and in that maze of possibilities: warmth, chill, bee stings, balm, sunlight, shadow, secrecy, revelation, freedom, capture.

They were not discovered. Minnie Neilor kept her eyes on the spontaneous color scheme of her half-finished macramé.

Later they parted, and out in the deep woods Charlotte changed her clothes again and smoothed the wrinkles that told a dress's tale of being stuffed in a knapsack. And yet her mother didn't notice. Charlotte was not sent to her room, or whipped with a slender branch from a birch tree. Two weeks later, Kane's father was transferred to Mississippi, a state whose very pronunciation recalled the hissing of the invisible snakes in the high grass. She never saw him again.

So many years ago, that kiss under the grape arbor. Back when she could still make words audible, back when she wore pink dresses and blouses with bishop sleeves.

Cotton hose. Secret lipstick. A touch of the cologne her mother no longer used. Back when her father could still smile. Back when her mother was alive and standing at the sink with her snap beans breaking and her husband's hands around her waist, his lips to her ear, their status as married people beating back any perceived disapproval from heaven above. Back when Charlotte herself still considered men to be capturable, pleasurable, wonderful things fully capable of helping her win her running battle with Belinda over who was the prettiest one of all.

The year 1940. Bees and grapes and the sharp old eyes of Minnie Neilor, gloriously turned away from the window.

Kane.

The press of lips. And a new—outrageous—use for the disregarded tongues.

But now as Charlotte sat on the bank, remembering that kiss, two words drifted over again from the conversation of Milo and Louise.

Soldier. Secret.

And suddenly Charlotte was back to that dark place in the woods, bordered by a tangle of honeysuckle. The struggle of that birth. And the baby's cry—she'd heard it now for over six years in her dreams, or in the distracted current of summer showers, or in the sound of a distant train or the immediate breeze through the scentless mimosa blossoms outside her window. Now she heard the cry again. It seemed to come from everywhere around her, from the sun and the water and from the mouth of Milo's catfish, which lay on the bank, dying.

Charlotte closed her eyes tightly, but the sound wouldn't go away. She shook her head violently, threw down her fishing pole and jumped to her feet.

"Charlotte!" her brother called to her as she rushed away. "Where you going?"

4

The soldier would not move. His body, pulled back from death, had responded not in celebration but with an absolute stillness. He did not speak, and his eyes would not follow voices or shadows or colors. He simply stared straight up at the hewn end of the hanging rope that still dangled from the ceiling beam.

The old doctor said Justin's knee was sprained from the fall, and rubbed it with turpentine and wrapped it with bandages. He gave him codeine for his pain, and also some quinine tablets.

"Quinine?" said Mr. Olen.

The doctor shrugged.

When Louise returned from the lake she served Justin a carefully prepared meal—tomato soup in a little ceramic bowl on a Hires Root Beer tray. He would not eat, nor meet her eyes. An angry red ridge circled his neck where the noose had tightened.

Louise hovered over him, flushed from the afternoon

sun and from rejecting Milo's kiss. She had never heard of anyone trying suicide, save for the woman who lived down the street from Milo's old house. One day the woman was squatting on her front porch, cleaning a gilt frame, and when her rag went dry and it was time for more turpentine, she drank the turpentine instead.

Suddenly. With her youngest child watching her in a pair of dirty diapers, and her husband working the slot machines in Leesville.

"The doctor says he knows it hurts, but you should try to swallow," Louise said to the soldier.

He shook his head. His hands were crossed over his heart as if protecting it from the dust in the room. Or the sunlight. Or perhaps from the steam of the soup, which he hadn't touched.

"Why did you do it?" asked Louise.

"Leave me alone."

"You'd be dead right now if I hadn't remembered the soap and the towel."

"Then you're to blame." He closed his eyes.

"Go ahead and sleep," she said. "While you're sleeping I'm going to clean up this room. And wash the floor. Daddy said I could."

It took her three hours to scrub the room. The baseboards, the closet, the windowsills. The beams of the ceiling. Dust rained down on the floor and she had to start over again. Justin slept through it all. A cobweb floated down onto his face and his next deep breath pulled the cobweb slightly into his nostrils. Louise peeled it off him and thought briefly of saving it.

Daniel came into the room. He was a small boy with astonishing blue eyes. The old doctor had cut Daniel's hair two weeks before while in a bit of a nervine stupor, and the mistakes were slowly growing out.

Daniel tried to smooth Justin's sheet.

"No, honey," said Louise. "Don't bother him. Go play."

Daniel raised himself on his tiptoes and peered at the motionless man. "Is he still sad?"

"Yes. I think so."

Louise finally finished the room to her satisfaction and breathed in the new smell of ammonia. She knew what had driven Justin over the edge. Not his unexpressed secrets, but all that dirt. She took a seat in a chair by his cot and watched him. How beautiful it was—this body that the noose could make writhe but not shudder.

Justin slept so deeply that Louise felt brave enough to go through his wicker suitcase, cataloguing the contents in her mind so that she could write them down later. A pair of leather shoes. Dr. Scholl's Zino-pads. A shaving mug. A razor and Gillette blades. Two white shirts. A military brush with a Lucite back. An Eversharp repeater pencil.

Louise closed the latches in disappointment. It looked like any suitcase whose function is to prepare a man to meet the world, not leave it. Her father had told her to remove anything sharp from Justin's room. She dropped the Gillette blades into her pockets and, after she spent a moment envisioning a bloody hole in Justin's neck, the repeater pencil too.

Over the next two days he showed little improvement. Louise read to him from an old *Life* magazine. She fanned his face. She brought him imaginative sandwiches and cold bottles of Coke on doilies cut from the mesh of an Aladdin's lamp. He ate only a few bites of the sandwiches, remaining in his reclining position so that she feared he would choke. Then he drank a few gulps of the Coke. It ran out the corners of his mouth, frothing like peroxide.

She could not help but think he must contain some uncontrollable guilt to live in such torment. Badness was such an exciting quality.

Louise knew only one other bad man besides Milo Gravin—and he was only fifteen years old. Her brother, Benjamin. From the age of twelve he had been a heartbreaker, taking the virginity of his first girlfriend and then pushing her, weeping, into a honeysuckle bush when she demanded his favorite hat to sleep with. He moved on to older girls, then to women. Married, single, divorced, widowed. News of his conquests rolled around the town, swung back around and reached the ears of his father, who only shook his head at this boy who considered kissing a sissy's chore, like sewing a torn shirt.

Sometimes Benjamin would light a kerosene lantern in his sweet potato barn and wait for the women to leave

The House of Gentle Men and pass through the backyard on their way to rejoin their real lives and families. When, dreamily satisfied, they stumbled past, Benjamin would crack open the door and call to them seductively from the soft light of his love den: "Hey! Hey! You sick of those kissy-boys in there? Those sissies? You want a real man? A man that's willing to put it in?"

Most of the women would shake their heads and hurry away. But here and there, others did follow the sound of that flutelike voice, did lie down with Benjamin in the languid smoke of his kerosene lantern and did have their newly-repaired hearts broken once again.

The other men in the house complained to Mr. Olen.

"Hey, can't you control that boy? He's bad for business. The women go home crying and word spreads."

But Mr. Olen would only shake his head and say: "He's young, he's young."

Louise asked Benjamin once why he felt sex was necessary. Wasn't it enough, she asked, to just lie with a woman and kiss her and tell her sweet nothings, like the men in the house? And Benjamin had snorted and said: "Are you joking? Do you know where those men go on their nights off? Straight into town for the dirty kind of loving. I bet you anything there ain't no kissing going on there. Just in and out and in and out."

But Louise didn't believe her brother, and secretly longed for a man with a few unexplained, unforgiven things. And that is why she was both horrified and secretly thrilled when she saw the soldier's legs dangling, throwing shadows high up on the wall. No man had ever hanged himself in this house. Bare-chested, no less. Here was a man with some get-up-and-go. A dissatisfied man, tormented by the bad thing he'd done.

What must it be like to kiss him.

But all this was decided later, after Louise discovered his dangling body and screamed, after the men rushed in to cut him down, after her father checked his pulse and the old doctor hobbled in to minister to him as he lay unconscious on the cot.

"Is he going to live?" Louise asked, leaning forward. The floor was sticky under her bare feet.

"Sure enough," said the old doctor, moving the disks of the stethoscope down Justin's chest. "He's got a good, strong heartbeat. Must not have been up there long."

"If I hadn't brought him his soap and his towel . . ." Louise said.

"See?" said Willy, a man with a pomaded mustache and an excellent kissing reputation. "Cleanliness does save lives, Louise."

The other men tittered.

"All right," said Mr. Olen. "It's over. Get back to your women."

Louise had edged closer to study the soldier. She opened her mouth to say something, but the boy, Daniel, had entered the room and was looking at the man with his miraculous eyes. A color of blue that could not be ignored, not even in a room full of near death. Justin turned his head and met the boy's stare. Daniel reached his hand out to him.

"No, Daniel," said Mr. Olen gently, taking his hand. "You need to go back to your room now. Louise, take him back."

When Mr. Olen turned back toward Justin, Louise snatched the noose out of the corner. She led Daniel down the stairs.

"What is that?" asked Daniel.

"It's called a noose. People use it to hang themselves."

Daniel pulled on her hand, stopping her. "Hang?"

"Daniel . . ." Louise bent down to him and lowered her voice to a whisper. "The soldier tried to hurt himself."

"Why?"

"Because he is sad, Daniel. Very, very sad." She thought for a moment, searching for a comparison. "Even sadder than Benjamin's women."

"Ohhhh," said Daniel.

Three days after the hanging, the shock still hadn't worn off Leon Olen. He sat in his office, amazed by it all. The sheer violence of the act—rougher than intercourse, wilder than fire—had left him disoriented. Guilt like that had to have a woman at its root. Like his own guilt.

Abandoned by his wife and aching with regret, he had come to Louisiana in the late spring of 1940 with Louise and Benjamin. Mr. Olen's father had died and left him fifty thousand dollars, and once he arrived he immediately set to work realizing his vision to establish a house where men could live in the service of unkissed, overworked, unappreciated, tired, sad, prematurely gray, widowed, nervously single, despondently married women. Sad women, starving for love, their bodies married to labor. No longer meant to be seen, but to do. Now these women finally had a house of their own, fragrant with affection, reeking of ammonia, sitting off the dirt road and surrounded by crape myrtle. A secret place to which they could flee and be women again, kissed and waltzed against, whispered to, touched with just the fingertips.

No charge. Just leave an optional donation in the syrup can before you tiptoe out in your only voile gown, drugged by courtly love and sleepy with forgiveness for the gender known as male.

In the interview room with Mr. Olen, they were allowed to describe two characteristics of the man they desired, and these wishes were accommodated on a first-come, first-serve basis:

"Thin. Brown hair."

"A gentle smile. Big hands."

"Five-foot-ten. A broken nose."

"Big front teeth. Glasses."

"Green eyes. Long lashes. A straight back. A nice rear end. White feet. Hairy legs—" ("Stop," Mr. Olen had said. "Ma'am, you only get two things.")

Sometimes the women got exactly what they wanted, and sometimes they had to have a little generosity of spirit, for there was only one man with big front teeth and not a broken nose in the house. But Mr. Olen tried his best, for he had let his own wife slip through his long fingers due to his sustained and dreamy neglect, and now could sit in his office and imagine women all over his house receiving what he should have given to his wife. Enough women, enough affection, attention, compliments, and kisses, would create the magic necessary to lure back his beloved, and provide the stage for the Second Chance.

The Second Chance was the name given to the occasion of his wife's return, and the vision of this hopeful reunion had grown so powerful through the years that he found himself more and more immersed within it. The colors in her dress, the curve of her eyebrows and also her waist, the smell of her neck and her habit of blinking her eyes rapidly and then opening them wide. The way her laughter seemed to stroke her own throat and send it purring. The slight turning in of one foot due to a childhood bout with polio. Sometimes the vision of this turned-in foot made him weep, remembering the peculiar sound it made on short grass, and the lovely and original way it climbed a winding staircase.

Because of his persistent visions and the persistent hope that accompanied them, he himself never serviced the women who came to The House of Gentle Men, although some of them openly flirted with him and said things such as: "I don't think I'll find a man in this house as handsome as you, Mr. Olen." He would blush and gently turn them down.

He waited. Year after year. Redemption going on in the rooms upstairs but none to be found in his office. Now this soldier had hanged himself, imperfectly. A shocking despair that Mr. Olen saw in his own life.

The young man moved him.

Early Friday morning the grounds were quiet. The love-drugged women had already slipped away, for according to the rules, no woman was to be left at first light.

But one was.

A blonde. Thirty-four years old. Twice divorced. Unlucky in love. One husband who hit her and another who told her he loved her and left in the middle of a hard winter. Now she had just awakened, wrapped in Benjamin's Indian blanket on the floor of the sweet potato barn, breathing in the smell of kerosene and cut grass and old sweet potatoes. Benjamin was sitting cross-legged in the corner, naked and smoking a cigarette. She blinked, realizing that the wolf that had seduced her the night before was merely a boy. And yet what a boy he was.

Benjamin looked at her. "Get out."

The woman stirred. "What?"

"You heard me. Get out."

"Why?"

"I have to go to school."

"But, Benjamin, I love you."

"Don't be stupid. I am young enough to be your son."

Inside the house, Mr. Olen was slowly making his way up to the third floor, a pad in one hand and a pen in the other. He found Justin staring at the wall and Louise hovering near his bed.

"It's time for school, Louise."

"I don't want to go. I'm his nurse."

"You have to learn things."

"I don't learn anything there. No one talks to me."

Mr. Olen's eyes were watering from the ammonia in the room. "Your work is done here."

She closed the door behind her, hard. Justin's eyes were still on the far wall. Mr. Olen watched him, remembering what his daughter had whispered in his ear when she had last kissed him good night: *You know right after he did it, Daddy? When the doctor was working on him? No one noticed but I grabbed his foot. It was warm, Daddy. Just like Grandma's. His feet want to live and maybe his heart does too.*

He took a seat in the bentwood chair next to Justin's bed. "How are you feeling?" he asked.

Through the years Mr. Olen had become an expert at talking to people who didn't reply. His haunted new recruits, his sullen daughter, his absent wife. And so he let the minutes pass. Wiped his eyes. Tapped his shoes on the sterile floor. Finally he leaned forward and said: "Please, Justin. Tell me why."

5

It felt like a rape. Lying on his back in a hot, stale room and being cajoled and urged and nagged into telling his worst secret to a stranger. His throat still hurt from the rope and some parts of the story were so difficult to say that he lapsed into mumbling. He did not look at the tall man sitting next to him, but sometimes turned his head to the wall and glimpsed the man's shadow, motionless except for its right arm, for Mr. Olen was frantically taking notes.

"I want to stop now," said Justin.

"No. Please. Go on."

And so he told him, all of it. Down to the temperature of the air and the gentleness of breeze and the grittiness of sand. Down to the chiggers, even.

Seven years, and the itch came right back. So much that Justin scratched at his neck as he spoke of it. He was eighteen years old, stuck in the unfamiliar woods of

Louisiana, a boy moving to a man's orders in the fake war. The war before the war. The Louisiana Maneuvers of 1941. The training soldiers divided up into the blue army and the red, both colors practicing against the yellow hair of the Germans. Crawling under barbed-wire fences. Marching on hot macadam. Sleeping on lawns, or in the woods, dreaming of colored snakes. Bathing in rivers. Fighting thirst with salt tablets and Lister bags. Blowing up railroads and charging through briars. It was lovebug season, and their black bodies were crawling everywhere. Clotting the headlights of jeeps. Finding their way into guns and boots.

Justin had heard that panthers stalked these Louisiana woods, screaming like women and dropping from trees. He listened for them at night, shamed by his own fear. The mosquitoes tormented him, great hordes of them. He took to rubbing kerosene up and down his arms, knowing he could catch on fire, preferring that horrible fate to the niggling sting. And the chiggers. Almost invisible, just a red dot moving up the socks. Sometimes he would press his cigarette against the swelling to try to burn them out of his skin. He still had scars from that torture.

The fear of it all. War and snakes. Uncertainty and chiggers. Death and warm beer.

None of it a good excuse.

When he came upon her she was already caught, and her body had already been rocked into the white sand of a dry riverbed. He knew the two men with her, the one who stood with his arms crossed, watching, and the one who pushed her curved fingers further into the sand with the motions of his heaving body. The soldier's bare ass was covered with chigger bites, and Justin remembered feeling more understanding of the soldier than the girl. Chiggers were tormenting his own body, whereas he had no idea what a girl must think whose blue dress was off and tangled in the remains of false indigo and whose body was sinking into churned-up sand. Her eyes were shut tight. She said nothing. She had long black hair. Pale skin. A red swelling near her mouth. A mole on her bare shoulder and one above her eye.

"I've already gone myself," said Marty, the one standing.

"Gone?" asked Justin.

"You need an explanation?"

"No."

"You gonna take a turn too?"

The other soldier, David, stopped and rose to his feet.

"Well?" said Marty. "We don't got all day."

Justin noticed the girl hadn't opened her eyes. Such a hot day. He itched. "Did you hit her?"

"Of course not," said Marty. "She's a backwoods girl. They know we're going off to kill Germans and they love that. This is her way of saying be brave for Uncle Sam."

Justin shook his head. "I don't want to take a turn."

David gave a short little laugh and zipped up his pants.

Marty said: "You maybe don't like girls? Maybe you like men? Blond hair, blue eyes?"

"It's not that."

"Look," said David. "She's willing." He turned to the girl. "Say something. Tell him to go away. Tell him to go across the sea and die lonely. Or just close your legs. Open your eyes. Wave your hand. And we'll go."

The girl didn't move.

"Well, boy," said Marty, "there you go. But you don't have to do anything you don't want to do. You always got your chiggers to keep you company."

Angry at the insult, Justin let himself believe that what they were saying was true, that she was willing, that all the girls in America were willing to lie down with them, for they were brave soldiers and better men than the Nazis.

He heard nothing when he'd finished with her. No birds. No wind. No planes overhead. Nothing crawling through the forest grass.

The girl lay motionless. Her eyes were still closed. Marty whispered, "What do we do?"

"What do you mean?" asked Justin.

"I think she'll remember me," said Marty.

"Nah," said David. "Her eyes were closed the whole time."

Marty leaned down and poked her arm. "Hey," he said. "Did you see me?"

"What are you talking about?" said Justin.

"Shut up," said Marty. "You knew."

"You told me she was willing!"

Marty ignored him, looking back at the girl. "Well, if she hasn't seen us yet, she's not gonna." He found the girl's blue dress and tore a strip from the hem. "We'll use this," he said. David held the girl's head and Marty tied the blindfold tight.

They walked away from her, found their base camp, continued with their war games and later with their war. North Africa, Sicily, France. The soil rich with atrocity, greater crimes than three eighteen-year-old soldiers could ever commit. And that was that. They never spoke of it. Marty was shot in the face and knelt down in the grass and waited to die. He covered his eyes and his blood came out between his fingers. And the other soldier, David, was hit in the chest by an 88 shell as he stood by a farmhouse in France, smoking a cigarette. Like the girl, he didn't see what was coming. Like the girl, he said nothing. Like the girl, when it was over he lay very still on his back.

In the fall of '44, Justin's unit moved from farmhouse to farmhouse, evicting the families and turning the bedrooms over to the soldiers. One night he slept in a bed too small for his body and looked at the picture on the night table. A teenage girl. About the same age as the Louisiana girl, with the same mouth and the same chin.

Four minutes. That was all he spent with his pants unfastened in some stinking little forest hopping with squirrels. A quick little crime, easily forgotten. But it wasn't. It buried the bigger battles of hedgerow country with a layer of white sand and a girl trapped on top of that sand, without speech. The blue of her dress and the white of her throat. *Shut up. You knew.* He looked with jealousy upon the faces of his comrades, who smoked Kent cigarettes and were haunted only by the prospect of sudden cowardice in the face of death. He felt separate from them, marked. This war was not black and white. And if good triumphed, then evil was mixed in with the good.

The nightmares began. Always the same nightmare culled from more immediate possibilities, as he slept under the intermittent explosions, his feet wet, his socks wet, shivering and unbathed. She was following him through the woods, with her shortened dress and hair that scattered sand. Her eyes now uncovered. He walked faster. She picked up her steps until she was right behind him. He would wake up shaking and look around. Fog sitting on the hills, the war quiet and getting ready to be loud again. Next to what he had done, the killing of Germans was a pure act, so pure that he never felt sorry for it, for this was what he was ordered to do. This was what all soldiers did, in broad daylight, where the world could see it. Not in some lonely corner of the dark woods.

After the war, he returned to Ohio and became a teller in a bank, the cleanest job he could think of. Something good and precise about quarters stacked together, and the combination of the safe. But his nightmares kept him up and made him tired the next day. He miscounted change and was blunt to the customers. He was fired after six months, and began wandering through the different states, and working a long series of temporary jobs. In postwar America, the soldier was welcome.

But all things soldierly left his hands shaking. He could not stand the melody of taps, or the dignity of the salute. And the sight of a flag in a front yard filled him with an old dread.

Seven years of nightmares, always the same, until finally he had come back to this land, scene of the small and monstrous crime, and had signed on with the chemical company, blasting the great stumps of longleaf pine that were left over from the rape of the land.

At dawn he would trudge wearily out to the chosen place in the forest of stumps, a little more slowly than the others, who talked and laughed with the cheerfulness of men who had outrun the dynamite blast the day before.

After the bulldozer had violently separated the stump child from the earth mother, Justin bore holes in the stump, slid in the dynamite sticks, packed the fuse with sawdust and then shouted the words that sent an electric thrill through the rest of the men.

"Fire in the hole!"

The flame that rode down the wick would die violently in approximately one minute. Range: one hundred to one hundred and fifty yards.

Justin liked the idea of removing all traces of a tree from the world. Remove the trees and the forests will vanish. And the riverbanks of white sand. And what will be left is a flat plain upon which one cannot imagine such a crime taking place.

One day he lit the dynamite and he didn't shout the right words. Instead he shouted, *Forgive me*. But the tone and the strength of his voice were right. The men ran for cover.

After the blast, the foreman looked at Justin in amazement.

"What did you say?"

"Nothing," said Justin.

After that, he could turn toward only one more place of refuge. House of redemption, house of peace. Where the men were happy. Where the girl bathed his feet. Where the noose tightened. Where the rope was cut. Where his knees hit the floor. Where he now shivered on the bed. Where even the clean ammonia scent was made thick and filthy by the sweltering heat. The closed window, the undiluted air. The girl, Louise, who made him imaginative sandwiches which he could not taste.

And still the same dream. The girl in the blue dress, following him, the blindfold lifted from her eyes but her dress still torn. Her feet bare. The dream merciless in its detail. Even the slight wince that fell across the girl's features when she stepped on a briar in her pursuit of him.

When Justin finished his story, he turned his head and saw that Mr. Olen's note-taking shadow had squeezed itself into the room's far corner. It was that late.

Mr. Olen himself sat regarding him thoughtfully. "You shouldn't have cut me down," Justin said. "Isn't this a house where no man is denied peace?"

"Not that way," said Mr. Olen at last.

"And you make the rules about finding peace? Are you God?"

"No."

"Then you should have just let me die."

"But you didn't. So what are you going to do now?"

"I don't know."

Mr. Olen sighed. "I know you want to work here. But I've got to think of the women. You're the wrong man for them."

"Are you thinking of your daughter?"

The tall man stood up purposefully. "I'm not condemning you, Justin. I don't know what's unforgivable or not. Depends on the woman. Depends on the god. You can stay until you feel better. But you can't work here."

Louise had been dusting the same baseboards all morning, running the cloth just up to the edges of the doorway of Room 21, pressing her ear against the door and then starting over. She could hear nothing of the conversation inside.

When her father finally emerged he seemed shaken, which was strange to Louise. Hadn't her father heard all things, and learned of every dirty secret another man could have to offer? He wiped the sweat from his pale face and sighed deeply. Louise glanced at his tablet. It was covered in writing all the way to the margins.

"Why aren't you in school, Louise?"

"I had a headache. What took you so long in there?"

Her father rested his long back against the wall. "It's none of your business."

"Is he going to work here?" She thought of Justin lying in there on his cot, the dark purple hues of his lids, his crossed arms, his sad breathing.

"No."

"Why not?"

He put his pen back in his front pocket. "He can't work here after what he's done. It wouldn't be right."

"You mean because he tried to hang himself?"

"No. Something else."

"But, Daddy, you told me this house is where a man gets forgiven."

"This is complicated. And private."

"What did he do that was so bad? You've let in murderers. What could be worse than that?"

"There are a few things."

"Then tell me, Daddy," she begged. "Tell me his secret before you lock it up in the safe."

"Justin's secret is not your concern. And neither is Justin."

Two hours after the sun went down, a thunderstorm moved in, flooding the air with a uniform sweetness and interrupting the kisses between women and men. The rain pounded on the dry grass, slid through the cracks in the roof of the sweet potato shack, and hit Benjamin's bare back as he moved on top of a redhead who had trained as a nurse in Lafayette.

A bolt of lightning jerked down toward a power line, and The House of Gentle Men went dark, as women took their lips away from their chosen men to sigh at sudden darkness as they had sighed at sudden love.

On the third floor, Justin groaned in his sleep, eyes shut tight. His dream was darker tonight. The woods and the sky and the blue of the girl's torn dress. She was following him again, the same girl who had followed him for seven years, as the Allies had tracked Hitler, as Hitler had tracked the Jews. Her step deliberate, her mouth covered by her hands. Moving through familiar woods.

Justin struggled on his cot until the sheet crept off his throat and moved down his body. He did not hear the door open, or the little boy walk in.

"Go away," he murmured, not to the little boy but to the woman in his dream. A bead of sweat sat between his eyes, trembling as if unsure of which eye to run stinging toward. The boy touched the side of Justin's face, his forehead, his chin, his throat.

When Justin opened his eyes, the room was pitch-black and the little boy was gone. Outside, the storm raged, but something was different. He felt fine. Justin fumbled for the matches and lit the kerosene lamp, which sent out a glow that reached two of the walls. He put one foot on the floor, then the other, standing up slowly and testing his knees. A little bit of peace, finally. A slackening in torment kept taut for seven long years. He reached up, feeling around the sore line in his neck, the legacy of the stretched rope. He felt hungry, and thirsty. Perhaps the girl, Louise, was still awake. He smiled a little. How she would jump to cook him something.

He opened the door and stepped out into the dark hall. He turned and squinted. A bright light was shining directly on his face. He shaded his eyes.

Mr. Olen was walking toward him, carrying a lantern.

When Mr. Olen was within five feet of Justin, he moved slightly to the side, and Justin saw who was behind him.

No longer a girl but a woman. Her dress not blue but yellow. Her black hair washed free of sand. Not in the woods but in the hallway. Seven years after the rape but still with the awkward steps of a girl.

There is no peace.

Justin's knees gave out. He fell unconscious to the floor.

6

The woman, Charlotte Gravin, looked at the stranger sprawled at her feet and clenched her tablet to her chest, rocking back on her heels a little. The thump he had made on the floor still resonated and she imagined the activity in the other rooms coming to an abrupt halt. Kisses freezing. Waltzes breaking off. Sweetness skidding to a stop. The man's eyes were shut, his feet bare. Already cowed by the events of the night and the unfamiliar house, Charlotte was not sure of the proper reaction. Therefore she only rolled her eyes as though men were complicated things who must be stepped over.

"Oh, my," said Mr. Olen.

He set the kerosene lantern on the floor and knelt down next to the prone body. "Just a minute, miss," he said reassuringly. "We'll get you to your man for the night. This one hasn't eaten in days. Don't know why he was up." Mr. Olen took the man's wrist and probed for a pulse.

Charlotte watched the scene from above. How supplicating was that prone body. How harmless. This man seemed to have no will of his own. Watching him, she barely breathed. The orange light of the lantern made the toes of her shoes glow.

Mr. Olen pulled one of the man's eyelids back, then the other. He looked up at Charlotte. "Good thing my daughter keeps these floors crazy-clean," he said. "What with this man's face being right down in it." He hesitated for a moment. "Miss? Can you watch him? I can't bring him around and so I have to get the doctor." And Mr. Olen jumped to his feet and ran down the hall without waiting for an answer.

And now the two of them were alone, on this night of her twenty-third birthday.

She knelt down next to him, listened to his breathing. A very slight moan escaping from his mouth. One elbow bent. One bare foot turned to the wall. A look of absolute torment frozen on his face. She surprised herself by putting a hand to his forehead. His skin was hot, and his sweat slid under the palm of her hand. She moved his hair back. His immobility so eloquent a sadness that she wanted to weep. Hollow-eyed. Red-lipped. Pale-faced. Bruises on his neck. Sweat on his skin and his hair in need of cutting.

Tired of the world. Mute like herself. And such a guilt on his face it reminded her of her own guilt. What she'd done.

She took one of his hands, opened it and spread his

fingers out smooth. She released them and they curled again. It had been so long since she'd touched a man, smelled his salty odor. The closed lids had a bluish tint. Stubble on his cheeks. Below her fingertips it felt like river sand.

After a few moments she heard Mr. Olen urging the old doctor up the stairs, then the doctor's cranky voice:

"Damn it, Leon, stop prodding! I'm seventy-six years old!"

"Hurry! Hurry!"

"Stop pushing me! If he dies before I reach him, then the hell with him." She took one last look at the fainted man and then stood up. Away from the light of the kerosene lamp, back into darkness. The doctor knelt down and opened a capsule of smelling salts under the man's nose. He inhaled and groaned loudly. The doctor and Mr. Olen carried him into his room.

Mr. Olen came back in the hallway, closing the door behind him. "Sorry about that, miss," he said to Charlotte. "That man hasn't eaten in a few days. But I'm sure he'll be fine. Now come with me. Your man is waiting for you at the end of the hall. He's a good, gentle man. You'll like him."

But Charlotte was shaking her head.

"What's wrong?" asked Mr. Olen.

She flipped back a page in her tablet and showed it to him.

BLACK HAIR. HARMLESS.

"Yes," said Mr. Olen, reading the words. "You wrote that when I asked you what you wanted in a man. And the man at the end of the hall meets those requirements."

I DON'T WANT HIM ANYMORE.

Mr. Olen shook his head in confusion. "But why? You haven't even met him."

I WANT THE FAINTED MAN. Charlotte tapped her pad for emphasis.

"No, you don't, miss. I mean, maybe you do, but that man doesn't work here. He's just here getting well. You see how weak he is."

I DON'T CARE.

"Believe me," said Mr. Olen. "That man is not for you."

YOU SAID I COULD HAVE ANY MAN IN THE HOUSE.

"Well, yes. But—"

Charlotte held her fingers up to his lips to silence him. She wrote something else on the tablet and handed it back to him.

SHUT UP.

7

Charlotte had awakened that morning from a dream about Kane and the grape arbor. In this dream Charlotte and Kane held each other, rolling on the fallen muscadines, their kisses breaking the silence with the same rhythm that existed in the buzzing of bees. Take away the kissing, the buzzing and the bursting of muscadines, and no sound would exist from the yard's other actions. A cow lowering its head. A dead ladybug soaking up water in the birdbath. And inside the house, the unraveling of an old woman's memory.

The grape arbor, and what went on under it, had been Charlotte's last great unpunished crime. A myriad of crimes, really: the forbidden kiss to the forbidden boyfriend, in the forbidden pants, while gathering forbidden stains, under the forbidden arbor, in the forbidden yard. And, behind the window that faced the arbor, the old woman with the bad memory and the sharp old eyes.

And yet no stings, no discovery, no swats from a birch stick, nothing. Scot-free. Clean as a whistle.

Charlotte had believed that this was a little gift from the world at large, something free thrown to her because she was young. Little did she know that punishments would follow quickly, within a year.

She now lived by herself in her grandmother's house. The old lady had died four years before after handing a cake to a neighbor, and Charlotte had moved in. A silent woman in a silent house, taking in ironing from the women in town to earn a little money.

As a child, she had often played in the shade of the live oaks out back. And now, returning, she saw herself as this same child, pretended to be her, skipped the recent past and lived in the far past. Her former friends never came over. They were all married now, and were raising children. Charlotte was nothing to them. She was single and mute, and appropriately so, for single women had no voice.

Charlotte threw off her sheets and put on her slippers. She was now twenty-three years old, and so she sat at the edge of the bed, waiting for the magic of her birthday to corral something outside in the world and bring it in to her. Anything. A song. Sunlight. A breeze. A red flower.

She waited but nothing came to her. The day's ordinariness deepened. So why not create her own miracle? Why not speak, after all these years? She opened her mouth. Nothing. No sound, no syllables, just the monotony of breath. And Charlotte realized that speaking was no longer a choice. She had forsaken sound and her punishment was not to find it again. Like other things.

At ten in the morning Milo knocked on her door. His hair was unkempt and he was wearing the same shirt he'd worn the last three times Charlotte had seen him. His pockets were weighed down by cigarettes. His jeans had a tear in the knee and his fingertips were black, as if from soot.

"Close your eyes, Charlotte," said Milo. "Okay, good. Now hold out your hand. Here's your birthday present."

Charlotte's hand clasped around something. She opened her eyes. A lamb. Perfectly symmetrical. Two ears and four legs. Two eyes. Milo had never carved anything this well.

"Know what?" said Milo. "I was going to give you another lamb, with horns. That way I thought it'd be special. But I saw the way Louise looked at it, and I figured, what the hell. A lamb is one critter that deserves to be perfect. So I whittled another one. Took me two days."

Charlotte nodded.

"You like it?" said Milo.

She smiled.

"That's cypress. Good wood. That lamb will last forever."

Milo had glued cotton on the back and sides to designate wool, and she petted the lamb very slowly with her index finger.

"I didn't know what to get you," said Milo, and the words began to spill from him. "You're hard to buy a present for and anyway if you don't like the lamb I can whittle you a calf because I've gotten pretty good at that or a cow although I usually mess up on the udders it's the little details of a creature that make the knife slip oh and you should have seen the mess I made of a blue jay but my next big carving is going to be a snake not a straight snake but a loopy snake which is harder to whittle you know like the snake that bit me on the finger when I was five and do you remember Charlotte how crazy Mama got and how fast that country doctor came . . ."

So many words. And today she resented them, because she had just discovered that words were not hers to make anymore.

Charlotte looked at her brother as he went on and on. She had heard so many rumors about him. That Milo loved the way a fire felt against his face. That he had tried to kill his first wife, not just when he found her in bed with another man, but on three different occasions. That he had once stabbed a dog for licking him on the mouth. That he broke his hands on trees and lost his voice whispering endless apologies. This was not the Milo she knew. She knew only Milo the boy, for just like Charlotte the girl, he had never grown up in her eyes. Here in her grandmother's house with no one to offer a worldly perspective, she could love him and see him as she pleased.

". . . and so I'm glad you like your present but I've got to go 'cause I'm gonna try to find a job today."

Charlotte raised her eyebrows at him, exaggeratedly so she wouldn't have to write on her pad. Milo read her expression. "I know I just got that other job last week. But some SOB was looking for a fight, and I gave it to him."

Charlotte sighed.

"I'll find work, Charlotte," Milo said. "Then your next birthday, I won't have to carve you anything. I'll buy you something from the store. A dress or shoes or anything you want. Okay, Charlotte? Okay?"

After Milo left, Charlotte waited the rest of the morning for other visitors, but everyone had forgotten her birthday, all those women who as girls had fought over who would be the one to throw her a party. Now Charlotte sat reflecting on just how much a voice is connected to the body's corporeal form. No voice, and the body slowly turns to the color of the wallpaper or the sky or the grass. A voice is the part of a person that turns people's heads. Charlotte no longer turned heads.

She roamed around the house and the backyard, feeling her loneliness growing. Everything and nothing needed doing. She stood near the hurricane fence out back and watched the shadow of her waving arms. She wished the shadow would extend into town, darken the tile floor or ivy plant of a childhood friend and make this friend remember her. All the friends were gone now, although Belinda occasionally called to gloat about her perfect husband and her perfect child. Still, Charlotte finally decided, Belinda was better than nothing on this rapidly fading day of her birth. She put on her shirtwaist dress and her saddle oxfords, took the cypress lamb in one hand and her pad and pen in the other, and set off for the long walk to Belinda's house.

She hated herself for giving in to the visit, for Belinda had grown smug. Every sentence she spoke somehow led straight back to that late-summer day of 1941 and her dreamy recitation of how she'd met her soldier of the sky while standing in a green meadow.

Richard Stanley. Tall, blond, and on the level of clouds.

In the summer of 1942, Belinda had taken a vow of silence until her pilot came home, no doubt to compete with Charlotte's disinclination to talk. Belinda became a martyr to the cause of war, wearing black crepe dresses and answering greetings or questions only with a sad smile. Somehow Belinda's silence was seen as holy, and Charlotte's as indulgent. Charlotte was, after all, the only female left in the household, and because she could not seem to attract a man, her duties were to her father and little brother, who needed a woman's touch and the comfort of a woman's voice.

The soldiers training the summer before had long since

gone, and more had taken their place. Like a plague that changes in content but not in form, they marched on, drank on, bathed on, shot each other with blanks, read their secret maps, died occasionally. That was about the time Charlotte began to truly hate Belinda, who was melancholy over her great fortune and hammered down by her perfect love. Belinda moved down the street in her black dress, a finger over her mouth, a mourner with no grief as a badge.

"The poor thing!" The other girls sighed. "She's so worried about her boyfriend. It's a terrible thing, this war." Deep down they detested Belinda too, and thought she was a simpering baby deserving of a hard slap and maybe a kick, but to admit to these feelings was to admit that they did not have great loves of their own to distract them from their hatred.

In 1943, Charlotte started working for the government, putting on her denim overalls and taking a bus to the military base. Charlotte and the others were in charge of keeping the parachutes perfect, for a flaw might translate into a dead soldier, a grieving mother, a war lost by another fraction. The women would spread the parachutes down huge tables, and under the fluorescent lights they would go to work, inch by inch, looking for holes and pulled threads.

Charlotte lost herself in her task, all that white silk, her fingertips running over it so gently. Never speaking a word, for if she spoke she would have told the truth: that she was not patriotic, that she hated the soldiers, that, yes, she did remember them dancing in her house while she played the piano and her father sang and her mother took her deep-woods religion out on the porch, but this memory had been buried by another one. As she worked she kept these words and all others to herself, inspecting the parachutes and at the same time imagining them tearing in flight, sending the soldiers spiraling down into the bleak wilderness, colliding with the ground with such an astonishing impact that their bones broke out of their skin.

Five dollars a day and all the falling, dying soldiers she could count.

In the fall of '44, Charlotte watched with the other women as Belinda's soldier of the sky came home. His first kiss loosened Belinda's tongue, and she was able to tell the surrounding world, with years of pent-up imagery, what their wedding would be like.

They were married in front of three hundred lightly clapping guests, Charlotte in the back, her title of Sole Official Mute reclaimed, but someone else serving as Maid of Honor because Charlotte would simply not do.

"I'm sorry, Charlotte," said Belinda. "But this is my wedding and I want it to be perfect. You can serve the coffee."

Little Ralph was born late the next summer and the love story was now complete. The whole town knew every detail, because to keep that story private would be a waste and a shame. The living room of their house was full of pictures: his blond hair, his European theater, a staged shot of Belinda waving up at his dazzling plane. The far wall of their house was reserved for their wedding photos. Every conceivable pose was represented: Belinda standing by his side, face-to-face, in his lap, behind, in front. Touching him and touching him and touching him, as if to administer fingerprints no other woman could remove.

He was a hero, of course. His most valiant act occurred after German shrapnel tore through his B-17 just as his crew was trying to drop bombs on a munitions factory. An oxygen bottle had burst into flame, and after the navigator had tried to urinate the fire out, Richard Stanley seized the bottle, and as it sizzled in his bare left hand, he found the nearest escape hatch and threw the bottle into the innocence of a passing cloud. For this he was awarded a medal of valor. For this his left hand was difficult to close tightly, ugly to look at and the color of warm punch. For this he had only phantom feelings in his palm when he ruffled his son's fine hair.

A year after he married Belinda, Richard Stanley was elected sheriff of the parish on the strength of his heroism, his fairy-tale marriage, his rich family, his blond hair and the high bones of his cheeks. Rumor had it that he had been shot down, captured by the Germans and held prisoner for a short time in Buchenwald. But Belinda never mentioned this part of his war, for the vision of her man dirty and eating soup from a big pot under armed guard was not nearly as romantic as the vision of the fire carried in his hands like a bouquet and then set free to the world. Although even this story had the ending chopped off: the part where the fire ravaged his hand, making it ugly and certainly less than perfect.

To know Belinda was to hear unending stories of Richard, and now Ralph. And this tendency to go on about her wonderful child and her impossibly brave pilot/ sheriff was almost too much for Charlotte to bear. More than that, she blamed Belinda for what had happened with the three soldiers. Blamed her fiercely.

But on this day, Belinda had to be tolerated, for there was no one else.

Charlotte knocked on the door.

Belinda was wearing a tea dress and a string of pearls. Her once-long hair had been cut short, revealing tiny pearl earrings that reddened the lobes of her ears. "Why, Charlotte," she said, "I knew you'd come by. Happy birthday!"

Charlotte nodded.

"Do come in. Richard's still working. A sheriff's job is never done. But he'll be so sorry he missed you. You know he thinks of you like a kid sister." She giggled. "I know we're the same age, Charlotte, but your silence seems to make you younger. And the way you dress. Sit down."

Charlotte took a seat on a long damask sofa while

Belinda went into the kitchen to make tea. Coming to Belinda's house always seemed to make Charlotte feel the weight of ten extra pounds around her hips, waist and ankles. Perhaps it was the easy give of the damask sofa, or the way Belinda peppered her conversation with sly little insults. Charlotte placed the lamb in her lap and sat with her eyes straight ahead, trying not to look at the pictures around the room. Her stomach still felt tight at the sight of a soldier, even a soldier of the sky dangling high above all women, made safe by the distance of clouds to earth.

The tip of Charlotte's finger moved down the lamb's back.

Belinda came back from the kitchen with the steaming tea and a square of candy.

"Divinity," she told Charlotte, handing her the candy. "It's my grandmother's recipe."

Charlotte bit down into it delicately. The sugar flooded her mouth, stirring up taste buds starving for the cool flow of words. She took the china cup and tipped it to her mouth, blowing on it severely before sucking at it.

Belinda frowned a little. "So how has your birthday been, Charlotte?" she asked.

Charlotte handed her the lamb that Milo had carved for her. Belinda set it in her palm to inspect it. "Isn't that cute? Is this from Milo?"

Charlotte nodded.

"He's done a good job. Are you sure he did it himself?"

Charlotte nodded again.

"Why the choice of the lamb?"

Charlotte shrugged.

"Well . . ." Belinda laughed gaily and handed back the lamb. "I admire his restraint. He must have been tempted to set it on fire. Of course, cypress fires smell so ugly."

Charlotte picked up her pen, hesitated, and then set it down again. Coming here had been a mistake, she decided, no matter how lonely she'd been or how in need of attention.

"What else did you get for your birthday?" asked Belinda.

NOTHING.

Belinda laughed again. "Oh, Charlotte. Even mute, you're such a card. Wait a minute. You're not serious, are you?"

Ralph came stomping into the room in his yellow sunsuit and ankle boots. Belinda seized him and pulled him into her lap.

"Look at his ankle boots, Charlotte. They're the kind the soldiers wear. Isn't that cute? I had them made especially. Ralph is my little soldier, aren't you, Ralph?"

Ralph reached for Charlotte's divinity.

"No, son, that's not for you. Run and play."

Charlotte couldn't help herself. She turned and watched the boy run out, a sudden ache in her heart. An unbearable guilt and longing.

When Ralph had gone out into the front yard, Belinda beamed at Charlotte. "I didn't forget your birthday. I never have all these years, have I? Even after the rest of the girls stopped giving you presents. But you're hard to shop for. Most women your age are married, so I could always give them a piece of china, or some linens, or a tea cart . . . anyway, this year I'm giving you two presents. One is nice, to be sure. But the other is very special."

Belinda disappeared into the back bedroom as Charlotte continued to drink her tea. Finally she returned with a gaily wrapped package and an envelope.

"Open this one first," she said, throwing the package in Charlotte's lap.

Charlotte immediately knew what it was. Belinda's specialty was making tiny pillows out of true lavender. A married woman's idle task. She had made so many pillows that they filled up the hall closet, and their odor reached all the way outside into the little herb garden she paid to have tended. Every one of Belinda's friends eventually received a pillow, to stink up her own house and make her own husband complain.

Charlotte unwrapped the pillow carefully and gave an insincere little gasp when it came into view. She smiled and wrote on her pad:

THANK YOU. I DIDN'T HAVE ONE.

"Of course you didn't," Belinda said sweetly. She handed the envelope to Charlotte. "Now, consider this with an open mind."

Something about the way Belinda's eyebrows arched felt like a warning, and yet Charlotte had no choice but to open the envelope. Inside she found four crisp dollar bills. She held them up to the light as though they might be something else than money. She looked at her friend questioningly. Surely Belinda did not think she was so poor as to need . . .

"That's what I hear is a traditional tip," said Belinda.

WHAT TIP? WHERE?

She giggled. "You know, Charlotte. At that house."

Charlotte shrugged her shoulders and arched her eyebrows, feigning confusion.

"Come on, Charlotte. I know it's not a subject that polite women are supposed to talk about, but no one can hear us. So don't play dumb. Your brother is friends with the girl who lives over there."

Charlotte stared at her, stunned. She felt tears coming, and fought them ruthlessly.

"Don't get mad. It's just that I thought you deserved some attention from a man on your birthday. And not that I would know, but those men are supposed to be very gentle. Full of nice kisses. Like the one you had under the grape arbor . . . was it eight years ago?"

Charlotte's pen bore down into her pad so that the words emerged as deep creases on the page.

I DON'T NEED TO PAY A MAN!

"Well, you still have a pretty face, but you are twenty-three years old. Which is still young, but not as young as—"

Charlotte began to write frantically as Belinda leaned forward to read the new words. **DROP DEAD YOU—**.

"Charlotte!"

Charlotte struggled off the couch with a mighty effort, for her body felt so big and clumsy that she could barely push herself up, and yet she did, the tea spilling down her leg and the divinity hitting the floor with a tiny thud. A tear escaped one eye, and Charlotte wiped it quickly as she stormed to the front door, past the rosewood side table, past the cabinet of Blue Willow china, past the porcelain bowl full of apples, past the pictures in their gilded frames, past the basket of dried oleander.

"Wait!" Belinda cried as Charlotte rushed into the street. "Don't tell anyone about my gift to you! I don't want anyone to get the wrong idea . . ."

Charlotte did not reply. She was carrying the tablet, the lamb, the cursed pillow and the envelope of dollar bills, and she didn't want to drop anything and slow down her progress. Down the road she marched, her saddle oxfords thudding along, until Belinda's protests disappeared behind her. Her dress felt heavy, her underarms wet. She took great lungfuls of sweet September air and then exhaled it with no relief.

Wicked Belinda and her wicked ways. What made Charlotte angriest was the thought that somehow Belinda had seen right through her—through to the fascination she had for that mysterious house. Through to her starvation for love. The gentle kind of love in whose power she had believed, until the day of the meadow. And had Belinda somehow seen what had happened with the soldiers? Did she know about that too? And were any of Charlotte's secrets safe from her?

Halfway home, after the street had turned into a path and the bushes of trimmed ligustrum had turned into wild woods, Charlotte stopped to consider her possessions. She tucked her writing tablet under her arm and threw the lavender pillow into a clump of brush, hoping that birds would peck at it and rabbits would sniff it and then leave their droppings in the creases. She put the lamb in one of the big pockets of her dress, then threw the envelope down on the ground. She stared down at it, a merciless pain in her chest suddenly causing another tear to swell and drop noisily onto the envelope. *I do not need to pay a man. I can have any man I want. If I wanted one.* She stomped on the envelope and moved on. She had walked only a few paces before she turned around and came back to it again.

She picked it up. Threw it down, picked it up. Threw it down, picked it up. She couldn't quite seem to leave it there. For on the shallow side of Charlotte's anger there remained a hunger and a thirst.

The House of Gentle Men.

Would they lie quietly on the bed? Would their kisses

be sweet grape-arbor kisses, secretive and yet pure and unforced?

Belinda's thoughtless gesture had a hidden boon. The money belonged to Charlotte, free and clear, to throw down on the street, to give to charity, to buy a kiss or two. Perhaps any love coming to her now would have to be paid for, and here were the first four dollars.

Charlotte stepped from the path, ducked behind an old hickory tree and cried. Crouching in the woods, feeling the heaviness in her stomach and hips. A formless woman shaking.

That night a great storm took out the lights throughout most of the parish. Charlotte stood before the window in the darkness, watching the rain. This, perhaps, was her sign. The lights were all out and no one was the wiser. When the rain slackened, Charlotte took up her pad and her envelope and slipped out the front door. She wore a yellow dress whose collar was out of fashion, but the dress was still pretty and Belinda had told her once: "Men only know what looks good. They don't care whether it's in style or not."

Charlotte's hair and dress were damp from the trickling rain when she arrived at The House of Gentle Men. She waited on the railway bench in the foyer, in near-perfect darkness brought on by the loss of electricity. A single kerosene lamp glowed from a little round table, so close to the hallway that only the hands of the nervous women around her were visible. Fingers played with fingers. Nails gently stabbed at palms.

After the tall man, Mr. Olen, had materialized in the gloom and led her into the office, she sat down in the channel-back chair and looked around. So much clutter. And pictures turned to the wall.

"How are you this evening?" asked Mr. Olen.

Charlotte shrugged and leaned forward to slide the envelope across his desk.

"What's this?" he asked as he opened it. "No, no. You don't give me any money. Whatever tip you leave is optional. You leave it in the syrup can on the way out, if you wish."

Charlotte felt silly. She wanted to say: *How was I supposed to know? The rules of this house aren't handed down from mother to daughter, to say the least.* But she wouldn't and in fact couldn't speak, and so she simply averted her eyes.

"Now," said Mr. Olen. "What kind of man are you looking for? You get two characteristics. You know, like hair color, body type, personality. Just about anything you can think of."

Charlotte scribbled something down and handed him her pad.

BLACK HAIR. HARMLESS.

After he read the words he looked at her for a moment. "Can't you speak?" he asked gently.

She shook her head.

"That's all right," he said. "The men here are very understanding. I think we can accommodate you. There's a man on the third floor who has black hair and is exceptionally gentle. His name is Matthew. That's a nice name, isn't it?"

Charlotte nodded.

"Do you have any questions?"

WHAT WILL THE MAN DO?

"Anything you want. Except intercourse. You see, the act of intercourse is violent by nature. Foreplay and afterplay are like pruning roses. Whereas intercourse is like blasting stumps out of the ground. Don't you think?"

WHAT IF I JUST WANT— Charlotte's hand hesitated.

"Want what?"

—A KISS?

"That's fine. Any other questions?"

Charlotte shook her head.

"The man I've chosen for you is very nice, very popular. His name is Matthew."

The word "Matthew" sounded nice to Charlotte, not as beautiful as "Kane" but a softer word, more gentle around the corners, sweeter in the vowels. Even as she followed Mr. Olen's lantern up the stairs, she imagined the longed-for kiss. And what a perfect night for it, with the thunder once more crashing outside and rain against the windowpanes.

But then events spilled on themselves, tripping in the dark. Jumbling up together. The pale man fainting. His whiskers under her fingers. The doctor breaking open the smelling salts.

Charlotte suddenly knew that this was the man she wanted. His silence mirrored hers, and his sudden swoon had removed any possible threat he might have carried deep within him. For what could make a man safer than the state of unconsciousness? The body still, the hands open, the legs quiet, the sex organ passive. In such a state a man was only a curve of the body away from being a woman.

Charlotte wrote on her tablet:

I WANT THE FAINTED MAN.

8

Louise had lain awake all night listening to the rain-
storm and thinking about the soldier. Now she
scrubbed the front and back porches of the mud that had
been tracked in by hurt women, and then out by women
newly liberated. Louise put muscle into the scrub, erasing
footprints and then the memory of those footprints. Real
specks and then the imaginary specks beneath them. Her
knees began to hurt from kneeling, and the small of her
back ached. She paused to dip the brush into the bucket,
dropping off dirt and picking up suds, wishing love to be
like the smooth surface of a porch, shining in plain sight
after the work is done. And wouldn't it be nice if the perils
of love could be frothed away, leaving only a sweet scent?

Daniel came around the side of the house and approached Louise with his fist held out, indicating a desire
to thumb-wrestle. She had seen him beat Willy once, his
tiny thumb up against Willy's huge one. David and
Goliath.

"You let him win," she'd accused Willy.

Willy had shaken his head. "No, I didn't. Believe me, that boy's thumb will trap you like a woman."

Now Louise pushed Daniel away very gently. "No, honey. Your hands are dirty. And I bet you've been playing with that filthy bullfrog."

"Please."

"Well . . . all right. Come here." She took a rag from the bucket and washed his hands and his arms until only the dirt on his elbows remained. "Let's wrestle," she said, and the battle began, their two sterile thumbs jockeying for position.

Her father came in from the garden, where he'd been brooding all morning long. Louise looked up at him and lost her concentration.

"Got you!" Daniel crowed.

"Guess you did, honey. Now go play." She watched him disappear around the side of the house and then peered at her father. "How is Justin?"

"He was asleep the last time I checked."

"I'll bring him up some soup later."

"You do that. But don't stay and visit."

He walked into the house, leaving footprints of clear water. He went to his office, sat down at the desk, cut a chaw of tobacco, chewed thoughtfully. That mute woman had made him sad. Perhaps because the silence that had emanated from her had been so angry and yet so full of need. He had felt and experienced this silence before.

Long ago, from his own wife, a curly-headed woman whose head had barely reached the crook of his arm. He hadn't realized how much his arm had grown used to that curly head nudging his elbow until the day she'd vanished with the man next door.

He hadn't hit her, ever, or raised his voice, but had simply been neglectful. Smart when it came to books, stupid when it came to a woman's hunger for the caress, he had assumed that his wife just needed a little attention in bed every now and then, a few kisses and some activity between the legs. How wrong he'd been, and when he'd finally decided to understand the woman, she was gone and he was left not only with a headstrong boy but with a girl who hated germs and who found men to be clumsy and thick in the head.

For months Mr. Olen had begged his wife to come home. Finally, having tried every other tactic, he wrote her a letter saying that in the hope of winning her forgiveness he was moving to Louisiana. There he would work in the service of ignored and taken-for-granted women like herself. He concluded the letter by pledging his undying love and begging her to come to Lousiana and witness his penance. As a postscript, he added that his brother would know where to reach him. Pleased with the mystery and the passion of the message, he left it in her new mailbox, packed up the children and drove.

And that was how it had all begun. He had never since been with another woman, and as an extension of his faithfulness, forbade every man in the house to have a woman either, convinced that this crowded celibacy would carry even further the force of his devotions. And yet no word from her, not in eight years.

And now this mute woman had come to the house and reminded him of his wife—deadly silent, the energy of anger unexpressed and yet swelling toward expression.

The notes Charlotte had written had also upset him. They seemed stark and sad. Words without sound, rough at the edges, yet pleading for a harmless man. Harmless. What a strange word to use. Equally strange was her desire for Justin. Mr. Olen had tried to reason with her. But no. SHUT UP. A message both weary and defiant, meant for him and for the world and maybe for the thunderstorm.

And so Matthew in Room 17 had gone without a woman that night, for Charlotte had disappeared into the heavy rain and the howling thunder, but not before writing one more message on her pad for Mr. Olen: I WILL COME BACK FOR THE FAINTED MAN TOMORROW.

Mr. Olen was worried over the health of Justin, and yet he desperately wanted to please this woman who so reminded him of his displeased wife. She had fled Mr. Olen's house, as his wife had before, but the difference was that this woman had promised to return. He sat chewing and thinking. Finally he decided that Justin owed this to him. Who knew why Charlotte wanted him, but how much energy could it take out of a man to bestow a little kindness and a few light kisses? Maybe it would do Justin good.

He spat out his tobacco, rinsed his mouth in the bathroom and slowly ascended the stairs.

The soldier was awake, under the covers, staring at the ceiling. Mr. Olen took a seat on a bentwood chair, one of whose legs was shorter than the others. The chair tipped. Mr. Olen adjusted his weight. "You sleep well?"

"No."

"How are you feeling?"

"Better. In fact, I wanted to tell you that I'm leaving this afternoon."

"You sure you're up to it? You were passed out cold for ten minutes."

"I know."

"The doctor said you should rest."

"The doctor tried to inject me with oil of peppermint yesterday."

"Well, he's old." Mr. Olen moved the chair a little closer. "The strangest thing happened last night . . ."

Justin did not ask what. He simply folded his arms and looked down at the small hills his knees made under the bedding. Mr. Olen watched him for a moment. From the very first time he'd talked to him, he'd seen himself in this man. In his haunted face and in the eyes, sad and faded from the strength of the torturing demon, which was really a woman-shaped memory that could not be beaten or blown into any other shape.

"I'll tell you what happened, since you're so curious," Mr. Olen continued. He had meant his words to come out jokey, and was surprised to find them slightly bitter. "You know that woman you fainted in front of? She was on her way to see Matthew down the hall. But when she saw you she told me that she wanted you."

The effect of these words on Justin was electrifying.

He flew out of bed, upsetting the kerosene lamp and sending it crashing to the floor, causing the chair to give under Mr. Olen as, startled, he rocked back too far and fell over backward.

Justin began throwing his clothes into his wicker suitcase.

Mr. Olen slowly picked himself up off the floor, rubbing his back.

"Justin?"

"What?"

"Calm down."

He kept packing. "Why did she say that? Why?"

"She didn't exactly say it. She can't speak."

"Can't speak?"

"She wrote it on a pad. And I was just thinking, you know, if you stayed one more night, maybe you could service her and then—"

He slammed the suitcase shut and began to pace back and forth.

"Watch the glass," said Mr. Olen, looking at Justin's bare feet.

"I don't care about the glass! And I'm not ever going to see her again. I'm leaving." He whirled around to face him. "And why are you even asking me! You said I'm unsuited to work here. And that's what I am. Unsuited."

"Sit down, Justin. Sit down on the cot. Please. All right. I know that's what I said at first, but perhaps I was being a little judgmental. In my head, I was putting my old sins up against yours, and I have to admit that yours made mine feel pretty good. But it's not right to compare."

"No," Justin said bitterly. "Go ahead and compare, if it makes you feel better than me."

"That's just what I'm trying to say! No man is better than another man. We all sin. And you know, I was a lot like you, before I came to this house and fired up this doctrine. I couldn't forgive myself. But I'm finding peace, slowly but surely. Every time a man kisses a woman in here, I can feel it. And each time, I come a little closer to healing, myself. And after that woman said she wanted you last night, I thought, Why not? This could be your chance for peace, too. Because I see the look in your eye, Justin. I know you can't wait to get your hands on another rope."

Justin did not reply but lay back suddenly, his head against the pillow.

"So," Mr. Olen continued. "Why don't you give this woman a try tonight? You'll show yourself that you can be gentle and loving. She needs soothing, I can tell. Someone's hurt her and you can fix her up again. Then you can leave, and maybe stay alive."

Justin stared up at the ceiling. Mr. Olen watched him, rocking back on his heels a little, feeling a shard of broken glass crackle under his shoe. Outside the window he caught a glimpse of a card game, a little sunlight. Brown leaves on the ground, birds moving through the tallow trees.

"Add this to your file," Justin said. "She was the one."

"The one?"

"The one we hurt back then."

"Are you sure?"

"I'm absolutely positive."

"That's why you fainted?"

"Wouldn't you?"

"Guess I would. And she didn't recognize you?"

"Read your notes again. Her eyes were closed, and then we blindfolded her."

Mr. Olen could hear his own breathing and the wonder in it. "You have to see her tonight," he said at last. "It's fate that she saw you. That's why all the lights went out. So the miracle could shine."

"It's not a miracle. It's my punishment. She's coming back to haunt me."

"That girl's been hurt. She needs someone. And you are exactly who she needs."

"I'm not going to kiss her. Or touch her. Ever again."

"Fine. I won't stop you. But she's coming back tonight. You leave before she gets here, and you're a coward."

"Then I'll be a coward."

"All right. But remember one thing." Mr. Olen leaned down to him. "You owe her this."

9

Charlotte sat before the mirror, brushing her hair. She had washed it carefully and while it was still wet she had rolled it in wire curlers, then opened the propane refrigerator and taken out a can of beer Milo had brought over one night and then forgotten to drink. Milo didn't need beer, anyway. It only made his fearsome temper worse, a temper directed at man, boy and tree but held in check for women—with the possible exception of his ex-wife, whom he'd tried to murder for all the accepted reasons.

Charlotte had put her head down in the sink and poured the beer over her hair. The smell of it—secretive and earthy—brought back memories of long ago, when beer had been used as a setting lotion in secret, for Charlotte's mother hadn't approved of beer touching her daughter—her lips or her scalp. In those days, primping was something that could lead to only good things. Marriage and children and more kisses, of course.

Now night had fallen again, and Charlotte stood up and inspected herself. Since the man had fainted right away, he probably hadn't noticed her dress, and therefore she could safely wear it once again. She turned around slowly, looking in the mirror. Then she drew out the tube of red lipstick she'd bought that day at the store and colored in her lips. All day long she had pretended that this was a real date with a real man, and the four dollars was nothing more than a prop for a perfect evening. She tucked the money in the pocket of her dress and walked out the front door.

Back at The House of Gentle Men, women had already begun to choose their courtly mates for the night, and the house was beginning to rock with gentleness, as room by room, kisses were asked for and received.

An old woman, who sold muscadine jelly out of her house and stored the jars in her dead son's room, now sat on the edge of a cot in Room 13.

The young man facing her said, "Do you want me to take off my shirt, ma'am?"

"No," said the old woman.

"Would you like me to put my arms around you?"

"Oh, yes. Please do that."

"Like this?"

"Yes, that's good."

"And would you like me to kiss you?"

"Yes. But right here." The old woman pointed to her

brow. "And say to me: 'Mama, it's your son. I'm back from the war.'"

Despite the fact that electricity had been restored, the men were lighting candles so as to cast a soft light on the lonely, not-yet-soothed faces of women who had managed to escape their families, children, dogs, cats, sewing, washing, ironing, spinsterhood or dead husbands' ghosts. Mr. Olen disapproved of the candles for reasons of safety, but had no way of knowing that the rooms were flickering with contraband flame.

Here and there, a little Glenn Miller music came on. Softly, so as not to disturb the people in the other rooms. Women sighed. Feet brushed the floors. Bodies swayed. Whispers moved into ears and displaced their motionless ether. Outside the house, the wind blew the camphor tree back and forth, and a band of mosquitoes arced away from the scent that drifted from the green leaves. The night was good for love, in the same way that some nights are good for fishing. The moon pulls at a certain angle, the air turns a certain flavor, the breeze releases a certain amount of sugar and salt. And men and women respond to the changes, and their angel souls rock inside their animal bodies like catboats in a furious sea.

A kerosene lamp went on in the sweet potato barn, and the light seeped out through the cracks in the boards. Inside the barn, Benjamin stood up and took his shirt off while a married mother of five remained on her knees.

"You have a nice chest," the woman said.

"That's what they all say," said Benjamin. He looked down at her. Twelve women in a month had made him weary. He was tired of women, for they were always sad underneath. They seemed to want from him things that he hadn't grown into, and this need made him cranky. He wanted to be a boy, and the women to be girls again. He wanted the sex to be easy and then break off forever. He wanted to climb a tree and have someone to climb with. He was tired of playing with Daniel and was lonely for the rougher sports of boys his own age. They didn't like him because of the rumors that swirled around his father's house, and because their girlfriends wanted only him.

"My husband doesn't care about me anymore," said the woman. Her head slanted to the floor and this gesture moved her curls. "After five children, a man looks at you like you're a farm animal."

"Why are you saying this to me?" asked Benjamin.

She unbuttoned her blouse. "I don't know."

Mr. Olen found Justin sitting on his bed, his face shaved, his hair cut and neatly combed, wearing a white shirt that Mr. Olen had seen on another man the day before.

"You borrow that shirt?" Mr. Olen asked.

Justin nodded.

"Who cut your hair?"

"Your daughter. This afternoon. She shaved me too. She didn't trust me with the straight razor."

"Smart girl. So you're not leaving tonight?"

"No," Justin said after a moment. "I'm not leaving. I'm going to service that woman."

"What made you change your mind?"

"I don't know. Maybe I decided that I do owe her this, no matter what it does to me."

"That's a good way to think of it."

"What do I do? How do I act?"

"Like a gentleman."

"And how do gentlemen act?"

"They wait for a stimulus and then they give a slow, careful response."

"Such as?"

"The woman holds out her hand. What do you do?"

"I don't know. Kiss it?"

"There's more to it than that. Take her hand gently by the fingers, bend down and kiss the hand just behind the knuckles, where there's more sensation. And say, 'You have the softest skin,' whether she does or doesn't."

"All right. What else?"

"Just do whatever she tells you. And don't make sudden moves."

"Sudden moves?"

"Well, I mean . . . don't grab her or anything like that."

"Like I did in the woods?"

"I didn't say that."

"Well, that's what you were thinking."

"Don't be defensive, Justin. It hardens the kiss." Mr. Olen reached for the doorknob.

"Mr. Olen? What's the woman's name?"

"You're not supposed to know unless she chooses to tell you."

"Please. This is no ordinary night."

Mr. Olen opened the door. Just before he stepped through the doorway, he turned around. "Charlotte," he said.

"Oh. I wondered about that all these years. For some reason, she looked like a Mary to me. I guess because in the Bible, Mary's so patient. And she looked so patient . . . on that day . . ."

Mr. Olen folded his arms. "Your eyes are turning red. Now's not the time to cry. She's due any minute now, and crying's going to ruin her night with you . . . you hear me, son? Be a man. Stop it."

Justin wiped his eyes.

"Button your top collar," Mr. Olen said. "Women trust men more who do that. They must think it makes them more civilized. I'm proud of you, Justin."

On the way downstairs, Mr. Olen ran into Louise, who was coming upstairs carrying a glass of orange juice.

"Where you going with that?"

"To Justin's room. Did you see how much better he feels? He let me shave him today, and cut his hair." Louise started to move past her father. He gently took her arm to stop her.

"Don't go up there, Louise."

"Why?"

"Justin's getting ready for someone."

"Who?"

Mr. Olen hesitated. "A woman."

Her hand jerked. Orange juice splattered on the stairs.

"What do you mean, Daddy? You said Justin couldn't work here."

"I changed my mind."

"Why?"

"A woman asked for him."

"What woman?"

"It's none of your business."

"This isn't fair! I'm the one that nursed him back to health. I don't want him to have a woman!"

"Well, he's going to."

"All right, then," said Louise. "If he can have a woman, then I'm going to choose him tomorrow night myself. I've got four dollars."

Mr. Olen's fingers tightened on his daughter's arm. "Don't you ever say that again," he hissed. "When the time is right, you can pick someone in the house, but you are never going to touch that man."

"Why not?"

"Because I said so."

"You're hurting my arm and that's not gentle." Mr.

Olen let go and Louise rushed downstairs with tears coming to her eyes. Justin servicing a woman. No, it could not be. And what if he liked touching her and dancing with her and breathing in her ear? Then he would be gone, just like her own mother was after she found someone she liked better than her father. Louise went to the kitchen, ran the water into a bucket and added a new cleaner she'd found at the dry-goods store earlier that day. Rich brown liquid hit the water and turned to healing suds. She found a brush and marched out into the backyard to Benjamin's sweet potato barn, and began to scrub it by the light of the spotless moon.

The sudsy water ran into the cracks. Inside the barn, the woman under Benjamin blinked. "What's that sound?" she asked.

"What?" said Benjamin. A drop of foam came through the cracks and fell on his bare back, sliding down to the crease of his buttocks. He rolled off the woman, wrapped his Indian blanket around himself and went outside.

Of course. His sister Louise, madwoman by night and by day.

"What the hell are you doing?" he asked Louise.

She did not stop her scrubbing. "I've been meaning to wash your barn," she told Benjamin. "It's a sight. It bothers me."

"Well, stop it! I'm busy in there."

Louise dipped her brush in the water. "Making more

germs, I'm sure," she said. "You make me sick, Benjamin."

"No, you make me sick! And you are sick!" Benjamin turned around and walked toward the porch.

"Ben, where are you going?"

"To piss on the porch."

"No! Ben, wait!"

He whirled around, shielding his eyes from a particularly vicious slant of moonlight.

"All right," said Louise. "I'm sorry. I'll stop cleaning your barn."

"Thank you. And go away."

He started to walk past her.

"Benjamin?"

The tone in her voice stopped him.

"What?"

"You know that soldier that hanged himself?"

"Uh-huh."

"Daddy's letting him have a woman tonight."

"So?"

"I can't stand it, Ben. I love him."

He peered into her face. "Are you crying?"

"No. Tell me what to do about him."

Benjamin's Indian blanket had slipped down his chest, and the moonlight tore at the faint patch of lipstick just below his collarbone. "Don't tell him you love him."

"Why not?"

"That always just makes me want to slap a woman."

"He's not you."

Benjamin laughed grimly. "All men are me, Louise."

Charlotte walked through the wet woods, her sandals collecting mud and mulchy odors on their soles. The path was wide—once used by cows and then by hunters—and the moon so full that the shadows of startled birds tripped up Charlotte's feet. She wasn't afraid. Her worst fears had already come true.

She walked on, kicking at the bed of pine straw that lined the path and noticing the black-eyed Susans and the way that their yellow color was soured by the moonlight. Something caught Charlotte's eye. A piece of torn cloth, hanging from a branch. Charlotte stopped and freed it. Gingham, perhaps. Somewhere a mother was scolding a girl, pointing down at where her dress was torn. Or maybe a hunter had simply left a message for another hunter. Or a friend was signaling a friend, or a brother a sister.

Charlotte smiled. For a week after her mother's death, this was how she would find Milo when he would run into the woods as far as he could, and then hide in some foxhole that the soldiers had dug and forgotten to refill. Milo had craved the hiding and the discovery, being lost and being found. To make sure his sister would know where to look, he would leave clues. Stones torn out of the ground and set with their dirty side to the sun. Branches broken. Marbles scattered. String around the trunks of trees. Tiny *x*'s carved in the bark with a bone-handled pocketknife. And torn cloth tied around low branches.

Milo would crouch down in the foxhole with his head covered, waiting for her, and it became clear to Charlotte that Milo wanted to be found only by his sister, for she was the size and shape of a mother lost, but gentler and more forgiving. And so for seven straight days Charlotte found Milo seven times, until some of his guilt let him go and some of his new manhood dissolved back into boyhood again.

In a watering hole on the far side of town, Milo drank his whiskey in two gulps. He looked at the bartender and pointed to the sticky bottom of his glass.

"Another?" asked the bartender. Milo nodded. The whiskey had made him hungry for company and he had words to share, plenty of words for everyone in the bar and for the people milling outside and for the people sleeping at home. And yet no one wanted his company, for ever since his mother and the air base had burned, rumors of fire had followed him everywhere. But here next to him was a man he'd never seen before, one who had been listening to him with seeming interest and good humor. Encouraged, Milo continued his story.

"So," Milo said, "I thought I loved this woman and I thought she loved me too because she said she loved me and she had a way of saying everything in a way that made you believe it and she had a mole on her face just like my sister 'cept my sister's got one above her eyebrow and this woman had one above her lip and anyway me and this woman had been married only a couple months and God I was so in love with her and then I come home one day she's in bed with a damn Redbone and I just went crazy everything just spun around in my head and I grabbed my shotgun and shoved it in her belly and pulled the trigger but nothing happened I'm telling you the damned thing didn't go off so I tried one more time to pull the trigger and still nothing so help me God."

The other man leaned away from Milo's whiskey breath and shot a look at his friend, who stood on the other side of Milo. The friend rolled his eyes. Milo didn't notice.

"So I ran outside and threw the shotgun against my work truck and it went off and blew the bird feeder to kingdom come and I just stood there with suet raining down on me and you know that was God saving me from being a murderer and from going to prison so my question is how come He saved me from being a murderer but He didn't save her from being a whore? You know I've been trying to figure out that one for a long damned time."

"You know what I think?" the man said slowly.

Milo drained the whiskey glass and set it on the table with a hard clink. "What?"

"I think you should have set your woman on fire. Like you did the air base. And your mama."

The man and his friend walked out of the bar. Milo

stood watching them, his mouth hanging open. He looked around. The other men were snickering and elbowing each other. Milo walked outside and caught up with the man who'd insulted him.

"Hey!" said Milo.

The man turned around and Milo punched him in the mouth, knocking out two of his teeth. And the cracking teeth felt good like the bark of trees and Milo hit him again and again as his face turned hot like an overfed furnace and Milo hit the man again to work off the heat and the man bent double and sank to his knees and a crowd gathered as Milo kicked him first in the stomach and then in the face and his boot rose up and the man's nose made the sound a pecan makes when the handle of a dull knife hits it and now blood splashed on Milo's hands as he jumped on the man and pinned him down with his knees while taking out his pocketknife and jerking his wrist to snap out the blade.

"I'll kill you," Milo said. "I'll kill you on purpose, you son of a bitch."

Charlotte arrived at The House of Gentle Men, entered the foyer and took a seat on a railway bench. In the darkness she could make out the forms of two other women, but she did not squint and try to catch sight of their faces. The house seemed alive tonight, trembling, and Charlotte imagined the rooms above her head and the bodies in them. The kissing and the sighing. Fearless women with peaceful men. Heaven on earth. She cradled her pad in her lap.

Mr. Olen came into the foyer and touched her arm.

"Come back to my office," he said softly.

Once they were inside, he closed the door behind him. He remained standing when he spoke to her, so that she had to look up to see his gaunt face and his solemn expression. "Miss," he said, "I'm glad you came back. I'm sorry we couldn't accommodate you last night, but tonight we have the man that you've chosen. The one that fainted."

Charlotte nodded.

"Is that still what you wish?"

She nodded again.

"Are you going to be all right?"

DO YOU ASK THE OTHER WOMEN THIS?

Mr. Olen smiled a little. So her fighting spirit had not been extinguished by what had happened to her that day at the riverbank. She was writing again. When she finished she held up the tablet and looked away.

DO I LOOK RIGHT?

"There's no right way to look," said Mr. Olen, but when she threw him an impatient glance he added hastily, "I mean, you look pretty. Very pretty." He led her up the stairs to the third floor.

At first, Justin did not answer the knocks. Then the door slowly opened. He kept his eyes down.

"This is the woman who chose you," Mr. Olen told Justin. "And now I will leave you."

Justin moved back so Charlotte could enter the room, then closed the door behind her. After a few moments he found the courage to look at her face, into her eyes. Green. A color once concealed from him by a strip of cloth torn from a dress. Now the eyes talked and the mouth sulked. And that mole just above her brow confirmed everything, made sure there was no mistake and no excuses. She seemed acutely uncomfortable to be in the room, and kept running her hand down her hip as if disappointed to find that her body had grown that particular curve.

"Hello," Justin whispered, and although he knew, he added: "What's your name?"

CHARLOTTE. When she finished writing she pointed to him inquisitively.

"Justin," he said. He kept his hands down, his voice low. He wanted to soothe her with this simple talk, to beg her forgiveness, to explain what happened to her, to admit he had no explanation. Sorry and sorry and sorry. He ached to touch her, to feel the edges of the wound her silence made.

She pointed to his neck and raised her eyebrows. He touched the bruises on his throat, where the hanging rope had tightened.

"I got in a fight in a bar," he said. "Someone choked me."

She frowned and scribbled.

BUT YOU ARE SUPPOSED TO BE GENTLE.

"I am!" he said quickly, realizing the folly of his own lie. "The fight wasn't my fault. I was attacked."

She seemed placated, and wrote: **YOU DO WHAT I SAY?**

"Yes."

She put her hands to her throat and made motions as if unbuttoning a shirt. Then she made two fists and spread them wide as if taking the shirt off.

"You want to take your shirt off?" Justin asked.

She pointed at him.

"You want me to take my shirt off?"

She nodded and he hesitated for a moment before he reached for his collar. Wasn't he supposed to kiss her hand? He started to unbutton his shirt and she stopped him.

"What is it?" he asked.

She studied him, biting her lip. Then she wrote some words down very carefully, in letters smaller than she'd used before.

WERE YOU A SOLDIER IN THE WAR?

Justin felt his heart speed up. "Yes," he said.

She looked terribly disappointed and backed away from him a little.

"Why do you ask?"

She looked at the floor.

"You don't like soldiers?"

She shook her head.

"Why not?"

THEY ARE NOT GENTLEMEN.

The bare scent of the smoke from the kerosene lamp was making Justin feel sick to his stomach. And the room was beginning to spin. He did not know how much longer he could stand in this room and play this game. But he remembered Mr. Olen's words: *You owe her this.*

"I know," said Justin at last, "that war creates monsters."

Charlotte wrote furiously.

YOU DON'T KNOW WHAT I KNOW.

"Do you want me to kiss your hand?" asked Justin desperately. "I'm told a lot of women like that, and I . . . could do that for you."

Charlotte stared at him for a long moment. Then she motioned for him to sit down on the bed.

He obeyed her. She stood before him for a few minutes, saying nothing. Then she placed her pad carefully on the night table, returned to him and put her hand cautiously on his shoulder.

I told myself you were willing, Charlotte. I lied to myself and made you part of the lie. It was hot and I was afraid and there was an army of chiggers moving through my skin, but I bring you no excuses. Only the truth. And the truth is that I knew. I could see the sand around you. It was torn up like the men who fell in Normandy. You heard my voice expressing doubt and you knew then, too, what a liar I was.

"It's all right to touch me," said Justin, and despite his best intentions, his own words sounded wicked.

And she, the woman, Charlotte, was no longer arching from a river of sand or even following him through an endless forest in his dreams, but was standing in front of him, very shy now that she had put down her tablet, and with her eyes downcast she was unbuttoning the first button of his collar. The backs of her hands were warm beneath his chin. She fumbled, bit at her lip. He looked at her and found that he could not want her, for he had already had her, and thus any arousal on his part, anything but total passivity, would take her back there to the place that he had originally put her.

How sin circles through a life.

She moved her hands down to the second button and to the rest. She unbuttoned the sleeves and slid his shirt off, which she carefully folded and placed on the bent-wood chair.

She picked up the pad and her writing was shaky.

TAKE YOUR PANTS OFF.

He had heard through his open window a man saying that some of the women wanted to watch a man take off his clothes, but this man telling the story had made it sound amusing, and Justin now felt only fear and regret. He took his shoes off, then his socks, then his pants, wadding them into a bundle and throwing it in the corner. He sat back down in his boxer shorts. The prospect of new words on the pad was suddenly dreadful, because they contained commands he would have to obey, whether he wanted to or not.

She patted the cot and indicated with her gestures that he should lie down.

He sat down on the cot again and leaned back until his head touched the pillow, lifting his feet. She sat down next to his hip. Looking at him. He lowered his eyes. The shame of a body bared by a stranger.

The man under Milo groaned and tried to buck him off, but Milo pressed his knees into the hollows of the man's arms. "You bastard," said Milo. He held the knife to his throat. "Dare me, dare me, dare me," Milo chanted. He wanted to kill him so badly, to watch the blood spray out of his neck. He was Milo the avenger. Milo the hero, defending his dead mother. He would teach those bastards to laugh at her memory . . .

"Uh-oh," someone said. "The sheriff is here."

Milo looked up as a car pulled up. Belinda's husband opened the door and sauntered over to Milo.

"Hey, Fire Boy," said the sheriff. "What you got into now?"

Milo turned his head just as the sheriff's boot caught him in the face.

The unkissed years. The inconsolable loss. Charlotte felt her senses returning to her in a rush. Had the scent of kerosene lamps always widened her nostrils so? Had they always thrown that daffodil color on the walls? She heard the sound of her own breathing, and even imagined that she could hear the breathing in the next room, and the next, and an old lady's murmur from a farther room: "My son, my son . . ."

Charlotte had chosen well this quiet man now lying on the bed in the position of a faint, who barely moved at all and when he did move, did so slowly and with caution. She touched his face, his chin, his nose, then rummaged through his dark eyebrows, stroking them until they tickled her fingertips. Her hand moved down to his throat, his chest, then to the slight depression in his belly. She was fascinated and soothed by the stillness of his body. When she touched the elastic of his boxer shorts he seemed to sense what she wanted and did not protest or move to stop her. She pulled on the elastic until it made an opening, bent down until her cheek nearly rested on his stomach and looked down at his privates. A tangle of black hair and the beige of a flattened penis.

She released the elastic of the boxer shorts, raised her head and heard the old lady's voice again, distinctly this time: "My son, my little boy . . ." And these words caused such a grief in her that she drew back suddenly.

"What's the matter?" asked the man.

She shook her head. A tear slid out one eye, dodged her fingers and fell upon his chest.

"I'm sorry," said the man, with such an aching regard that it made another tear fall. "Do you want me to touch you?" he asked.

Charlotte hesitated and then nodded. Very slowly, he

raised his hand to the back of her head. Charlotte leaned forward until her head rested against his bare shoulder.

"I'm sorry." His breath on her neck.

His fingers moved in her hair, stroking her scalp, rubbing smooth and then smudging her long-standing belief that men were violent and cruel. His bare shoulder cool beneath her lips. They turned on the bed. Five new fingers moved through her black hair, joining the others. Her mouth met his in a sudden and trembling kiss, like the grape-arbor kiss, but now nothing was forbidden, for all things forbidden had been explored and then paid for.

The sheriff kicked Milo again.

Charlotte closed her eyes.

Blood came out of Milo's mouth as his head hit the macadam.

Charlotte sighed. Another kiss, longer. Endurable tenderness.

The sheriff picked Milo up by the hair.

Justin murmured something. A breath, a blink, another kiss.

My son, thought Charlotte. *My son.*

10

An hour past midnight, the house grew quiet. Men and women spoke in whispers, embraced wearily or fell asleep in each other's arms as the candle flames flickered and died. Mr. Olen dozed with his feet up on his desk, dreaming of his absent wife. The old doctor snored. Louise lay on her bed with her arms crossed in the position of a corpse, grieving over Justin, tears running down her face.

And the boy, Daniel. His nose to his bedroom window. His eyes scanning the backyard and the woods beyond. Surely by now Benjamin must have broken some new woman's heart and thrown her from his sweet potato barn. Surely by now she needed comforting. Daniel left his room and quietly tiptoed down the hallway to the back door.

When he was four years old, Daniel had discovered his most remarkable gift. One night, restless and bored, he stole out of his room and crept past Benjamin's barn and into the forest—a wildly disobedient act for an angel, but a mild peccadillo for a Southern boy. It was July and the locusts were rattling. He heard a rustle in the brush and he froze. Willy had told him that panthers roamed the woods and that these panthers liked to eat little blond-haired boys: "They have a scream like a woman. And they'll drag you back up a tree and maybe they'll swallow you whole. You can't thumb-wrestle in a panther's stomach, you know."

Daniel heard another rustle in the woods and spun on his heels and ran pell-mell back for the house, tripping over a discarded gin bottle on his way through the yard. Once safe on the porch, he sat with his knees together and stared into the woods, breathing heavily. Along with the rustle, he thought he'd heard something else. A sigh, or a moan. It didn't sound like a panther. Very gingerly, Daniel made his way back into the woods, creeping along carefully through the ferns that licked at his chest, peering up at the twisting branches of the oaks and cedars. Again he heard the moaning. Full of sudden terror, he turned around and ran, his pajamas catching on branches, his bare toes stubbing on rocks.

He fell right over a grown woman who had been curled up under a great tangle of honeysuckle vines, weeping. If the footprints she had made had been visible, they could have been traced back to the sweet potato barn, where Benjamin sat with his legs crossed, smoking a pilfered cigarette.

Now the woman wept for twin shames—the shame of loving such a young boy, and the shame of having this boy cruelly reject her.

"I'm tired of you," Benjamin had told her. "Get out."

"But I love you."

Benjamin had finished his cigarette, put it out on the wooden floor and taken out another one. "Do you have a match?"

At that time, Daniel was not accustomed to hearing women cry. Quite the contrary, for late at night, when they passed by his room as they left the house, Daniel could hear their contented sighs and little girlish bursts of set-free laughter. Thus he had begun to think of women as permanently satisfied creatures, elusive and pretty-smelling, the rush of taffeta, the whisper of long hair, the slide of spectator shoes on a smooth wooden floor.

And now this sad woman, out in the dark woods. Daniel crawled toward her, his knees brushing wild phlox, his fingers burying in the cover of pine straw left over from winter. A bug creeping up his arm with equal stealth. The woman was curled like a new baby, alone and abandoned. Starlight had filled her tears and pulled them down to the line of her chin. She closed her eyes and more tears fell. Daniel saw the curl of her figure and knew even at his young age that this particular posture displayed some specific agony. At the same time, he felt himself both burdened and freed by some mysterious light, as though a rainbow had concealed itself in his last gulp of breath and then expanded very gently inside him. He moved his face down to hers and kissed her on the cheek, softly so as not to startle her.

The woman opened her eyes and stared into two spheres of a blue she had never seen before. The astonishing and peculiar shade of intangibles: a bend in a children's story, a Samaritan's dreams, the knowledge of a single sparrow falling. The stare and the sweet kiss took all the pain from her. She looked down in surprise at her body, which trembled from the blessing, and when she looked up again the boy had vanished. She sat up in the forest, blinking, the scent of the cedar trees powerful and the locusts barely heard. Her longing for Benjamin had suddenly metamorphosed into a motherly concern, and she wondered if Benjamin was getting enough to eat, if he was cold in his sweet potato shack, if he was afraid of the dark, if there were bruises on his arms or chiggers in his socks.

Then she rose to her feet and picked her way home through the woods, bringing this new peace and calmed-down love with her. The next morning she made the best pot of oatmeal she had ever made, sweet with the acceptance of her limited life. Her husband and children didn't notice any of it: the new glow, the oatmeal, the quiet smile.

And so a cycle began, made of a man's best impulses and his worst ones. Hurt by the world, women would come to The House of Gentle Men. Kissed, stroked and complimented, they would leave through the backyard. Seduced and then thrown away by the wolf Benjamin, more damaged than they'd been before, they would fill the woods with their mournful weeping. Discovered and cured by the touch of the angel boy, they would return to their lives, newly comforted and full of bliss. They never spoke of him, never told a soul, for they could never admit to anyone why they were out crying in the woods.

Daniel loved the women. Felt a peculiar empathy at their abandonment. Felt motherly toward them in their grief. Sometimes he wished the healing was reciprocal—that they could kiss him or touch him and take away his loneliness, for he knew that these women had something that made them different from Louise. They were older and their scent had a nurturing quality. They were bigger in the breasts. Larger at the waists. Their voices were deeper. But because they were thrilled by the sudden soothing of their own sorrows, they forgot to kiss him back, or remove the tangles from his hair, or notice the scratches on his bare feet. They forgot to nurse his fear of panthers. To warn him away from five-sided leaves and snakes with shovel heads. To explain why his bullfrog would die someday. Their heads spinning, they could only stumble back home, away from him.

Daniel would watch them leave and be filled with sorrow. In his motherless house he ached for a mother. For although he received much love in the house, he often fell into the calming smoke of near sleep without a lullaby. Sometimes he asked questions and no one answered him. Some of his scratches healed without Band-Aids, and once, his fingernails grew so long that his four front teeth had to play mother and shorten the nails themselves. The men in the house ruffled his hair and swung him around by the arms, but the gentleness they had for women did not extend to little boys. And though Louise tried her best to look after him, she lacked some vital quality that Daniel felt but could not put into words.

Once, he had found a bluebird lying on the ground after a spring storm, had picked up this wounded bird and felt its last heartbeat in his hand. He had carried the bird to Louise, who had cried out not in sympathy but at the bird's dirtiness. She had taken it from him and buried it quickly, and somehow Daniel knew that a real mother would have cared about the last heartbeat and not so much about the filth.

Sometimes he asked the men in the yard about their mothers and to a man they quieted down, put their flasks back on the table, looking off into the woods, for although their demons were gone and they were forgiven of their crimes, every one of them had some sad memory of their mothers. They were either dead, or sick, or not speaking to them, or had knowledge of their actions and were heartbroken.

As the years passed, it was always the same. After the women were drawn to the house and to Benjamin's barn, Daniel was drawn to them. And Benjamin kept him busy.

*   *   *

Now, an hour past midnight, the house quiet and Charlotte and Justin busy kissing each other good-bye in Room 21, Daniel opened the back door and stole out through the backyard. He heard his bullfrog croaking over in the wading pond that some of the men used for soaking their feet, but now was not the time for playing with frogs, or building tepees out of cane poles and sheets, or swinging on the low branches of trees. The light was on in Benjamin's barn. Had he ruined a woman tonight yet? A few steps into the woods and Daniel heard the moans. He found the broken woman on a bed of clover, behind a huge mulberry bush, and knelt down beside her. A tired-looking woman with yellow hair and a few early wrinkles around her trembling mouth.

"Benjamin, Benjamin," the woman cried.

Working with an otherworldly patience, forgetting his fear of panthers and bobcats and large twisting snakes, Daniel kissed her sobs into a smoother pattern. Wiped the tears from her eyes. Spoke to her softly. Finally the woman took out a handkerchief and wiped her face.

"You don't know what it's like to be abandoned," she told him.

Charlotte opened the back door to The House of Gentle Men and stepped into the darkness of the backyard. Her four dollars were still in her pocket. Justin had told her not to leave a tip.

As she stumbled through the yard, disoriented by the events of the night, she heard a soft, muffled voice call from a rickety barn: "Hey, ma'am? Aren't you tired of being treated like a queen? Don't it wear you out a little?" The door of the barn opened, revealing a bare-chested boy holding back a surge of yellow light. His pants were zipped but not buttoned at the top. "Come on," the boy called. "Come over here. I know what you really want."

Even from a distance she could see, or perhaps just sense, his wicked smile. The barn radiated just-completed sex. Charlotte paused, annoyed by the sudden intrusion of her reverie. The wind blew. A bird fluttered in the dogwood tree. A dog barked at the sudden wanderings of a grasshopper. Charlotte's mind whirled.

"Admit it," called the boy, lowering his voice to a whisper. "You want more."

Charlotte was suddenly filled with a rage at the presumption of this boy and the kind of male he represented, for she felt as though she'd just stepped from a coop of sweet and amorous chickens and run into a wolf. She shuffled through the pages of her tablet, writing furiously, then held up the pad for the boy. He peered at it, took a step closer.

"I can't read that in the dark," he complained.

Charlotte threw the pad down and began to run, across the rest of the yard and into the woods, as Benjamin crept forward to retrieve the pad. He read through the words on the other pages: WHAT HOUSE? DROP DEAD YOU—

BLACK HAIR. HARMLESS. I WANT THE FAINTED MAN. SHUT
UP. A KISS? THEY ARE NOT GENTLE MEN.

Then the last page, the page meant for him: YOU
DON'T KNOW ANYTHING ABOUT WOMEN.

Benjamin lit a cigarette.

Charlotte slowed down when she reached the edge of
the woods, continuing with a slower gait and an easier
breath as she found the path and took it around a curve.
She stopped by a large mulberry bush. Was that the sound
of crying? No, it couldn't be. And so she walked on,
unaware that she had passed within four feet of a sad
woman and a little blond-haired boy.

Charlotte's anger at the wolf from the barn was fading.
After all, he was just a silly child, with little knowledge
of the world's true state. Not like Justin. He was familiar
enough to be called Justin, wasn't he?

Kisses from the fainted man. Sweet and tender, sad
beyond depth. Primary colors. The temperature of au-
tumn. Quiet as a footstep. Tasting of a summer pear.
Scented like a pillow. History leaping from man to
woman. Tragedy. Joy. Every gesture gathered in the
mouth, negotiator between the savage body and the noble
mind. Sex without war. Love without dread.

In his softest hour, a man is mostly woman. Gentle
hands. A calm pulse. A rushing slope of mercy steepened
by a kiss.

The hours had moved but Charlotte did not want to

leave. The two of them would pause and then begin again, their lungs growing clumsy with held-in breath as the kiss lasted. Finally the kerosene lamp went out, and they kissed in total darkness, the eyes resting and the skin hot. She thought with fiendish glee of Belinda, who had so cruelly thrust those four dollar bills into her hand, as if to say, *Poor Charlotte.*

No poverty here now. She would see that Belinda knew this.

Now the dollar bills rustled in her pocket as she floated through the woods, a woman aware of the exhaustion of her body and the chill of her feet, but nevertheless rejoicing. Charlotte took an easy pace as her mind moved back to the quiet room on the third floor, back to the ecstasy of the beckoned kiss. She closed her eyes as she thought of it, which caused her feet to stray to the edge of the path and her dress to catch on an old blackberry vine.

Her dress ripped. And her eyes flew open. And the joy left her body, for the sound of cloth tearing had brought back that moment on the sandy riverbed. *Did you see me? What are you talking about? Shut up. You knew.* Undistinguished voices in the undistinguished woods, after this extraordinary crime.

At first she had pretended that it hadn't really happened, and she could go on, brush herself off, wear cologne and the formerly denied lipstick. The swelling near her mouth had gone back down to nothing, and after a week or two Milo had stopped asking her questions. Now she could go back to the way things were, could flirt with the remaining men on earth, now that the soldier of the sky was taken by the fortune-drenched Belinda. But suddenly she did not want to be a girl, least of all a woman. Women seemed too soft to her. Their sweet girlish voices incapable of the scream needed to summon aid. Their dresses inadequate armor. Their slim crossed legs at Sunday teas a vain attempt to guard the point of entry.

When she no longer had to soak her panties in the zinc tub because the monthly blood had ceased, she had told herself that perhaps the blood went hand in hand with the voice. Her silence begetting a change in the flow.

Now Charlotte inspected the tear in her dress and moved on. The night birds called. The branches of trees rubbed together with a whispery friction. And Charlotte walked faster, remembering things but defiantly, carelessly, forgetting them again.

Milo lay on the floor of the jail cell. Blood had dried in a line down his chin, and one side of his face was swollen where the sheriff had kicked him. He moaned slightly and closed his eyes. "Mama," he said. She was alive again, and her voice was not as it had been. It was a caress, a whisper, full of love, no fear, nothing urgent or wild. "My sweet boy," she said, and reached for him through the flames.

11

Louise had been tormented all night long by the thought of Justin rallying his starved body to minister to a woman. Louise needed ministering too. Like all the other women who had come to this house, she had been hurt by a man—a man named Leon Olen, whose distracted, overeducated mind and whose tendency to spit tobacco juice in cups meant for drinking had driven away her mother. Whose houseful of boneless love had never won her mother back and was never going to. Whose habit of sitting night after night, his oaken desk bearing the weight of his crossed legs—one asleep, one awake—while he waited for her return, seemed stupider as the years progressed. And whose latest harebrained plan, whatever it was, had now resulted in Justin holding another woman in his arms.

Hadn't her father told her that Justin wasn't fit for any woman? Then why had this woman come to his room? And who was she?

All night long she had pondered these questions, tortured by the creakings of the house and by a faucet dripping at teeth-gritting intervals. Twice she had crept up to the third floor and moved down the hallway, past the doors that held back sighs and whispers, and stopped in front of Justin's room, listening. She could hear nothing, even when she pressed her ear to the door. And this absence of sound drove her into a fury.

Morning had found her in a terrible mood, a throbbing behind the eyes and a contempt for the men she now served oatmeal. She hated their little jokes, their sleepiness that they wore like a badge of honor as, glutted with good deeds, they added sugar to their steaming oatmeal. Benjamin's words came back to her: *You know what they do on their nights off. In and out and in and out.*

Hypocrites, she thought. She moved around the butcher-block table, slamming down bowls in front of each man, sloshing the contents, cracking one of the bowls so that a trail of oatmeal slugged down the table.

"Louise?" said Mr. Olen.

"What?"

"Could I please have another bowl without the big crack in it?"

"Of course, Father." Mr. Olen noticed the bitterness in her words and shook his head. He had spent the night dozing intermittently in his office chair, waking up to wonder what was happening in Justin's room. The beauty of it thrilled him. Sin and redemption twirling into one body. Wrongs made right. And the woman who came back.

Louise wiped the oatmeal off the table, went into the kitchen and returned with a replacement bowl for her father and a smaller bowl for Daniel. As she stood over the sleepy boy whose light hair was in disarray, her angry expression relaxed.

"What's the matter, boy?" said Willy. "You have nightmares about Louise boilin' the germs off your pet frog?" He pushed Daniel a little on the arm and then ruffled his hair until it stuck out in all directions.

Louise ignored Willy, giving Daniel a kiss as he picked up his spoon. "Good morning, sweet lamb," she murmured.

Daniel's unwashed hands were still sticky with the invisible tears of the married woman he'd kissed in the woods. He blew on his oatmeal with the weariness of all nocturnal healers.

"Daniel," said Louise. "Did you—"

She froze. Justin had come into the room.

The other men stopped talking and stared at him too. He looked sallow but with a bit of new color in his face, a tiny light in his eyes. A hint of a smile, and his pants hanging a little on his waist. He took a seat at the table and looked around shyly, as if he had no idea what to make of this group, or of living people, or of the bright world. His gaze stopped when it reached Daniel. He sat transfixed by the boy's eyes, a look of wonder on his face.

Louise realized Justin was looking at him for the first time with a clear head. He had seen Daniel only once before—the night he'd lain on his cot insensate after the unsuccessful hanging.

Mr. Olen cocked an eyebrow. "You sleep well?" he asked Justin.

Justin dragged his eyes away from Daniel. "Not really," he said, and the other men laughed. Word had traveled through the house that Justin had been with a woman.

"Got any tips to report, soldier?" asked Willy. The men laughed again.

Louise slammed down a bowl of oatmeal in front of Justin. A clot of it leaped to his face and hung there. He wiped it off with the back of his hand.

"Louise," said Mr. Olen.

"What?"

"Be a little more careful."

Justin picked up his spoon and began to eat, very gingerly. A man tasting food and finding it to be good, and necessary. The other men watched him. So did Louise.

Benjamin came dragging in, his hair sticking out all different ways, walking like someone wounded. He sat down across from his father.

"You know you're not supposed to wear your union suit to the table," said Mr. Olen.

"Come on," said Benjamin. "Who's embarrassed by a

little underwear? Not Louise. As long as it's clean underwear."

"Shut up," said Louise.

Benjamin ignored her. "How is everyone?" he asked loudly. "Are your fingers sore from rubbing on tired muscles? Your lips bruised from your sweet kisses?"

The others laughed, as good-naturedly as could be expected for men who provide the foreplay for a younger man's sex. "You'll learn about women soon enough, boy," one said.

"I know all about women that I need to know. Like, they're the ones that are supposed to be sore the next morning."

"Benjamin!" said Mr. Olen.

Benjamin looked down the table. "Oh, no," he said, looking at Justin. "You too, soldier? I was hoping that you'd turn out to be a man."

Louise took a spoonful of hot oatmeal and dropped it in her brother's lap.

"Damn it, Louise!" Benjamin shouted as the men laughed again. He jumped up from the table, oatmeal clotting on his cotton leggings. He pointed to his crotch. "You trying to boil the germs off it? You want to scrub it down with lye?"

"Benjamin," said Mr. Olen.

Louise had to leave the room because she felt tears coming, hot and pure. Not because of the stupid antics of her brother, but because of the look on Justin's face. Someone had been with him and it showed in his eyes.

Louise had found him that night he tried to hang himself. Had made lightning-quick note of his dangling feet. Had saved him. And he had never even thanked her. Now someone else had saved him again, in a different way, and this was the saving that mattered to him. Louise had simply dragged him back into the hateful world. Someone else had to come along and make that world less hateful.

But she deserved Justin.

Thanks to her stupid father, she had been given this life and had been denied the proper amount of boyfriends, much like her family had been denied rubber and cloth and sugar during the war. Now the war was over, and shoes and love were no longer rationed. And, after all, hadn't she endured enough tribulation for living in this house full of woman-pleasing fools?

Once, when she was eleven years old, two girls named Ladonna and Ethel had cornered her at school, behind the coal bin.

"My daddy caught my mama coming to your house," said Ethel. "She got beat and so did I, just for standing there."

Louise was taken aback for a moment. No one had spoken of the house to her before. She gathered her wits and said bravely: "So? I just live there. I can't account for what goes on."

"I heard every man in that place is a sissy," said Ethel, and Louise did have to silently agree, for those were the days before Benjamin was old enough to break women's hearts.

"Your daddy must be a prize," said Louise, "since he can't please his own woman." This insult invited the cat-like screech and graceful leap of tiny Ethel, followed by the heavier Ladonna with her balled fists and hairy arms and hard punches.

They fought then, two against one, punching and scratching and biting. Suddenly Louise found herself with her fingers buried in Ethel's kinky red hair. In one smooth motion she lifted Ethel off the ground and flailed her body around back and forth, hitting Ladonna with Ethel's legs.

"Aaaaaah!" Ethel shrieked, a redheaded devil with pig wire for hair. Louise kept swinging her around. Ladonna looked stricken. She had never before been pummeled by her best friend.

"You're hurting me!" Ladonna screamed at Ethel. Louise released Ethel and she fell on the ground. Later that day, Louise went home, took off her dress and soaked in the bathtub, as the water turned gray with the runoff of coal powder.

Just one of the many indignities of living in this house. She had poured a spoonful of oatmeal on her brother's crotch, but really she wanted to dump a bowl of it—scalding-hot—on her father's head.

★　　★　　★

Louise sighed as she finished the dishes. It was nearly noon.

The old doctor came in the kitchen for a drink of water.

"How's that soldier?" he asked.

"Better, I guess."

"Maybe he needs more nervine to calm his spirits. Or Lydia E. Pinkham tonic."

"Isn't that for female troubles?" asked Louise idly.

"Hell if I remember. Couldn't hurt." The old doctor filled his glass at the faucet. "Once I had a blister on my gum for a month."

Louise went out on the porch, took off her shoes and stepped down into her outside shoes, the clunky brogans whose soles she reluctantly allowed to touch the filth of grass, squashed pill bugs and the cigarette butts of the men who sat out in the backyard. They played pinochle and gin rummy. One man whittled. All of them were drinking, sipping at their cups. They had learned that the women who came to them were generally tired of whiskey kisses and wanted something pure. And so the men did their drinking at this time of day, in order to let the sensation and the smell leave their bodies by dark.

Justin sat under the camphor tree away from the others, staring off into the woods.

Willy motioned her over.

"Hey, Louise," Willy said softly, "do we have some competition now?"

"You mean him?" Louise nodded toward Justin.

"Yeah, him."

"I don't know. Ask Daddy."

"You know what I think?" said Willy. "I think he ain't competition at all. Seems too quiet. Too wrapped up in himself."

"No," said Willy's sidekick, Ray. "He's too *tied* up in himself. As in a noose." The other men guffawed, falling silent when Justin looked over.

"Aren't you funny," said Louise crossly, and went around to the front yard to find Daniel. He was standing by the road with Benjamin, who pointed at something in the grass.

"Kill it. Kill it," Benjamin was saying. Daniel backed up a little.

Louise came closer until she could see the unkilled thing. A caterpillar, yellow and black.

"Stomp on it, Daniel," said Benjamin.

"Don't make him kill that bug," Louise said. "It's innocent."

"Come on. I'm trying to teach Daniel not to be a sissy. Little boys are supposed to stomp on things that don't deserve it. It trains them for war."

"The war's been over for three years."

"There will be other wars," said Benjamin. "Daniel's going to shoot people in the head."

"No, he's not. If he ever goes to war he'll be a doctor, saving people's lives."

"He'll operate on people's guts and be in shit up to his elbows."

"Shut up. Shut up or I'll punch you."

"You want Daniel to be like them?" asked Benjamin, nodding toward the house. "There ain't a man in there."

"Justin's a man," Louise said quickly, before she could stop herself.

Benjamin raised his eyebrows. "You still have a crush on that soldier, Louise? The one too stupid to hang himself?" Benjamin began dancing around in the road. "Louise and Justin sitting in a tree, W-A-S-H-I-N-G," he sang.

"Benjamin!" Louise shrieked. She pushed him down.

Benjamin lay on the dirt road, his arms and legs spread like any angel's. Louise turned around and stomped back into the house. She heard her brother's voice behind her. "Daniel," he said. "Men are always getting told to behave. Don't listen, boy."

Louise climbed the staircase to the third floor and stole into Justin's room, determined to find out the identity of his mysterious guest. She closed the door behind her and looked around carefully. No dust on the floor to collect a small footprint, no way to tell whether the woman had worn spectator shoes or sandals or penny loafers. She glanced out the window quickly. Justin dozed in the sun with his head down and the shadow of a branch stuck behind his ear like a pencil. She put her face down near the floor, every sense heightened in the search for clues.

Hair, a chipped fingernail, a strange scent, a dried tear, a piece of unfamiliar thread. She had seen her father hone this meticulous craft when she was a little girl and her mother had disappeared for the afternoon, with no note and no sign of preparations for dinner. Her father had moved like a cat through the bedrooms, nose to the floor, then on to the living room, shaking the pillows of the couch for answers.

Five days later, a blue sock her father found behind a door finally led him to the culprit, but by then her mother was living with the man in a shotgun house bordered by a field full of ribbon cane, and there was nothing her father could do about it.

Louise pulled back the sheets of Justin's cot, studying the depressions on the mattress, not missing a curve or a pinch. She knew that sometimes a body leaves a good story on a bed, full of twists and turns. Down near the foot of the bed the fitted sheet was rumpled, a sign of restlessness by one or both parties. Louise moved up to the middle of the cot and pressed her nose to the mattress, discovering the faint scent of roses. She had washed these sheets the day before on a scrub board, then hung them to dry in an unscented breeze. Had this woman worn rose cologne, as Louise's mother had?

Under the pillow she found her best clue—a very long strand of hair. Curled at the end. Coarse. Jet-black. Louise closed her eyes. Most women had a shorter cut now, a style pulled from the big cities. But in this parish there did live a woman who had dropped away from the world, and neither read its magazines nor dressed in its fashions. Charlotte the Mute. Milo's sister. And now she could see the woman flying toward her in the hazy woods, long hair tangled, hands outstretched to push her down for the crime of bathing a stump.

Holding the strand of hair as if it were some live and primitive creature, Louise realized the feeling her father must have had as he crouched behind the door holding the blue sock. The grim joy, the deep and bitter satisfaction, of finding the culprit too late.

Later that night, as Louise wept on the porch, Daniel came to her. Frogless, slingshotless, stickless. Minus his building blocks or the skates which, frustrated, he often tried to navigate down the broken dirt road. His toys had dropped at this sudden new healing to be done. He bent down and kissed her cheek. Touched her throat and mouth. Ran his wrestling thumb over her brow and under her chin. And as the tears stopped and Louise felt a temporary flood of peace, she gathered him in her arms and held him close.

"Honey," she said. "You need to go inside. The women are coming soon."

But she did not release him, just yet. Were it not for her Daniel, she could not lead this life.

12

Louise had found him in the woods one day, when he was just a little baby, so young to the world that the dried bit of umbilical cord—a pacifier from his absent mother's womb—still clung to the pinch in his belly.

For this discovery she owed her eternal thanks to a giant oak stump, upon which the baby lay wrapped in a printed cloth. She was on her way to do some swimming in the crystal blue water of Lake Swane when she saw the child. She bent over him, astonished by his face and his existence and the colorless tears sliding out of his stunning blue eyes. A silent weeping, as if out of respect for the quiet forest. She did not want to pick him up, afraid that touching him would make him disappear.

She looked around as if expecting to find the mother hovering nearby, foraging for berries or for water. She saw no one. The two of them were alone, and the forest was silent.

She tried breathing on him first. Just a little bit, and

then a full whoosh that blew a tear off his face but did not make him vanish. She snapped her fingers. Neither the sound nor the shadow dispelled the magic of his human form. Encouraged, she slowly extended her pinkie finger—the kindest and least intrusive of fingers—and gently stroked his pale nose. She kissed his brow once, twice, then the all-affirming thrice. He was real. An angel come to earth.

Immediately she decided on a name. "Daniel," she said, and another tear ran down his face. When she tried to move him the sap from the tree stump sucked at the cloth that swaddled him, and she had to free him corner by corner before she scooped him up and rushed back to the house.

Her father was amazed, then appalled, at the presence of the quiet baby with the beautiful eyes. He turned the tiny body from side to side, then held him up to the sun until the light came through the fuzz on his head.

"Unbelievable," he whispered.

Mr. Olen tried to make Louise put an ad in the newspaper, nail up flyers. Even ask around. But to Louise, Daniel was a gift from the God who had taken away her mother. Like a bully stealing a quarter and then buying you a cupcake with it.

"He wasn't wanted, Daddy! He was lying on that stump where the big paths cross. He's ours, fair and square."

"We have to tell someone."

"Who? We can't even tell people about ourselves."

Finally her father gave in. Daniel would remain with them, growing up in the house, playing alone in the yard, forgetting the scent of his real parents—if he'd ever known it at all.

All secrets should be kept clean, and Daniel was the cleanest, most powdery, most sweet-smelling barely glimpsed secret in the parish. Louise raised him herself, first on goat's milk and later on soft food. She rocked him at night, sang to him, rubbed paregoric on his sore gums and combed his pretty hair.

Benjamin was already training himself in the belligerent and manly arts. He complained: "A boy ain't supposed to be that clean! You'll ruin him, Louise!"

She only smiled. "Angels can't be ruined, Benjamin. He touches the world. The world doesn't touch him."

"I'm going to take him out and roll him in cow shit, Louise."

"You do and I'll break all your marbles."

As Daniel grew, Louise despaired that this angel stayed as dirty as any other boy. Arm by arm, leg by leg, she lost the battle over cleanliness until she gave up and concentrated on keeping his teeth brushed. But her concessions to his dirt-collecting habits did not extend to his freedom. She made him stay around the yard and in the very edge of the forest, where the dogwoods bloomed. So afraid was she of his discovery that she would not let him play past the first fifty yards of the dirt road, or be seen on the front porch past dark.

Benjamin was appalled that Louise wouldn't let the child roam wild in the woods, like a boy was meant to.

"Someone will take him away from us," said Louise.

"Why? He's just a boy."

"Look at his eyes. People will know they're angel eyes and steal him."

"Come on," said Benjamin. "You're keeping him a prisoner here. He's never even been fishing!"

"What if someone sees him?"

"We'll sneak along without anyone knowing. Like Indians."

But Louise remained adamant in her refusal to let Daniel go. It was up to Benjamin to release him when Louise turned her back. He took the little boy's hand and led him into the winding paths of the wild woods, happy to finally have a friend. It became a game to Benjamin, hiding this boy from hunters and drunks and forest rangers and various people wandering through the woods.

Once, they roamed very deep into the woods and came upon a drunk wallowing in the pine straw. Benjamin grabbed Daniel's hand to pull him into the bushes, but Daniel broke away and went to the drunken man. Knelt down beside him. Took his hand. Touched his cheek, which was sticky as any boy's. The drunken man looked at the boy and his mouth fell open at the sight of him.

"Get away from him, Daniel," Benjamin said. "He stinks."

He pulled the boy away and the two of them plunged back into the brush.

The man stared after them, trembling, astonished by the boy's miraculous eyes and by the mercy in his touch. He had given up God years ago, after his wife had died horribly, but now he was not so sure that God did not exist. He rose to his feet and staggered home, the woods blurry green and filled with meaning. This man, Charlotte's father.

In time, under cover of night, Benjamin's brokenhearted women saw Daniel too, although they kept this angel a fierce secret from the world. They didn't think of him as a boy, but as a miracle sent down by someone who knew the hearts of women and took pity.

Forgiveness in the body of a child.

Often they touched the spots on their arms and throats and faces that the boy had kissed. He couldn't be real, they decided. Along with this realization came others: that their dull lives could shine with heaven; that chores could be glorious; that throwing scraps to a hungry dog was love; and tending a garden was love; and soaking a white shirt in bluing was love; and kissing the forehead of an aging parent who mixed small talk and prayers in crazy patterns was love—and that they were born to this love, as satin is born to the long, slow stitch.

The men in the house were more accustomed to Daniel. They saw him at the breakfast table every day, ruffled his hair and asked no questions about who he was or where he'd come from. For they were men who understood the value and necessity of secrets. They showed him how to play cards and, later, how to whittle. They swung him by the arms and feet. But sometimes when they looked into his eyes during a quiet moment, they would see something there that left them awed and humbled.

Louise's lamb. Her pet and son and brother. A secret she had kept from everyone all of these years—even Milo. That was the reason she had gone in the woods with a pail of soapy water and a brush. She had wanted to bathe and baptize the stump that had given her this miraculous child.

Charlotte Gravin, madwoman and mute, had knocked her down.

And now was taking away the soldier she loved.

13

Justin and Charlotte kissed. As crape myrtle faded. As sneezeweed bloomed. As acorns fell. As the air cooled. As deer season drew closer. As, deep inside their shells, pecans began to lose the color green. Confederate rosebushes still thrived, but all through the parish, arbors had dropped their muscadines, and the bees had flown away. Still, it didn't matter. Up in Room 21, the man and woman kissed with no grapes or bees to kiss under.

After the first week, Charlotte began to move Justin's hand over her body, little by little. She tested him, letting go of his hand to see if he would move it on his own. He did not. His fingers clung to her wet skin, waiting for guidance. She slid his hand inside her blouse, under her brassiere. Felt the heat and the pressure of his hand on her breast. Needed his hand there, and on the small of her back, and on the side of her face.

Charlotte no longer waited for him on the railroad bench in the foyer with the other women. Instead she entered the house through a side door and climbed the back stairs to Justin's room. Late at night, she went out the back door, across the backyard and into the woods, where a little boy sat waiting for hurt women to make themselves known. Charlotte never saw him. Her eyes were on the stars and he was hidden in the brush.

Justin would not let Charlotte pay him, and sometimes the other men of the house complained that he did not contribute to the huge syrup can whose contents were divided amongst them once a week.

"He only has one woman to serve!" Willy complained to Mr. Olen. "And he doesn't make any money."

"How is that your concern?"

"What do you mean? Why should he get special treatment?"

"Because he's redeeming himself."

"Aren't we all?"

"Not like he is."

"This is a fascist kissing establishment!"

Mr. Olen was quite a bit taller than Willy, and when he spoke his voice came down on him with more severity than he'd intended. "It's not all about the money, Willy. It's about the banishing of demons. You do remember your demons, don't you, Willy?" And Willy had quieted down, for his demons had indeed once been bountiful, and now lay recorded in detail in the basement safe.

If the truth were known, Mr. Olen was almost as thrilled as Charlotte by the new developments. This was the magic he'd been waiting for. The spark that his wife could see from a distance.

He sat behind his oaken desk. The women were upstairs, the house was gently creaking and, by the sound of it, his daughter was washing a wall close by.

He cut his tobacco, pushing it to the little pouch habit had created on the side of his jaw.

A knock.

"Come in," he said.

She closed the door behind her. Her wellness amazed him. And her height. Good love had grown her at least three inches.

He leaned over and quickly spat out the tobacco, ashamed to still have the habit she'd hated so much. He straightened back up.

"How are you?" he said. A dull question whose lack of magic he hoped would not show in her eyes.

"I'm well." She looked at the backs of the picture frames arranged along the sideboard. "Why are they facing the wall?"

"Because your face is on them. And if I could, I would turn clocks to the wall, and refrigerators, and radios, and jars of mustard, because your face is on those too."

She nodded as if she understood.

"You look younger than your pictures," he said. "Without me you've grown prettier. Wives whose husbands are stupid eventually take on the homogeneous look of women ignored. I've seen enough of them come in here."

She sat down and straightened her skirt. He saw that one of her feet was turned slightly toward the other.

"How are the children?" she asked.

"They miss you."

"I miss them."

They looked at each other for a few moments, a stare made softer by the low lights. Finally she said: "I've come about business."

"Business?"

"That's right. You're a proprietor now. You have something to offer."

"You mean that you are here for a man?" he asked.

"Yes," she said. "That's what is done here, right?"

"I suppose."

His eyes watered and his lip found his sharpest tooth when he looked at her red dress, and at her young face. The chill of her long absence had kept her beauty fresh.

"What kind of man do you want?" he said at last. "You get two characteristics."

She hesitated. Finally she smiled. "Professorial," she said. "Snoopy. And impossibly tall."

He gasped. "Truly?"

"Yes, truly." She smiled. "I know that's three, but I wanted to make you sure of my point."

He walked around his desk, went to her. Sank down on his knees. She moved her legs apart so he could come in closer, so close as to feel her breath and to count the teeth revealed by her smile.

"I love you," he said. His fingertips very carefully touched her lips. And her face. A face unweathered by the years without him, so that when the time came it would be his face, to know again.

"What brought you here?" he asked.

"I saw the spark in the sky," she said. "The spark made when a terrible crime unwinds itself around its forgiving victim. I followed the magic here. Because I am mother to your children. Because I am your wife."

Never mind that his wife would never speak this way. It was his dream. The vision he had, night after night, cutting his tobacco in his quiet room. His wife more eloquent, more lovely than she had ever been.

Justin, whose miracle contributed hope to the fantasy, did not have to contribute to the syrup can.

One night Charlotte brought her cypress lamb to Justin's room. When she crept out early the next morning, an hour before dawn, she left the lamb on the night table. Now a little bit of Charlotte stayed in the room.

Justin studied the lamb, stroked its head absently. He had begun to eat again, and slowly his strength had come back to him. But he had not shared his life with Charlotte—any details of his history—for he knew that nothing could be said before he told her the truth, and this he was unwilling to do. Sometimes he caught the stare of the tall man, Mr. Olen, who raised his eyebrows at him but so far had not approached him with the question Justin felt sure was on his mind: *Have you told her yet?*

Justin wasn't sure that he loved Charlotte, only that he was drawn to her, to the very silence that he'd forced into her all those years ago. And he knew that it relieved something in his soul to lie beside her and let her hands move his.

His harmlessness so natural one would never suspect. And perhaps that is what he loved.

During the day, Justin sat out with the other men, their laps catching bits of the weak October sun. Justin's legs didn't stretch out quite as far as the others'. His laughter was rarer. His eyes darker. His face still colored with one demon—the demon of the untold truth.

Louise watched Milo skip a stone in the lake. One, two, three, four, five.

"You see that?" said Milo. "Five skips." He turned to Louise and she could see that the side of his face had completely healed. For the past month, Milo had insisted that he'd fallen from a tree. But Louise knew that was a lie, for a shame glowed on Milo's face that trees could not elicit.

"Very good, Milo." She sighed. Absently, she ran her hand over the quilt Milo had spread out for her, so she didn't have to touch the dirt underneath.

"Charlotte's not coming," he said.

"Too bad," said Louise.

"Aw, she don't come fishing too much anymore. She's been sewing."

"What's she making?"

"A dress, I guess. But you know what, Louise?" Milo knelt down next to her. "I heard her talk the other day."

"Really?"

"Just one word. 'Damn.' She said it while she was sewing. I think the pedal got stuck on the sewing machine. I don't even think she knew she talked out loud."

"That's good," said Louise, irritated at the whole subject of Charlotte, whose lamb now stared down from the end table whenever she cleaned Justin's room. As if the lamb held Charlotte's place for her during the day. Louise wanted to throw it down the chimney of the kerosene lamp and watch it flame with a pestilential odor.

"She's acting different," said Milo. "You think she's got a fellow?"

"I don't know." Louise was suddenly angry at her father for swearing her to secrecy about the goings-on of the house. She longed to tell Milo that Charlotte indeed had a fellow, the very same fellow whom Louise loved madly.

"You know what?" she said instead. "I think Charlotte's just been quiet all these years because she likes the attention."

"What?"

"You heard me."

Milo leaped to his feet. "Louise!" he shouted. "Don't you ever say that about my sister! You don't know what she's been through! You don't know! I don't know! I should punch you!" Instead he seized the quilt and pulled it out from under her, in a quick jerk, so that Louise felt her bottom hit the hard edge of the unbathed world.

"Milo!"

He whirled the quilt over his head and threw it in the lake. Louise watched him, frightened but oddly thrilled by the violence that had so suddenly entered his body.

Milo turned back around. His face red. His teeth bared. Eyes of an animal. He dropped onto his knees and stared at Louise, trembling. He put his hands around her throat.

"What I really want to do is choke you, Louise."

Louise's voice was calm, although her heart raced. "You can't choke me. I'm a girl."

After a moment, Milo's hands dropped. He sat back on his haunches and let out his breath. "Someone hurt her," he said. "Don't you see? She came out of the woods one day with her voice gone and her mouth all swelled up."

"Really? When?"

"Long time ago." He looked at her. "You tell anyone and I'll kill you, Louise."

Louise didn't see Milo for a long time after that day at the lake. He had made her a little afraid, and besides, her passion for Justin had driven her into frenetic cleaning sprees. The House of Gentle Men had never before experienced such sterile fits, not even on the birthdays of Louise's absent mother.

Ammonia. Lye. Pine oil. Dutch cleanser. Octagon soap. The glass in the windows squeaked and the doors swung silently from the hinges. The curtains stank of suds and starch. Spiders crept in, looked at the sterile baseboards and went somewhere else. Birds flew into the windows and had their blood and feathers scrubbed from the glass almost before they slid to the ground.

Under the vigilance of suds and brushes, unrequited love is a pain that lessens but does not die. Louise had learned that lesson eight years before, but still she mopped, wiped, dusted, scrubbed, washed, starched, polished. Germs can die in so many ways, and hearts be soothed.

The only item saved from the scourge of hot water was the hanging rope, which Louise would not clean despite its greasy filth. After all, it carried the scent of Justin's neck and also the essence of his secret. Here was proof of his tormented life and also proof that she had saved it, after she had burst into the room and found his feet making shadows higher up on the wall than they had a right to. From time to time she pulled the rope out from under her bed and stroked it gently while she imagined his neck in it, his sorrowful eyes bulging, his body turning, writhing and warming in the kerosene lamplight. She would put the rope away, get up and wash her hands, lie back down and repeat the process again. The thrill of contamination. The bliss of cleanliness.

Although the sterile scent of the house kept the men and women mindful of the rules and the love courtly, the men began to complain to Mr. Olen that the aroma of pine oil fought their Old Spice, and that the waxed floors ruined the timing of their languorous waltzes.

Mr. Olen had noticed the frenetic activity as well. He walked into the kitchen and stood in the steam rising from the hot floor. "Louise," he said, "you're cleaning too much. The men are complaining. And you shrank Benjamin's best shirt."

"Benjamin is a dirty boy," replied Louise. "No telling what kind of germs he's growing out in his filthy barn. He licks the doorknobs in front of me just to get my goat."

"He's a normal boy. Normal boys aren't clean."

"You're telling me."

Mr. Olen rubbed his eyes. The ammonia had turned them red.

"What's the matter, Louise?"

She threw the mop in the bucket and swirled it around. "Nothing."

"It's not right to clean so much. It's not . . . healthy."

Louise leaned down and wrung out the mop. "And when did that start, Daddy?" she asked, not looking at him. "When did it start?"

And Mr. Olen did not answer her, because he knew.

14

Back at her house, Charlotte finished the last stitch on the dress and held it up to the window. Light moved through navy crepe. Her foot was tired from pumping the pedal on the old Singer sewing machine. She went over to the mirror and held the dress up to herself. Last night she had not visited Justin but had stayed home, her dreams ruined by the wire curlers she'd slept in. Now her long black hair hung in waves down past her shoulders.

She put on the dress, applied some lipstick and some rouge, then a double layer of nail polish, the color of her lipstick. Indeed, she'd found the two of them side by side at the drugstore in town.

She looked in the mirror. She was ready now for her newly arranged self to prove its devastating point.

"Why, Charlotte!" said Belinda when she answered the door. "I haven't seen you in ages! You look beautiful! What a pretty blue dress!" She moved closer and whispered conspiratorially: "But the hemline's a little crooked. I guess it's hard to see in that old dark house you live in. Anyway, come in, come in!"

She guided Charlotte to the sofa. "Please sit down. I'll make some tea." She disappeared into the kitchen.

Ralph came running in, his hard shoes clattering against the floor. He seized Charlotte's pad. She pulled it away from him and he grew quiet, gazing up at Charlotte, batting his long lashes. Charlotte felt a deep, drawing pain, looking at him.

Belinda returned. "Water's boiling," she announced. "Oh," she added, noticing Ralph. "Isn't he a dear? He was my nurse yesterday. Look." Belinda turned her head so that Charlotte could see a dark bruise, the size of one square of a checkerboard, at the line of her jaw. "This is the stupidest thing possible, Charlotte. You'll laugh! I was walking in from the garden the other day, thinking about how much I missed my husband, and how lucky I was. I ran right into the door! But Ralph rubbed some ice on it for me. Didn't you, Ralph?"

Ralph reached for Charlotte's hair.

Belinda laughed. "No, honey. She's our guest."

Ralph paid her no attention.

"Charlotte," she said, "you have no idea what it's like to look at a little boy and think, 'He's my son!' It's just a miracle. I see myself in him sometimes, but mostly I see Richard. It's almost as if . . . oh, it's hard to explain to someone who's never had children. I do hope you have your own someday. It's not too late. Really, it's not."

Charlotte shrugged, fending off Ralph's fat little hands, which smelled of taffy.

"Ralph, go play. So what brings you here, Charlotte? What's been going on in your life?"

This was the moment Charlotte had been waiting for. She picked up her tablet, started to write, then thought better of it. The moment that Belinda's face fell had to be perfect. Charlotte opened her purse, slid her hand down into the pocket on one side of it and pulled out a wallet-sized photograph of Justin, taken in Paris right after the war had ended. She handed it to Belinda.

"Hmmm," said Belinda. "He's very handsome. Who's this?"

MY BOYFRIEND.

Belinda eyes opened up a bit. "Really? I've never seen him around these parts. Where did you meet him?"

Charlotte shrugged and took back the picture.

"Come on, Charlotte. We're friends. Don't be coy with me."

I MET HIM ONE NIGHT AT SOMEONE'S HOUSE.

"Where? Who introduced you?"

Things were not going well. Charlotte felt her face blush hot, and she felt trapped here, with the teakettle whistling from the kitchen and Belinda paying it no mind as she leaned forward with her eyes big and her lashes unnaturally long.

WHY ALL THE QUESTIONS?

Belinda read the words and seemed to be preparing an answer for them when suddenly she burst out with a peal of laughter. "Wait, wait!" she cried. "He isn't one of those men at that house, is he?"

Charlotte looked away.

"Why, Charlotte, you did use that four dollars after all! And I thought you were angry at me!"

Charlotte seized the pad and scribbled furiously.

HE DOES NOT CHARGE ME. HE IS MY BOYFRIEND.

"Of course he is. I suppose that's part of their charm. Making every woman feel special."

HE DOES NOT SEE OTHER WOMEN!

"All right, all right," Belinda said soothingly. "There's no need to get upset. But, Charlotte, surely you must know that you can't go around announcing that this man is your boyfriend. Not when you can't even talk about that house in public."

HE IS A GOOD MAN.

"I'm sure he is. But, Charlotte, even you can see that going to the house is a great shame, can't you? It's a place for desperate women."

I AM NOT DESPERATE!

Belinda leaned forward. "Tell me something. What's it like over there? Is it true that the men do nothing but kiss and stroke and whisper? How very odd. And is it true that they've . . . you know . . . removed their manly parts?"

Charlotte struggled off the couch.

"Charlotte! Don't go! The tea's ready." Belinda followed Charlotte out the front door. "Please!" she called after her. "I'm just trying to protect you, Charlotte!"

Once home, Charlotte pulled her dress over her head, washed her face, yanked her hose off so carelessly that they tore. Her date with revenge had not gone well. Belinda had not eaten crow, not one greasy bite of it. Charlotte moved moodily from room to room, dusting, straightening pictures. After a while she realized that the snide Belinda hadn't put her in such a state by insulting her new boyfriend.

No, it was something else. Something that really had nothing to do with Belinda.

Charlotte walked outside, climbed on the old bicycle that she used to ride past marching soldiers and rode through the woods, deeper and deeper until she found the place where two big paths converged, a well-traveled place where people would be sure to pass.

The giant oak stump was still there.

She leaned her bicycle against the tree and ran her fingers gently over the stump, remembering the anger that had flooded her body when she'd discovered the silly girl, Louise, scrubbing the stump clean. Now everything was gone. Whatever slight scent of him that might have remained there.

She sat down on the edge of the stump, stroking the rings in the wood.

Milo had been right when he'd reported her spoken word to Louise, for indeed, in the past days, words had begun to grow in her, rising up inside her like water rose in Milo's Coke bottle when certain habits of the air reduced or strengthened themselves. Good fishing. Good love.

She wanted to talk so badly, even though talking led straight back to the world at large and the world at large led straight back to her earlier memories and she didn't know if she could revisit them, not ever, for the agony had been there all along. She could not forgive herself for what she'd done, and the feeling would not go away, like the soldiers who had kept training and training and training in the shadowy woods.

Charlotte felt the tears begin.

"My son," she said.

"My son."

15

All those years and the stump was still there. And the words finally said aloud—*My son, my son*—told Charlotte that words, unlike her boy, still belonged to her.

A week after she'd visited the stump, Charlotte opened her front door and stepped off the porch. The air was crisp, but not cold. The night newly black.

Milo sat under a porch light whittling. "Hey, Charlotte," he said. "I didn't have nothing to do so I came over here. Where you going?"

She watched him whittle as he waited for her to write down her answer. "To see someone," she said.

Charlotte watched Milo's blade bite deep. Too deep. He dropped both knife and stick and jumped to his feet. "What did you say, Charlotte?"

"I said I was going to see someone."

"Charlotte, you can talk! You can talk!" Milo's mouth fell open wide. "My God, Charlotte," he whispered. "It's a miracle. I've prayed for this." He touched her face. "Say something else."

"I don't have anything to say."

"Sure you do."

"How are you?"

"Good. Say something else."

She shrugged.

"How did it happen?" he asked.

"I don't know."

"You just woke up and—"

"It was time," she said.

"Hell, yes, it's time! Let's celebrate! Let's go into town!"

"No. I have to meet my boyfriend."

Milo's eyes opened wider. A moth quit flirting with the floodlight and dove at his face. He brushed it away. "I knew you had a boyfriend!" he said. "What's his name?"

"Justin."

"Justin? He from around here?"

"No."

"Where did you meet him?"

"At the house."

"The house?"

"You know. The house near Ober Road."

Milo's face darkened. "Charlotte," he said. "What are you doing there? That house is for bad girls."

"That's not true."

"You're paying him?"

"No."

"Charlotte, it's not right. If Mama were here she'd—"

"Well, she's not here, is she?"

Charlotte started to walk away.

"Charlotte?"

She turned around. "What?"

"Say something else."

"Good night, Milo."

"Good night."

Milo watched his sister leave. He sat back down on the chair for a minute, ignoring his whittling. He was used to women moving from whole things to ruins. His mother was a strict Baptist woman and then ashes. His sister could speak and then was a mute. His wife, a saint and then a whore. Now something was moving in the other direction. Charlotte was healing. Now she could speak, and he felt with this miracle a sense of his own innocence restored.

Milo flicked his lighter under the tip of the whittled stick until it caught fire, then sat staring into the flame. Ever since he had watched the soldiers training in the woods he had wanted to be a hero, and yet he could not protect his own mother or even his own sister, who had come out of those same woods that September day with a torn dress and a new distaste for words. At that moment she had given Milo a new dream—to find out who had hurt his sister and to take revenge. Like heroes do.

Now that Charlotte could talk, perhaps revenge was no longer necessary. And yet Milo still yearned for it.

He blew out the flame and walked into the yard. He found a cedar tree and gently stroked its trunk.

Charlotte entered The House of Gentle Men through the side door and climbed the stairs to the third floor. The look on Milo's face had been priceless when he'd heard her speak. Now her throat still itched from the recent conversation. Part of her wanted to forget the words and go back to the silence, but once silence is disturbed all things will change.

With words she could grow closer to Justin.

With words she could describe the three tragedies and the crime she threw at God in response to them. And then Justin could tell her what to do. Her faith in him was endless. His magic had brought her speech back, and now he could help her find her little boy.

As she reached the third floor she heard Mr. Olen's voice drifting down the hallway. He was saying, "You'll like the man you've chosen. Blond hair, blue eyes. Just like what you asked for." She turned the corner and saw Mr. Olen coming the other way, a woman by his side.

Charlotte stopped dead in her tracks, staring in disbelief.

"God!" Belinda said. Her hand flew up to the string of pearls around her neck. The pearls broke. The beads clattered to the floor.

"What's wrong?" said Mr. Olen.

Belinda whirled on Mr. Olen. "You said it was anonymous here!"

"Yes, yes, it's supposed to be . . ."

"Supposed to be! You *jackass*!" Belinda ran down the hallway toward the back stairs.

"Wait!" Mr. Olen shouted.

Belinda marched across the backyard, her purse clutched in one hand, her face burning. Fighting tears. The heels of her court shoes rutting the dark grass. Four one-dollar bills in her beaded purse.

Discretion, the tall man had promised her. No one would be the wiser. Except for Charlotte, it seemed. Now everything had popped like a bubble. Her pride. Her privacy. The man she had picked for the night. Blond hair. Blue eyes.

The door to the sweet potato barn opened. "Hellooooo," a voice called.

Belinda stopped in her tracks. "Who's that?" she demanded.

The door swung open wide. In the orange-colored light, Benjamin stood bare-chested. He had unbuttoned the top half of his union suit, freed his arms and pushed the suit down around his waist. Now the cuffs of the empty sleeves almost brushed the ground. His hair was disheveled and his smile was wicked.

"It's me. The only man on this property," he said.

Belinda, fighting tears, was in no mood for conversation. "You're no man. You're just a little boy."

"Little? Ma'am, won't you take a closer look, here in the light?"

"You horrible little boy!" Belinda shrieked. "How dare you speak to me like that! And showing yourself to a woman in your underwear. How crude!"

Benjamin scratched himself near the crotch. "You tired of those kissy boys in there?"

"It's none of your business."

"Why you leaving so early?"

"Because," said Belinda, "they told me this house was *discreet!*"

"Was what?"

"You know. Private."

"Sure it is. You got lots of women who'd rather not be seen. Like you, I'll bet."

"I wasn't here about a man. I'm in the pillow business. I was just here delivering a pillow."

Benjamin took a step forward, then held the door open with the toes of his bare foot. "You're not a good liar."

"I'm telling the truth. But it's none of your business."

Benjamin pulled a cigarette out of one pocket and a book of matches out of the other. He lit his cigarette and took a long drag. "So your husband's not pleasing you."

"I'm not married."

Benjamin laughed. "You sure as hell are. I can tell, just by looking at you."

"My husband is a very prominent man in the community, smarty. When he hears about your insolence—"

"Yes. Why don't you tell him? And tell him where you were tonight."

"He wouldn't be angry. He's a perfectly understanding man."

"Then why are you here?"

Belinda had no answer to that, and so she walked up to Benjamin, slapped him in the face and then disappeared into the darkness. Benjamin stood there, amazed. Women had cried on him, kissed him, run their nails lightly down his back, composed songs for him, made him pies, knitted him socks. But not one of them had ever slapped him. He held his face, staring at the ruts Belinda's shoes had made in the grass. He was not used to this kind of woman coming out of the house, neither love-drugged nor compliant, but angry and unsoothed.

A cloud moved away from the moon, leaving the backyard lit. Benjamin noticed something in the grass. He picked it up. The woman had left her beaded purse behind.

He went back into the sweet potato barn and sat down cross-legged on his Indian blanket, thinking about her. Stroking the latch on the purse but not daring to open it, having been raised to treat secrets as sacred things. He glanced around the barn and noticed the tablet the mute woman had left behind, and which he had saved because it sounded mysterious. It lay on the ground with the last passage on it clearly visible under the light of the kerosene lantern.

YOU DON'T KNOW ANYTHING ABOUT WOMEN.
The words mocked him.

Charlotte lay with Justin, the room warm and the cypress lamb's shadow, made restless by the flickering light, large and quivering on the wall. Justin felt Charlotte take his hand and move it down lower on her body.

"Are you sure?" he asked.

"Yes," said Charlotte.

He sat up in the cot. "Charlotte," he gasped. "You spoke!"

She nodded. There was a story she needed to tell him. Several stories. But she had to plan it carefully. What to reveal, what to hide. She didn't want to lose him.

The bobcats lay low and the snakes burrowed. The birds circled and the squirrels moved higher, for the woods were filled with soldiers that summer, learning how to fight by fighting each other in the greatest of pretend wars, the Louisiana Maneuvers. The fake Blue army against the fake Red army. American against American, because there was talk of war and the young men needed the practice. They bathed in streams. They dug foxholes. They slept in yards and dreamed of cooler nights. They washed their faces with water splashed from their helmets—gear left over from World War I. They came with duffle bags, horses, half-tracks, pigeon vests. Dog tags and rations. They were a little better equipped than those who had trained the year before, in 1940—real guns instead of broomsticks—but they were disoriented, hot, thirsty for water and beer and far from home.

Before it was all over, some of them would die. Heart attacks, drownings, accidents, snake bites. And one soldier hanged himself from the limb of a sycamore tree and fled forever from the heat and the dancing bugs. A soldier here and a soldier there, cut down in the battle before the battle, the war before the war. Sent back home with promises to his family that he had been as brave as a real soldier could be in a pretend war.

In town, the stores were packed with fighting men, as were the barbershops and the bars. The threat of war made them thirsty for Mexican beer, which they threw on each other when the nights stayed hot.

A fight between the regular army and the National Guard had to be broken up by the house band striking up the national anthem, which forced the men to stop fighting for the required salute. One soldier, denied his tenth beer, drove his tank up to the saloon and butted open the swinging doors with his gunnel until the bartender reconsidered.

At curfew the men would stagger back to their base camps for another night under the stars, in a land that disoriented them, among strange creatures and crawling bugs.

The army that moved through Louisiana knocked limbs off pecan trees, ran sheep to death, dug foxholes and forgot to refill them. They crowded the streets for hours on end with their horse cavalry. They set off explosions that made nervous countrywomen drop cakes. One night the drunken men took down all the signs and barber poles in town and stacked them by the railroad depot. No one cared. The town was brimming with patriotism and starving for commerce. Soldiers had money and bullets for the Germans. They were heroes before the war began.

Many of them were Yankees, and some had never seen a cow or a chicken. They stared at the pigs running through the front yards of camelback houses, swore at the mosquitoes, scratched at the chiggers. A young private killed a snake with the butt of his rifle and proudly showed it to the woman—Lorraine Sands—whose yard he had slept in the night before.

"See, ma'am?" the private said proudly. "You won't have to worry about your kids being bitten now."

"That was a king snake, idiot," Mrs. Sands replied. "King snakes kill poisonous snakes. I hope a copperhead crawls in your sleeping bag tonight."

The soldier turned white, and after Mrs. Sands had calmed down she went inside to call her best friend from church (who could be reached on the telephone after three long cranks and two short ones) and tell her about the stupid Yankee who did not know a friend from an enemy.

"My God," Mrs. Sands said into the phone, "he'll kill the English and shoot marbles with the Germans once he gets overseas."

Charlotte's mother thought this was very funny, and when she put down the phone she repeated the story to her husband.

Charlotte was at the piano, laboriously revisiting the "Toreador Song." All day she had been playing it to the

distant sound of marching hooves on the macadam road
that led into town. She paused, heard the punch line and
her father's laughter.

Then the sound of a kiss. The same kind of kiss she
had practiced the year before under the muscadine vines.
Charlotte resumed playing, contemptuous of her parents'
open and guiltless love.

A short time later her mother would be kissed by fire,
all over, with the same quiet smacking sound.

Late in the summer the soldiers began to sleep on
Charlotte's lawn, on their blankets or in pup tents fes-
tooned with mosquito netting. Charlotte had Belinda over
for the night, and the two of them watched the soldiers
through the chintz curtains of Charlotte's bedroom.

"What color hair do you want? What color eyes?"
Belinda whispered. There were five hundred thousand soldiers out there in the dark. Plenty to choose from.

"Black hair. Gray eyes," Charlotte said.

"Blond hair. Blue eyes," Belinda said.

They raised the window and pressed their noses to the
screen. Late summer came into the room. The faint scent
of moonflowers and the sound of crickets. Light snores
from chigger-ravaged men. Charlotte and Louise smiled.
With all these soldiers around, they were safe from the
Germans, and from the prospect of becoming someone's
spinster aunt.

★   ★   ★

Charlotte and her friends went scavenging in the woods, browsing through the old encampments. Souvenir-hunting. They found canteens, duffel bags, a pair of boots, a field jacket, cigarette butts and one condom still in its packet. These things they gathered carefully and brought to the attic in Belinda's house, where they arranged their treasure. Each of them wanted to marry a soldier, one who would have gladly died in battle but did not. Instead this pretend soldier returned from the war with all his disciplined habits, to marry her and treat her like a queen.

The girls closed their eyes and imagined the Americans in battle. Charging. Yelling patriotic slogans through white and perfect teeth. Dignified even in the pitch and roil of war, as they would also be in peacetime, making love on cotton sheets. When the girls opened their eyes in Belinda's attic, they could almost see the Germans lying around them, dead.

The attic was insufferably hot in the August heat. Sweat ran down Belinda's face. "Those men out there need us," she said meaningfully. "They itch. They've got scratches on their arms. They're lonely. And their clothes need washing."

Charlotte laughed, loud enough that Belinda frowned. "I'm not going to just be a nurse to a man," she said. "Or a maid. True love is when a woman is equal to a man."

"You're just saying that because your mother is the boss of your father," Belinda said.

"She's not the boss," Charlotte returned hotly. "He makes rules too."

But truly, in her mind, she wondered why her father was not like the other men. His gentleness seemed off course here, out in the woods. He was softer than her friends' fathers. More pliant. When Charlotte played the piano, he joined in, his tenor a silky thing. Other men would laugh to hear him sing, or to see him wash the dishes.

Later, he would be quietly scorned for not dying in his wife's place. Something was wrong with that family, people would decide. These men who let their matriarch go up in smoke.

Milo and his friends lost interest in skipping stones and killing snakes. Now they wanted to be soldiers.

War and its prospects thrilled them, filling the woods with a deadly sense of tragedy and meaning. They divided themselves into two armies of three boys each, and fought against each other more ruthlessly and with less concern for safety than the soldiers themselves. Each side pictured the other as Germans and thus worthy of considerable malice and fear. Milo led the Red army, and his archrival, Tom, led the Blue one.

They moved from tree to tree with their broomstick rifles, fighting pitched battles and trampling the wild palmetto. Milo painted his face with mud, and because he owned nothing olive drab, he wore another ugly color.

He moved in slow motion, a pocketknife in his belt and one hand outstretched in front of him, as he had seen soldiers do. He crouched, then sank onto his belly, collecting pine straw in his belt buckle as he inched along the ground. The movement of a squirrel made his heart stop. Initials carved in a tree became German code. In this dreamy confusion, in a world half America and half Europe, half war and half peace, half playground and half bunker, enemyships were struck up between boy and tin can, boy and bush, boy and bird. So many enemies, and the supper bell just around the corner.

One of the boys drew the short stick and shimmied up a black gum tree to dump flour down on the boys, which was meant to designate the strafing from enemy planes. Milo crept forward on his belly, a sack of old pine cones over his shoulder, which he would hurl like grenades when the time was right. His own age—twelve—disappointed him in a way that a girl hadn't yet. He wanted so badly to fight, to carry a real gun and ride around in a tank.

A clot of flour hit Milo's face, blinding him. He wiped his stinging eyes. From the top of the tree came a high-pitched voice: "You're dead, Kraut."

Milo's friends/enemies took him to an abandoned sawmill, to an old concrete kiln that had become their clubhouse, and tied him up with a rope that one of their fathers had once used to whip a horse.

"Tell us where your army is hiding," they demanded.

Milo shook his head.

They stripped his shirt off, and Tom whipped him across the chest with bull nettles.

"Tell us," they said again.

Milo knew the value of a secret, even a pretend one, and so he remained silent as a stone, a burning agony spreading across his chest as Tom continued to whip him. Milo's lips pursed tight. Sweat ran down his face. He was proud of his defiance, of his silence. This same stubborn refusal to share words would later grow in his sister Charlotte, for entirely different reasons.

All around the parish, all around the world, there were little spaces full of secret things. Charlotte and her friends had the attic. Milo and his friends had the kiln. And Milo himself had the toolshed, out in the back of the house, so leaky and full of holes that blue jays would sometimes flutter in Milo's face when he opened the sagging door. All the good tools had been moved to a new, waterproof shed on the other side of the lawn, a fine shed complete with asbestos shingles. The old tools had remained to rust. There was no floor, only the hard ground, a few scattered pieces of pine straw and a weed or two.

The privacy of failed shelter. The House of Milo.

One day Milo entered to find a surprise. A carrier pigeon had somehow grown tired of its route and had defected to the old gun cabinet at the far end of the toolshed. A message was still tied to one leg, although the pigeon would not let Milo get close enough to untie it.

And so the pigeon and the mysterious message remained. The pigeon had come closer to being a real soldier than Milo ever had, and Milo took it as a sign. Instead of flying to the powers that be, the pigeon had detoured into Milo's shed. The toolshed became Milo's war center and the pigeon his general. Worthy of a salute, which it never returned. As the days passed, it began to favor the leg holding the message, in the way that old soldiers favor knees that harbor buried shrapnel. It sometimes cooed softly, for the other pigeons, perhaps. For the cool fall months. For peace.

Milo found the yellow braid from a cavalry hat and wore it in his belt loops, creeping through the woods with his face covered by a piece of torn mosquito netting. When he returned to the shed he reported all he'd seen and heard to the pigeon, in a whisper, sweat running down his face.

The Maneuvers went on. Mosquitoes and heat and snakes, and rumors of Patton coming to join them. The soldiers trained in this unfamiliar country, growing used to the shape of the trees, the force of the legends, the local dos and don'ts, the vagaries of Southern women, the word "pop" as opposed to the word "soda," which they drank on friendly porches in their dress khakis.

Milo and his friends watched them train. The soldiers

would blow up a section of railroad, build it back and then blow it up again. Once, something went amiss with the procedure and a huge oak tree caught on fire. Milo's eyes lit up. He imagined war itself as one great fire, men running into the flames, heroes rushing out again. Even the straw hair of the Germans seemed to be made for good kindling.

Sometimes Charlotte's mother had the soldiers over and cooked for them, not because she cared that much to have them in the woods, but because the other women at church had begun to host dinners, and Charlotte's mother wanted bragging rights for her own dinners. Chicken, rice, black-eyed peas. The soldiers tried not to bolt their food. Their eyes opened wide at the Southern cooking. This amazing taste in the middle of this bug-roiling, heat-shimmering land over which black-eyed Susans had spread like a carpet. Some of them had gone to the barbershop in town to be clean for the table. Their hair was slicked down with Wildroot Creme-Oil. They had shaved closely and smelled good.

They sent shy looks in Charlotte's direction.

It had been almost a year since the kiss under the grape arbor. Now grapes were ripening and falling in arbors all over the parish, and wild out in the woods. Charlotte was hungry for another kiss, which would buzz like a bee and soothe like the pulp of a grape.

Her mother was so close to dying, and yet had no

way of knowing. And so this small flirtation annoyed her. She cleared her throat and sprinkled salt on her yellow squash, still bound to the ordinary gestures of the living.

No one knew or would ever know, but had she lived she would have mellowed. Would have giggled more. Would have turned a jump rope for her grandchild, slowly but surely, the loop of that jump rope as perfect as she had once expected her children to be. She would have sat in the sun and basked in the mercy of a finally understood God. Not the God of wooden rulers and peach-tree switches and raised eyebrows, but the God of forgiveness and love.

But these things would not happen. She would die a disapproving Southern wife and mother, with half the silver polished and her apron soaking in the sink.

"Ma'am," said a soldier, looking at Charlotte's mother. "This is the best eating I've ever done."

The other soldiers murmured their agreement. Their hats off and their backs straight. Charlotte watched their lips.

After dinner her mother left the room, and went out on the porch to add starch to a willow tub of steaming water. This was her signal that the gaiety could begin, and that she would thoughtfully turn her back while Charlotte played the piano and the soldiers and Milo and her father, and even some girls from down the road, sang and danced.

Roll out the barrel, and we'll have a barrel of fun. I

wish I was in Dixie, away, away. Milo danced with the soldiers, his hair ruffled by their brotherly fingers. Over his ruffled hair they placed an army-issued cap, too big for him. It fell down over his eyes but he wouldn't remove it.

Spinning round and round, Milo was in the ecstasy of war, whirling in a musical confusion that both terrifies and exalts. Charlotte played faster and her father laughed.

Charlotte looked over her shoulder at the men. Too many to choose from. Perhaps that was what war was for—to thin out a woman's choices. Make it easier for her. This sacrilegious thought made Charlotte's fingers slip off the F-sharp. No one noticed. Milo was too happy to be dancing with the soldiers, and her father was too busy singing.

One day Milo and his two-man army discovered Tom's secret hideout, a tiny shack at the far edge of the Burgess property. Inside were crudely drawn maps, a set of rules for Tom's two men, two warm bottles of Orange Crush and an empty pack of Lucky Strikes.

"We have found the enemy's fort," Milo told his friends. "Now there's only one thing to do."

"What's that?" asked Brian Loften, Milo's palest friend and least supportive recruit.

Milo smiled. "Burn it," he said.

The wind kept putting out Milo's match, and Brian Loften sighed in relief.

*　　*　　*

August was ending, the attic was hot and the hair looping through Belinda's fingers was wet with perspiration. She had a story to tell, about the day she found herself standing in a meadow in her new gingham dress because she felt pulled to that meadow. Just a feeling she had when she woke up that morning. The heat turned her face wet and cool, and the grass was an endless green. A bee landed on Belinda's hand and she did not disturb it, but let it crawl up her arm.

Her new life began as a sound: the hum of a plane engine. The plane dropped out of the clouds and came so low over the tree line that the birds in the highest branches were frightened away. Belinda raised her head and saw the plane's underbelly. She waved. The plane circled back and dipped lower over the meadow, so low that Belinda could see the outline of a pilot. She waved again and the plane suddenly darted away. But Belinda knew that there had occurred some understanding between girl and plane, between soldier and civilian, between sky and earth, between steel and the pale skin of a waving hand. Sure enough, the plane came back. It passed over once more, and Belinda saw a tiny parachute making its way to earth. It fell into a clump of goldenrod, which Belinda was allergic to but never mind. She plunged into the yellow weeds and picked up the parachute, which really a white handkerchief attached to an empty grapefruit juice can. Inside the can was a note:

HELLO. THIS IS A SILLY WAY TO MEET BUT I FEEL THAT HEAVEN SENT YOU. WHAT ARE YOU DOING STANDING IN A FIELD IN THE MIDDLE OF NOWHERE? YOU ARE BEAUTIFUL. MY NAME IS RICHARD. WILL YOU MEET ME ON SUNDAY IN THIS FIELD? WEAR THE SAME DRESS.

And so Belinda went to meet her soldier of the sky. Wading through the grass in his dress khakis, he was no less magical. Blond hair, blue eyes. Six-feet-tall and a soon-to-be hero. They talked. They held hands. They embraced. They kissed among bees and Johnson grass, Belinda holding back the sneezes of her allergies the way a Baptist woman would hold back her fits of laughter.

The other girls sighed. The attic so hot. Charlotte felt the urge to cry, for Belinda's kissing story was better than hers. A meadow better than a grape arbor. A soldier of the sky better than a pious red-lipped boy who dreaded Armageddon. Even meadow bees were somehow more romantic than the grape-arbor kind.

Belinda smiled. "He is mine. We are in love."

Milo came back from playing war games and opened the door to his shed. His pigeon lay dead on the ground inside. Milo fought tears. He knew that soldiers die in war, and so do birds, but he was unprepared for the motionless pose and the feathers that suddenly seemed randomly attached. He bent down on one knee, thinking. Burial was for pet birds who never did anything special or brave. His bird was different. Its funeral called for flame, for heroes and fire belonged together. Milo left the shed, returned with the can of gasoline his father kept under the front porch.

It was five o'clock.

Inside the house, Charlotte sat before the pier-glass mirror, watching tears slowly roll down her face, impressed by her own weeping. She hated Belinda, who now owned the best legend of girl and soldier and had won, hands down, the competition over who could find the best fairy tale and bring it to life. She imagined Belinda and her soldier, flying together across Europe, kissing among clouds even as her soldier dropped fire on blonder men. A soldier elevated by war and by his plane. Fighting for freedom. Patriotic. Blue-eyed. Weightless.

Kane's civilian kiss was nothing compared to a kiss from a soldier, and so Charlotte cried before the mirror.

Outside, Milo knelt over the body of his bird. The anointing of valor. The bathing in glory. Fumes began to fill up the shed, and Milo's eyes watered. The gasoline soaked through the feathers and ran onto the ground beneath it. It ran across the dead bird's eye, but the eye did not blink. Milo considered untying the message from the bird's leg and reading it. But in the end he decided against it. The message would remain a secret, as would the bird, as would what the bird meant to him. He stood up slowly, stooping a little so that his head would not bump against the tin roof, and took a book of matches out of his pocket.

Charlotte's mother went to the stove to check on the consistency of the rice, looked in the sink to see if the stains on her apron had loosened, and threw a glance in the direction of the far bedroom, where her daughter was weeping in secrecy. She opened the cabinets and pulled down the dinner plates, folded the napkins, stirred the gravy and growled at the lumps. Lately she'd been feeling discontent, for she was tired of soldiers sleeping in the yard, tired of the summer and the hounds that seemed to multiply each year around the porch. She was tired of her old shoes and her new permanent. She wanted to lie down and sleep for months. In her mind was the cobwebbed mass of things undone and enough idle thoughts to unravel through three different countrysides. Dinner was almost ready and she wondered where her husband was. And Milo.

She went down to her daughter's bedroom and opened the door without knocking. Charlotte looked up from the mirror. Two tears were halfway down her face, and she wiped them away quickly.

"What are you crying about?"

"I'm not crying."

"Where's Milo?"

"I think I saw him playing around the toolshed."

"Get ready for supper." Charlotte's mother went into

the kitchen, checked on the gravy and parted the curtains so she could look out into the backyard.

It couldn't be.

Black smoke and fire. All the hot colors—orange and red and yellow—were using the old boards as platforms to leap at the blue in the sky.

Petty thoughts and middle-aged irritations vanished from her body. Her mind froze. Her hands flew to the doorknob and jerked it open.

"Milo! Milo!" she shouted. "Milo!"

She slammed the door behind her and rushed through the yard, gone mad from the sudden drama, her feet pumping, her arms thrown out in front of her, hurtling toward the shed and the possibility that her only son was dying inside.

"Milo!" The rusted latch on the shed door had been made new and hot by fire, and it burned its shape into her palm as she yanked the door open and plunged inside. She dropped to her knees, moving quickly through the shed, covering every space with her frantic hands even as her breath scorched the back of her throat.

In the far corner, near the gun rack, she put her hands out and touched the cotton shirt she had ironed that morning. Inside the shirt a body shivered. She seized her son and pulled him back through the shed door and into the yard, where the grass was still green and the dogs weaved and barked.

Her curly hair was heavy with flames, as was her cotton dress. Milo fainted on the grass while his mother twirled around and around, flames making kissing sounds but otherwise covering her so quietly, that inside the house, Charlotte watched two more tears fall down her face and sighed at her lot in life.

The woman danced. She danced. While the chickens muttered in the tin coop and the cows looked shyly her way and ashes floated toward the standing water in the ditch by the road.

Life is a riot of failed space. Hiding places found, or diminished, or destroyed. Milo's shed burned while his mother twirled and he lay in a dead faint.

Milo's father pulled into the driveway and saw the smoke. He leaped from his car, rushed to the backyard and found his wife on fire. He tripped over Milo running to her, got up, took her in his arms, carried her to the edge of the yard and dropped her down the well.

A quick-thinking man with a wife already past quick thinking. Already in heaven with the God she feared. Laughing at herself now. Laughing with God over her earthly dread of Him, her frantic efforts to please.

Later, the neighbors would immortalize Martha Gravin as a woman who loved her children dearly enough to die for them. They would bring over divinity candy and peach pie and stews and smothered chicken, and sing "Amazing Grace" so loud at her funeral that the preacher raised his eyebrows. All the while asking themselves the same private question: Did Martha Gravin not have the stupidest son in the world? Who had made a funeral pyre of a dead pigeon in a closed space? With gasoline, no less?

She was gone, and the absence of her strict and practical ways somehow made the grief of her family that much more unbearable. Mr. Gravin sat in his easy chair hour after hour, his hands over his ears as if shielding them from the high-toned buzz of events best forgotten. If only he'd come home a few minutes earlier, if only he'd kept a better eye on Milo, if only he'd put the gasoline on the top shelf in the garage, where Milo couldn't reach it . . . Mr. Gravin picked up a bottle one day, took a few deep gulps of its contents and found that it made the flames around his burning wife the bland yellow color of a box of ant bait. He drank some more and his wife stopped twirling. He drank some more, and a little more, until the bottle was empty, the well out back contained only water and his wife was kissing him in the green and shrineless yard.

Milo began wandering farther and farther into the woods, hiding. He had killed his mother, the woman who had cooked his favorite meals and cut his hair and helped him find catalpa worms to use for fishing. He wondered if she forgave him, or if his sister did, or his father. At night he dreamed of a pigeon that wore his mother's face.

Charlotte herself was haunted by the fact that if only she had realized what was happening, she might have reached her mother in time. But while the terrible event unfolded she had sat before her pier-glass mirror, crying her eyes out over Belinda and her soldier of the sky. Still, into Charlotte's mind-numbing grief came the magic of Belinda's story with all its clouds and clover and promise and its one tiny parachute falling from the sky. Because Charlotte thought that things could not get worse, because she believed that she was owed some miracle in a green field, because she did not understand that sometimes a tragedy attracts another in the same way that a dress attracts a plane, she went into the meadow one afternoon to look for her own perfect man.

17

Belinda was to blame. It was her myth that inspired Charlotte, motherless by two weeks, to put on her prettiest blue dress and her clip-on earrings and go to Belinda's lucky meadow to watch the sky. Like Belinda, she would find the man of her dreams simply by looking pretty and looking up.

She was sixteen years old, with no one to tell her what to do. She could wear lipstick. She could set her hair with beer. She could drink that beer. She could listen to big-band music, and to Negro jazz. She could kiss any man she wanted to. Her mother's pull on her was weak now, made fragile by the sheer distance from heaven to earth. And yet she knew that she would have given it all up in a second—music beer red lips even the kiss of a man—to see her mother sitting on the bank, holding a cane pole and asking God to let her catch a nice little goggle-eye.

Charlotte was brushing her hair when Milo came into the room. He was cowed and quiet, a bandage still on his face from the burns. More on both arms. The shrine to his mother growing in the corner of the backyard.

"Where you going, Charlotte?"

"To Lowe's meadow."

"Can I go with you?"

"No, Milo. I have to go by myself."

"What for?"

"Can you keep a secret?"

Milo nodded.

"I'm going to find a pilot. Like Belinda's pilot."

"That why you put on lipstick?"

"Yes."

"Mama wouldn't want you meeting men like that."

She looked at him. "I know." She felt her eyes well up and tried to keep the tears from running down her face, fearing that they would upset Milo and send him running back to work on the shrine. "But Mama's gone. And I need a boyfriend, Milo. I'm really lonely."

He nodded. "I'm lonely too."

This new boyfriend would be found between two odd-shaped clouds. Charlotte was sure of it because, as the days without her mother had passed and rumors of Belinda's great new love had sifted into their house with the Bundt cakes and the covered dishes, Charlotte had begun to feel that the magic would come around again, dropping suddenly on her head like the flour her brother used in his war games. And so Charlotte walked through the woods, down the paths and over a dry riverbank, through a grove of hardwoods until finally the path opened onto a vast rolling meadow, dancing with the colors of wildflowers, humming with bees.

It was all just as Belinda had described. Charlotte waded out in the middle of the meadow, ignoring the prospect of snakes. She stood near a clump of Johnson grass, staring up at the sky.

The sun moved. The clouds passed. The grasshoppers spat the color of vanilla extract. The birds flew by, but nothing bigger or louder or more promising. And still Charlotte stood, waiting, until she knew that the plane wasn't going to come, for her rival, Belinda, had already grounded all the fairy tales to be had in that blue, shining sky.

It was late in the afternoon when Charlotte, tired and hot and discouraged, went back into the forest and headed down the path toward home.

At the riverbank the soldiers found her.

They seized her arms from behind and forced her to her knees, then onto her back. The hands over her eyes stinging them with loose sand. One of the soldiers hit her, hard, across the mouth. The two of them handling her like a doll, turning her to one side to unzip her blue dress and pulling it down her body, the hem of it catching briefly on the buckle of her shoe, polished into a shine that could be seen from a passing plane. They mumbled among themselves. By their unfamiliar accents, she knew they must be soldiers. Northerners, training for the coming war.

She kept her eyes closed as they took their turns, and then she heard the sound of one joining them. His the most hesitant rhythm. His the gentlest voice. And yet she hated him the most, for arriving late and not saving her, but finally deciding to take his turn as well. A human joining two animals out of a freedom of choice.

She wondered, sometimes, if the shape of her body was still in that bank, unfilled by time, and if it still told her story to everyone who passed, a tale made more obscene by the paw prints of some wild animal that trailed through the depression in the sand which was posed like a snow angel defiled by other angels. See where the arms flailed? And the knees held down those arms? And the face turned away? And the feet kicked?

And why should Charlotte herself speak when that depression in the ground described events so eloquently? For it is by their leavings that events truly speak: wineglasses left on a table, bullets spent on a battlefield, a low place in a riverbank where a girl once lay.

She would have imagined that one tragedy would protect her from another, for she believed, at the time, that tragedies don't travel in pairs. Soldiers wounded in battle rarely get food poisoning too. Little boys trampled by horses don't, in quick succession, lose their favorite dog to a hunting accident. And girls whose mothers burn up aren't pressed down, two weeks later, into a riverbed of sand.

Charlotte had stopped speaking at that very instant her body was speaking for her, and when she had worked the blindfold off and found her way back home, her brother was the first one to receive her gift of silence. Milo had been working on his mother's shrine. When Charlotte came out of the woods, he rose to meet her, wiping the dirt off his knees. He stopped dead in his tracks when he saw her face, her torn dress, the disheveled hair that just a few hours before had been full of curls and shine.

"Charlotte, what's the matter? Where have you been?"

She shook her head.

"Your mouth is all swelled up." Suddenly a look of understanding crossed Milo's face. "Did that pilot you met in the meadow hurt you, Charlotte?"

Charlotte's eyes filled with tears at the thought of that mythical man, so different from the ones she had met.

Milo's eyes turned red. He'd always had a temper, but watching him now, Charlotte saw that his anger had become more masculine. Like a chin growing whiskers, it had aged. "What did that pilot do to you, Charlotte?" he screamed. "I am going to find him and kill him! I'll protect you! I'll kill them all!"

She reached out her hand to her brother, but he had already hopped the fence and was running into the woods. She stood watching him. The difference between soldiers of the land and those of the sky wasn't something she wanted to explain.

A few months later, Milo tried to burn down the air

base, out of his newly found hatred for pilots. And it was this second burning—not accidental, but deliberate—that made him an outcast.

She couldn't feel sorry about it. She felt sorry about too many things by then. Sorriest of all that she'd trusted God. Now she wanted to shout at Him: *You have sent two terrible things, now where is the third thing?* And when the third thing came—the baby growing in her womb—Charlotte knew that it must be a demon. And that it must die.

She lay in a space bordered by summer honeysuckle. Her back against the pine straw. Knees in the air. Panties around one ankle. Her eyes wide open to see treetops, squirrels, birds. Her white thighs that didn't match the woods. The unbearable pain of giving birth, like a lifetime of guilt collected in rhythmic spasms. Her screams drove a dragonfly from the nectar of a nearby thistle. No name to call out. The three fathers off killing and being killed in a land as bloody as the ground beneath her rump.

The baby was so perfect that even cutting the cord seemed a reduction of his beauty. Eyes the most stunning blue she had ever seen, filled with light. She shaded his face with her hand and still the light shone, as if the color itself was bursting with a secret, not a bad secret but a heavenly one.

The sugarcane knife was still in her hand. It trembled. A few quick thrusts, without thought, and she could start over again. No one would ever have to know. But the baby's eyes stopped her. No demon could have eyes so blue. No demon could send such a peace flowing through her just by lying in her arms.

She buried the knife with the umbilical cord.

Charlotte hid in an old sawmill for two days, nursing this child among abandoned machinery. Sweet milk and a bittersweet longing. She couldn't keep him, for he would require an explanation and this she stubbornly refused to give. For the shame on the riverbank she had made private and deeply quiet, like this boy, and in a sense, the shame then belonged to her. To share it would make it real.

On the morning of the third day, she went to a giant oak stump on a well-traveled part of the forest and laid the baby down. He was wrapped in the cloth of a cotton feed sack, the printed kind that women had used to make dresses for themselves during the war. The baby cried out once and was silent. Charlotte made her way back home, sunlight pouring down into the forest and drying the tips of her breasts. Now she had thrown a crime back at God. Her own crime. She felt bitterly pleased, and yet at the same time she felt her heart might break.

"Where have you been?" her father demanded.

Charlotte looked around, found a tablet and wrote: I GOT LOST IN THE WOODS.

"Lost," he said. The explanation seemed to appease him. How simple. Daughters get lost in the woods, wives burn up, well water goes bad, spring turns into summer. He sucked on his pipe. "Get washed up, then."

Milo ran into the bedroom as she was taking off her shoes. "You're back! You're back! You're back!" he shouted, and whirled and danced as his boyhood moved through him for the first time in months. "Now we're a family again!"

A family. The words broke something in her. That baby on the stump was her family. Her blood. Her boy.

She ran from the room, past her father, into the back-yard, out the far gate and into the woods, Milo calling behind her. She ran blindly, branches scraping her face, her bare feet catching on brush. Once she fell down, and when she rose back up, tiny pieces of broken pine straw clung to the wet places on her dress where her breasts had leaked milk. By the time she reached the stump she was gasping for breath.

Her baby was gone.

Vanished. Taken by a fisherman or a hunter or by a taunted, riled-up God.

Charlotte walked through the woods all day, hunting for signs, wondering what to do. Whom to tell. In the end she told no one, went back to hating the soldiers because that hatred felt better than longing for her son. The thought of the boy left her weak as she went about her chores, stirring the starch into the clothes, throwing millet to the chickens, pulling weeds in the front garden. The silence in her was unbearable, and she fought the urge to run from house to house, shouting all her stories and all her grief. And above all, shouting, "Where is my son? Who has my son?" She remained alert for news. Who in the area had found a little boy? She never heard anything, although once could not stop herself and ran out into the road when she saw the minister's wife, who knew everyone's business, strolling by. Charlotte wrote down on her pad:

I HEARD SOMEONE FOUND A BABY. TRUE?

The minister's wife shook her head. "Found a baby?" she said, confused. "I haven't heard of anything like that. Where did you hear that?" And Charlotte had turned and fled back into the house. The next day she'd gone back to the stump and very carefully looked for clues. A bit of cloth, a thread, a strand of hair? The footprints of whoever had taken him? Nothing. Just the absence of the thing that was hers.

Charlotte wanted to tell Justin all of this.

To lie down beside him in darkness and put her mouth to the black cave of his right ear, talk into it until her history fluttered there, adjusting to its new home like a bat adjusts to a dark new space. And the reason for her long silence would finally be known to just one person, which was all that would be needed.

Justin would grieve upon hearing the first story. A girl separated from her mother by a spiraling flame. This girl who had to take her mother's place, stand in those ashes and raise her little brother.

And how would Justin react to the second story?

He had been a soldier too, but surely his loyalties would lie with her. Armies change, but love is forever. She would take him to visit the scene of the crime and horror would fill him, as it did the American soldiers when they saw Dachau and Buchenwald after the war. Justin would hunt down those three soldiers, one by one.

But first things first.

In the darkness of their room, as the wind blew and trees shimmered red and gold out in the woods, and pine cones dropped on the forest floor with the sound of small gulps, Justin pulled his ear away from Charlotte's mouth.

"Really?" he whispered. "That happened to your mother? How old were you?"

"Sixteen."

"My God. Where were you?"

"In the house. Crying about other things."

"How did your father react?"

"He lost himself."

"And your brother?"

"He ran off into the woods, hiding in foxholes. I had to find him. It's always been my job to find Milo."

Sorrow in his eyes. He was wounded for her. What was old to her was new to him. She stroked his face. This had gone well. Three more sorrows to be told: the story of the riverbank. The quiet swelling. And then the new crime she had committed all by herself: the giant oak stump, the baby waving its arms.

Justin would forgive her.

18

Louise arched her back and then pressed hard on the nylon brush, urging it across a gnarl in the wood of the porch. The wind picked up, blowing strands of pine straw on the porch and chilling her wet hands. She paused, sinking back on her haunches. The odor of the porch—wet clean wood—entered her nostrils. The scent no longer soothed her. Upstairs, her soldier was dressing after his night with Charlotte, who had apparently shrugged off her silence and could now speak, according to Milo, who had literally danced when he'd told Louise.

"It's a miracle, Louise! A miracle! Charlotte's getting better!"

The lake shone behind them. Louise, who did not care to hit the dirty ground again, had simply nodded.

"I know the secret of Charlotte's happiness," Milo had added. "It's a man. He lives at your house. Why didn't you tell me, Louise?"

Louise shrugged. "I'm not allowed to tell."

"What do you think of that?"

"Of what?"

"Of Charlotte being with one of those men."

Louise pretended to think about it. "She should find someone else."

"Why?"

"Because the men and women there—it's strange. They aren't normal couples."

"I know what you mean. But me and my wife were a normal couple, and I almost blew her head off. Anyway, it don't matter what you and I think. Charlotte's happy. And she's talking. That's what I care about."

Louise shrugged again. She did not tell Milo that both Justin and The Soldier Who Hanged Himself—the man she loved—were one and the same. In the battle for Justin's heart, Milo would be on his sister's side.

"He's coming over for lunch on Sunday," said Milo. "I'm going to meet him."

"I would ask him some things," said Louise.

"What things?"

"Well, maybe he's done wrong in the past. Something terrible." (Louise pictured the safe, locked tight, bulging with secrets. Someone should punch holes in the top. Secrets should breathe.) "Maybe he wouldn't be safe for Charlotte."

"Safe?" Milo laughed. "Any man who lives at that house is gonna be safe. They're all a bunch of sissies."

Louise leaned over to Milo. "All men have a little badness in them," she whispered.

Milo looked at her. "Sometimes, honey," he whispered back, "a woman can be just as evil as a man."

Benjamin stood next to the porch with one foot raised, hesitant to step where Louise had just scrubbed. He did not want to torment his sister, but only because he needed her advice. He had spent the past two nights alone, too preoccupied to lure in the satisfied women who stumbled across the grass, for he was consumed with the vision of the single unsatisfied woman who had called him a boy and slapped him hard across the face. Women were supposed to be soft, sleepy, compliant, weepy, clingy. *But I love you, Benjamin.*

Out of the darkness she'd come, her eyes blazing in the light that poured from the barn, her jaw clenched. This woman was different. Sleepy she was not, but bristling with anger. Teeth showing. Eyes shining.

Through the long night, he'd sat and thought about the exchange of dialogue over and over: *They told me this house was discreet.* Every now and then he'd pick up the beaded purse, weighing it in his hand, trying to discern the objects inside by feel. Lipstick? Keys? Marbles? Surely she would have missed her purse by now.

Just before dawn, he'd read once again the mystery of the words on the mute woman's pad. The fractured and sometimes hostile poem.

I WANT THE FAINTED MAN.

SHUT UP.

A KISS?

YOU DON'T KNOW ANYTHING ABOUT WOMEN.

"Porch getting clean?" Benjamin said to Louise.

Louise looked at him suspiciously. "Why do you ask? You want it to be extra fresh before you stomp on it? Or blow your nose and fling snot on it? Or spit on it?"

"Come on, Louise. I've never spit on it. Well, just that once. I was aiming at a tin can."

"Go away, dirty boy." Louise went back to scrubbing.

"How's your soldier?"

Louise scrubbed harder.

"Come on, Louise. You can tell me."

She looked up. Soap bubbles were running down the backs of her hands. "Why do you want to know all of a sudden?"

"Because I'm your brother."

"What do you want, Benjamin?"

Benjamin sighed. He pulled at a metal button on his corduroy jacket, ran his fingers through his hair. The fidgeting that forms a question. At last he said: "Can I ask you something?"

"What?"

The long silence made Louise pause in her scrubbing. Her brother had a distinct red color on his face.

"When you look at me," he said, "do you see a man or a boy?"

"Neither. I see my brother."

"Well, pretend that I'm not your brother. Man or boy?"

"Both," she said finally. "An in-between creature."

"Oh. What makes for a man?"

"Well . . . men shave."

"I do too."

"I mean every day. And men take care of their hair better than you."

"Okay."

"And dress better. And tuck in their shirts. And let bugs live. And eat with their hat off. And read the paper. And smoke pipes. And they don't spit in their palm and then look at it . . ."

"All right," said Benjamin. "Shut up. That's enough." He felt irritated. Humiliated. He desperately wanted to wipe snot on his hand and then touch her porch, to teach her a lesson for telling the truth. He half raised his hand to his nose, then thought better of it and walked slowly back to the barn.

"Benjamin!" Louise called after him.

He turned around. "What?"

She pushed her damp hair out of her eyes. "When you look at me, do you see a girl or a woman?"

Benjamin's sad eyes lit up. "I see a big germ," he said. He closed the door to the sweet potato barn and opened the woman's purse. He found a small wallet containing four dollars, two buttons in the change purse and a card that read, in dainty gold letters:

BELINDA STANLEY.
PILLOWS OF TRUE LAVENDER.
113 MAIDEN LANE.

19

This old shack is a firetrap itself, thought Belinda's husband, Sheriff Richard Stanley. He pounded on the door again.

"Open up, you little asshole!" he demanded.

Finally he heard someone fumbling with the lock. The door moved enough for a head to stick out. A pair of half-open eyes regarded him distantly.

"Hello, Fire Boy," said the sheriff. "Sleeping late?"

"What the hell do you want?" asked Milo Gravin.

"I want to talk to you, so get your ass out here."

Milo kicked the door open and stood there with his arms crossed, in a pair of old corduroys, bare-chested.

"You got two minutes," said Milo.

"Really?" asked the sheriff. He punched Milo in the face. Milo stumbled back into the filth of his house, recovered himself and rushed forward with his fists clenched.

The sheriff drew his gun. "I wouldn't strike an officer of the law if I were you. Better stick to trees, son."

He watched as Milo slowly lowered his fists.

"That's better. Now put a shirt on." Milo turned away and began hunting through the clutter inside the house for a shirt. The sheriff holstered his gun. He had nothing but contempt for people who lived this way. Garbage on the floor and rusted tools around the yard and every shade of dog shit known to man within stepping distance.

Milo buttoned his shirt and moved past the sheriff into medium sunlight. His nose had started to swell. "What did I do now?"

"That depends on where you were last night."

"I was here. Working on my car." Milo pointed to an old Chevrolet whose hood was propped open with the lower half of a cane pole.

"Sure you weren't running around somewhere?"

"I didn't leave here all night."

"Someone set the First Pentecostal Church on fire last night. Took out three pews. Know anything about that?"

"No."

"Got a little itchy for a blaze?"

"No."

The sheriff sighed and took a cigarette out of his shirt pocket. His lighter flared. He watched Milo's eyes widen at the sight of the tiny flame.

"You like that, don't you?" the sheriff said after a long inhalation.

"No."

"I heard different. I heard you set your mama on fire

way back when. During the Maneuvers. With soldiers in the woods, all around you, training for war. And you. Burning up the very women we went over there to protect."

Milo's face turned red. The sheriff watched his hands clench.

"Go ahead, Milo. Hit me. See what happens."

The sheriff waited.

Milo turned around and punched the wall.

"Yes, that's it, boy. Take it out on wood."

Milo glowered at him and rubbed his knuckles so hard they cracked.

"I guess you know I was in the war," said the sheriff. "I was a fighter pilot."

"I hate pilots."

"I know. Heard you were burning down the air base while I was getting shipped across the seas to get my ass shot off by flak every day or so. You know how long the average B-17 lasted in 1943? Eleven missions. A pilot pretty much knew he was going to die. And if he did, his buddies fought over his short coat. I knew all that. And yet I fought. That's what heroes were made of."

"I was too young to fight," Milo murmured.

The sheriff caught the look of sudden longing in his eyes and went in for the kill. "Yes, that's too bad. You could have pranced around burning things. But do you know what? Even if you'd been old enough, it wouldn't have mattered. You'd have gone over there and played soldier boy a little, maybe killed a couple of Germans. But you would never have been like me. Because you ain't hero material. And you never will be."

"I would've fought just as brave as you!" Milo sputtered.

"Just as brave? Just as brave? You can't even talk, son. You gotta let fires do your talking for you. Like the fire you set in the church."

"I was here all night."

"Of course you were. Anyone here with you?"

Milo looked away. "No," he said.

The sheriff sucked his cigarette with exaggerated power, so that the orange color bit hard into the tobacco. He exhaled as he studied Milo. He held out his left hand to him, palm up. "Look at that," he said. "It's not so much fun when you're the one burning. Try feeling a woman's breast with a hand like this."

Milo rubbed his knuckles. "I was here all night."

"Well, we'll see about that. Because you've been lucky. You were practically caught red-handed burning down Sid Havens's ribbon cane patch. But the truth is, Sid Havens is even more of a son of a bitch than you are. So maybe he deserved what he got. But setting a church on fire is different. Let me tell you something, boy. In Buchenwald, *innocent people burned*. Never again. Not in this parish. I'll kill you next time. And you know what else? It really ticks me off to know that I fought for my country, got shot down, got treated like a dog in Buchenwald, just to come back here and realize I fought to save people like you. At least the Germans were clean."

The sheriff finished another cigarette as he drove back toward home. He had wanted to toy with Milo Gravin just a little longer, maybe find a way to needle him further about his mother or his temper or the way he lived. But he had to get back to Belinda. She had been acting strangely lately, or so it seemed to him. She no longer rushed to the door to meet him when he came home from work, but waited a second or two. She did rub his tired shoulders after a hard day's work, but stopped half-way down his spine instead of at the small of his back. A very slight change, really. But noticeable.

He had first seen her at a distance, the sun in her hair as she waved from a green field, and now he began to feel that distance coming back. And their two worlds—sky and earth—once united in marriage, had begun to pull away from each other very slowly; and when he awoke in the middle of the night, the dark form that was her body was a little farther down on the mattress.

That girl whose parish had seized him as a hero was fully capable of betrayal. This he knew, for she reminded him of another girl he'd met in the summer of 1944.

Funny, what goes through your mind.

After the Plexiglas from the fusillade had been shat-tered by flak, after his waist gunner was dead and his navigator too, after his plane had lost its bomb-bay doors and two engines, after he had bailed out and was sailing through the air toward the French countryside, he thought of a limerick:

There was a young girl from Madras
Who had a beautiful ass
Not rounded and pink
As you probably think
But with long ears, a tail and eats grass.

The limerick seemed hilarious to him, especially in the context of the war and the falling ashes and the frenetic beating of his heart. Especially because what was supposed to be a milk run had turned into such a disaster. Just bomb a railroad-marshaling yard, he was told, and then he could fly back to the base. Look at pinups in *Yank*. Smoke cigarettes. Heat up dinner on a stove that was actually a glycol tank. See if Belinda had sent him a letter.

Now he repeated the limerick as details pushed through the geography beneath his dangling feet: trees, houses, fields, tractors.

And a girl.

She stood in a green field, waving him over. Dancing a little. The sun in her hair. He hit the hard earth, and the limerick went black for a stanza or two. When he regained consciousness he was looking straight up into her adoring stare.

"American?" she said in a thick accent.

"Yes," he said. "American."

She helped him get out of his parachute and his fleece-lined aviator jacket. Knelt down beside him, touched his face, ran her fingers through his hair. Richard Stanley had seen American and English women look at him this way. Now this French girl. One of his legs hurt fiercely, and so he sat there and let her touch him while he tried to get his bearings. He looked to the right and the left. A few cows grazing. Some trees and a red barn.

He was thinking about hiding in that red barn when the girl took his hand and kissed it. She smiled, turning his hand over so she could kiss it on the other side. But she didn't. Instead she stared at a palm ravaged by fire.

Putting out that flaming oxygen bottle had won him the Medal of Honor. Now it was about to cost him his freedom.

There was a different look in the girl's eyes now. A contempt for his imperfection. She rose to her feet and started walking back across the meadow while Richard began to drag himself in the direction of the barn.

When she reached the fence, she ducked under it and ran out into the road beyond, waving her arms. "American!" she screamed. "American!"

The Germans took him to the Fresnes prison in Paris. On a warm August night, he and the other prisoners were

packed in old 40 and 8 boxcars for transport to Buchenwald. Then the long trip began.

The threat of typhus.

The unbearable heat.

The occasional fainting of a pregnant woman.

The heat drove him mad. The odor it made out of
breath and tears and excrement and the lavender cologne
of an old woman who had died in the far corner. He
hated the frightened people around him, hated their language and their arms and legs and the backs of their necks
and their unwashed hair. *There was a young girl from France,
a traitorous girl from France* . . .

At Buchenwald they took his clothes, his watch, his
Benzedrine pills and his Zippo lighter, then shaved him
from head to toe. They gave him a uniform—a pongee
shirt and a light pair of denim pants—which he found out
later had belonged to a Jewish prisoner who had been
executed.

Two weeks later, he saw a man set on fire for throwing up his goulash soup. He turned away, sickened.

The glance of a Russian POW.

The screams of the burning man.

A pile of bodies by a bunker.

The busy sound a fire makes.

A cloud overhead.

A French girl had found him imperfect and sentenced
him to hell for it. And he could not stop thinking of his
girl, Belinda, who waited for him in America. Who had

also waved him down from a green field. The sun in her hair. Already making a myth of him. Would she betray him too?

The war had been over for three years now, and Buchenwald had given up its secrets. The crematoriums, the gallows, the rooms whose center drains pulled down blood. The jars full of organs. The shrunken heads that served as paperweights. The lamps whose light glowed through the eagle tattoos of Russian POWs. The bodies piled up in square-shaped stacks.

It was all over, and he was no longer a prisoner but the sheriff of a small Southern town whose wife had been acting strangely.

He pulled into his driveway.

"Belinda," he called as he walked through the door, "I'm home."

The air was murky with the scent of lavender, and immediately it made him queasy. Belinda drifted in from the kitchen in a gauzy dress, her smile looking like something forgotten entirely and then remembered at the very last second. It had that slipping quality. She kissed him on the cheek.

"How was work today, Richard?"

"It was fine. What have you been doing?"

Belinda stepped back, then forward, as if each sentence came with its own proper distance. "Making pillows."

"I could tell from the lavender stink."

"I'm sorry. I'll open a window."

"Never mind. What else did you do today?"

"I took Ralph over to see his little friend."

"What friend?"

"Nathan."

"What time did you get back here?"

"About one o'clock."

"Then what did you do?"

"I took a nap."

"Then what?"

"I did some baking."

"And you didn't leave again?"

"No, I didn't. I've been here all afternoon."

He hated her manner. Skittish and nervous and light on her feet. Moving her arms too much, her pale hands as distracting as sudden light.

"Get me a lemonade," he said.

Later that night, he stood bare-chested before the mirror, studying himself intently. Belinda sat on the bed behind him, brushing her hair.

"In Buchenwald, the doctors injected me with something green," he muttered. "My chest turned black. I wonder what it did to me."

"It was probably just some medicine, dear," Belinda offered.

He turned around. "Yes, just some medicine," he said. "The Nazis were very concerned about people's health.

They'd lay out syringes full of concentrated phenol. You know what that does?"

"No."

"It kills you."

"Oh."

"Come here. I want you to feel my chest and see if one side is bigger than the other."

"Don't be silly, Richard. Your chest looks fine."

"I said, come here."

Slowly Belinda approached him. She put her hands on each side of his chest.

"They feel the same," she said.

"One's not bigger?"

"I don't think so. And even if it was, that would be all right. A lot of women have one breast that's bigger than the other."

He grabbed her wrists, his ruined left hand applying steady pressure, his right hand squeezing so tightly her fingers turned purple. She groaned deep in her chest and he pulled her closer.

"Belinda," said Richard Stanley. "Tell me something. *Dear.* Do I look like a *fucking woman?*"

20

Charlotte stood at the stove, remembering the old days when she had helped her mother prepare a Sunday meal for the soldiers. The thought of soldiers still prickled her skin, but the act of cooking contained no fear. Peeling the potatoes, flouring the meat. Watching the okra float to the top of boiling water. Pulling the heavy tea bag out of the bubbling pot.

The doorbell rang.

Milo rose from the couch. He had on his good khakis and a clean white shirt.

"You must be Justin," Milo said as he opened the door, holding out his hand to the dark-haired man.

"Nice to meet you," said Justin.

Milo showed Justin around the house. "That's Charlotte's room." Milo's obvious delight at having a guest was making his words spill forth frantically. "This used to be my grandmother's house and boy she was a card you know when she was ten she killed a rattlesnake with a slingshot and she just kept that spunk for oh about eighty years and when she finally died it was after two years in bed but I still miss her because even though she was Baptist she was fun and so anyway Charlotte moved in here and myself I live in a little place way off on a dirt road it gets kind of lonely especially because I don't have a wife no more not since the day I came home and found her in bed with someone else the whore but I have to tell you she had a pretty ass and that probably saved her life a time or two . . ."

Milo led Justin to the living room. "See that piano? Charlotte used to play when the soldiers were here and I used to dance with them. But I want to show you something else." Milo squatted down and opened a cabinet by the fireplace. "See this?" He pulled out a stack of tablets and handed them to Justin.

Justin read the first page.

TO THE STORE.

NO, TODAY.

BECAUSE I SAID SO.

DOES NOT.

TWO O'CLOCK.

Spare words that made their own poetry.

"That's from 1945," said Milo, looking over Justin's shoulder. "I date 'em. There's about a hundred tablets in there, and a lot more than that in the shed."

"Why do you save these?"

Milo shrugged. "Oh, I don't know. It's like saving part of Charlotte. She's special. But you know that, right?"

"I know that."

Milo took the tablets from Justin's hands and put them back inside the cabinet. "I guess what I'm trying to say is that you rescued my sister. You brought her voice back. Now she doesn't need these tablets."

Justin shook his head. "I don't think it was me."

"Sure it was. She started seeing you, the words came back." Milo stood up and stretched. "Come out on the porch. I want to talk to you, man to man."

Milo whittled on a gaunt stick of willow as he spoke. ". . . and so I tried to kill her with a pump shotgun, but it wouldn't go off. Isn't that something? I should be in prison right now."

"That's something," said Justin.

"They say I tried to burn her house down too, but that's just a damn rumor." Milo whittled off another slice of willow. It twirled as it fell to the porch floor. He leaned back in his bentwood chair. "So what's it like in that house over there?"

Justin shrugged. "It's a place to live."

"Is it true that all the fellows over there are happy?"

"Most of them, I guess. Wouldn't you be?"

Milo hooted. "Hell, no, I wouldn't be happy. Not if I couldn't ever put it in." He lowered the chair. "Tell me something else," he whispered. "I hear that house can chase off a man's demons."

"That's what I hear," said Justin.

"It chase off yours?"

"Some of them."

"You were in the war, right?"

"Yes."

"That's funny. Charlotte don't usually like soldiers. You guilty about the war? About all the men you killed?"

"That was a guilty time for everyone," said Justin.

"I ain't never killed anyone," said Milo. "At least not on purpose."

Justin didn't answer him.

"Something happened to my sister," Milo said suddenly. "A long time ago. That's why she stopped talking."

Justin reached down and picked up a willow shaving. He smoothed it like a feather.

Milo dropped his whittling stick, put his knife back in his pocket and then lit a cigarette. The match fell down on the wooden planks, trailing smoke. "Everyone thinks it was because our mother died," he said. "But I don't think so."

Justin nibbled on the end of the wood shaving, then put the whole thing in his mouth. Crunched it like candy.

Milo's words slowed and took on a serious tone. "Some pilot got her the day she stopped talking. She went to meet him in a meadow. When she came back she was all wrong. Her mouth was swelled up. Her dress was tore and her eyes didn't have no light and her hair was full of sand. I asked her what happened and she didn't answer me. She didn't talk again until just here recently."

Justin didn't answer. He let out his breath and stared into the sun.

"For a long time," said Milo, "I hated pilots. Tried to burn down their air base to get them back." Milo stood up and began to pace, back and forth. "But you know what I'm thinking? I'm thinking Charlotte's happy now, so maybe it don't matter anymore. Maybe it's all over."

Justin spat out the fragments of willow. One of them landed on his knee. "Do you really think so?" he said.

"Could be," said Milo, "that a man can be guilty for something a certain number of years, then he's finished. Like prison."

"Like prison," Justin said.

"No!" said Milo suddenly, and when he looked at Justin his eyes were blazing. "It's never gonna be over! If I ever meet that pilot I'll kill him, Justin. He should burn in hell for what he did."

After the meal, Justin and Milo sat on the couch and listened to Charlotte play "Für Elise" on the piano. The higher notes were delicate, sweet. The lower ones harsh.

"Play 'Alexander's Ragtime Band,' " said Milo, and she began.

Justin felt his heart stop.

Why had he not remembered until now? The living

room full of soldiers. The little boy dancing. And the girl playing with her back turned. He hadn't really noticed her then, consumed as he was by trying to be polite to the host of this strict Baptist house while chiggers were tempting his fingernails to scratch in indecent places. But it was the same girl. Playing the piano or cringing in the woods, under the spell of two different rhythms.

He had heard her music before he had taken her voice.

Milo slapped Justin's knee.

"Ain't she good?" said Milo.

Berries turning red and white. The trees almost empty of birds. Cardinal flowers still alive.

Stepping on brown leaves, looking up at green ones, Justin let Charlotte lead him by the hand. "Where are we going?" he asked her.

"You'll see." No playfulness in Charlotte's new voice.

"Why don't we go back to your house?"

"Not yet, Justin."

A soldier never forgets his surroundings. Justin felt sickened by the familiarity of the woods around him. The scent of pine needles and mulch, the consistency of the ground beneath his feet. The sudden cry of the few remaining birds. All that was missing was the heat and the chiggers and the mosquitoes, and he would be right back there, with his army haircut and his civilian pride.

"Here we are," said Charlotte. She let go of Justin's hand and leaned against a pin oak tree, staring at the riverbed. White sand, a few footprints. Two old Jax beer bottles stuck down in the sand. A burned-out campfire over to the right, which could have been a week old, or a year, or a generation.

"I wanted to tell you this," said Charlotte, "because you gave me my voice back. I owe this to you, this story, if we're going to be together."

"You don't have to tell me anything. The past is the past."

"No, it isn't. The past stays with me."

"You can tell me this story later."

"Listen to me, Justin. You'll have to excuse me if I say this wrong. I'm not used to words after all these years. But I'm tired of this part of the woods. I see it in my mind, over and over." She pointed. "You see that place on the riverbed? Somehow I thought it would still have my shape. But it's all filled in. I wonder how long it took to fill in."

Justin sat down on a fallen log. He had felt nauseated ever since he'd listened to Milo's threats and Charlotte's piano music, and now his heart was pounding and he could not catch his breath. *Stop. Stop. I know this story.*

". . . and so I went to the meadow to find him," said Charlotte. "It had worked for Belinda, and so I guess I was thinking that meadow was magic. I put on my blue dress and I curled my hair and I stood looking up at the sky for most of the afternoon. The sun was so hot. Sweat took my curls.

"You know, once I found a dead bird, and I thought that if I really believed, then that bird would come to life again. So I thought that if I believed in the plane, then it would come. And that since my mother had died in such an unlucky way, maybe she'd passed her luck over to me. Silly, right?"

During the Maneuvers I saw five soldiers go down in a river. I rescued one of them. Pressed on his chest until he opened his eyes and drooled water like a baby. I am not all bad . . .

". . . and after a few hours I just gave up and started back home. I was so hot and I also remember that beggar lice covered my ankle socks and the hem of my dress . . ."

I couldn't sleep at night. I don't know how I made it through the rest of training, because I'm certain that I didn't sleep at all . . .

". . . and they held me down. There were three of them. I could smell the kerosene on their skin. Isn't that what soldiers used to do, rub kerosene on their skin to keep mosquitoes away? One of them had gargled with Listerine; I could smell that too. And this is so crazy, Justin, but a few grains of sand went in my ear and that itch was almost more unbearable than . . ."

And Marty fell with his hands over his eyes, and David died a week later. And you can't cover horror with horror, for horror is opaque and I could see right through it at the thing I'd done. I'd killed lots of Germans but that didn't matter; that was just my finger on a trigger, they had not surrendered, Charlotte, not like you had . . .

". . . and when I took the blindfold off they were gone. I had to shorten my dress later by two inches, and the funny thing was that Mama wasn't there to disapprove. I went back to her grave and nothing had changed on it. If you think of a grave as an expression on a face, then Mama's face never changed from what happened to me. Sometimes I wonder if she was there. You know, looking down? And saying, 'Charlotte, I know about the soldiers and the lipstick too. I know all of it.'

"By then I was quiet. There were chores to be done, but almost no chore needs talking. And you can get by with just whistling when you're calling in the dogs. I liked writing things down on a pad. Sometimes I would write a message to God and it was always hateful. Justin?"

Justin leaned over and threw up between his legs. Vomit splashed on his shoes, splattered his socks and the cuffs of his khakis.

Charlotte put her hand on his shoulder. "This doesn't change anything, does it, Justin?"

Several miles away, on the pretty side of town, Benjamin Olen stood in front of Belinda's house, one hand holding the beaded purse and another hand on his unsettled stomach. He had no idea what to say to her, and the premonition filled him that one wrong verb would lead to another slap in the face. And yet he could not turn around and go back home. Where his sister scrubbed every flat thing. Where the women begged him for love. Where his barn had begun to feel lonely and dark.

He walked up the flagstone path to the front door, past the fountain grass, the tall ferns and the cement fountain in the shape of a swan. In his mind he practiced going over his words one more time; then he rang the doorbell, shifting on one foot, licking his lip and finding no bristle above it.

The sight of Belinda sent a quick electric chill through him, tingly waves that she flattened with the look on her face.

"What are you doing here?" she whispered.

"I just came to return your purse, Ms. Stanley."

"How do you know my name?"

"Same way I know your address."

"You looked in my purse? Give me that!" She seized it from his hand.

"Now get out of here right now!"

"But . . . I'd like to talk to you."

"Boys don't talk to married women. Go! Vamoose!"

"Vamoose?" he said. The word had an exotic quality that amazed him. "I just wanted to say—"

"You don't understand. If my husband—" She stopped, and Benjamin saw the spark die in her eyes.

A car with the word "Sheriff" written on the door was pulling into the driveway.

Belinda stepped through the doorway and pulled the

door closed behind her. "Stay here, stay here," she whispered frantically. "Be quiet."

The sheriff removed his hat as he came up the walkway. Late-afternoon light played upon his blond hair. He looked at Benjamin. "What's going on here, Belinda? Who's your little friend?"

"He's just a neighborhood boy."

"A neighborhood boy? I've never seen him. Does he live underground?"

"He came to return my purse." Belinda's smile looked strange, the teeth bared unevenly. "I dropped it on the way back from Mother's the other night. This young man found it and was nice enough to bring it back."

"What other night? When did you go to Mother's?"

"Tuesday," she said quickly. "Remember?"

"Why would you bring such a fancy new purse over to see your mother? You want to impress her that bad? Or did marrying me not do the trick?"

"The purse was new. I wanted to show her."

"And you liked it so much you just dropped it coming back? Is that your way of saying how much you like something? Are you planning to drop your son on the street someday?"

"No."

"No? You sure? Because you like him, don't you? You like to show him off, don't you?"

Benjamin looked in Belinda's eyes. They were wide open and alert.

"Please, honey. It was a mistake. I just wasn't thinking."

"Why haven't you mentioned it to me?"

"I forgot. I've just been so busy lately, and—"

"I'm the *sheriff,* Belinda. You don't think I could have found your purse?"

"No. I mean, yes."

The sheriff grabbed Belinda's purse. Benjamin watched him hold it open with his ruined left hand while he rifled through it with the nimbler fingers of his right hand. The sheriff pulled out Belinda's card and read aloud: "Belinda Stanley. Pillows of true lavender. One-thirteen Maiden Lane." He looked at Benjamin. "You see, my wife and I work together. I keep the parish safe and she keeps it stinking of lavender. Isn't that right, Belinda?"

Belinda hesitated. "Yes," she said carefully, looking over at her herb garden.

"What?"

"Yes."

The sheriff suddenly laughed. "That's one thing you'll learn about women, son," he said to Benjamin. "Sometimes their little hobbies cover up things. I have a friend whose wife makes soap. Know what she needs all that soap for? To scrub down after she cheats on him. Aren't women something?" He laughed again, and one lid closed over one blue eye in a lightning-quick wink. He smiled. Big white teeth. Like the Germans Benjamin had seen during the war, in propaganda films.

"Yes, sir," said Benjamin.

"You want a reward?"

"A reward?"

"For bringing back the purse."

"No, sir."

"Then please accept our thanks. And, son?" The sheriff leaned down to Benjamin and put his mouth to his ear. "You ever find my wife's purse again, bring it to me, not to her. Don't you ever be seen talking to her again. She's a married woman and you're just a stinking little boy. You understand?"

The spray in his words tickled Benjamin's ear. "Yes, sir," Benjamin said.

The sheriff and Belinda went inside and closed the door behind them.

Benjamin stood there for a moment, his fingers hooked through the loops of his pants. Licking his lips. Half boy and half man. Or perhaps two-thirds boy and one-third man. Tickled relentlessly by the fine hairs of boyhood, frightened by the words of the sheriff, scratchy from the new wool sweater that had moved no one's heart, Benjamin kicked at the heads of the chrysanthemums on his way to the street.

21

Sunday ended with a sweet and chilly darkness, and the windows of The House of Gentle Men began to glow with light. The occupants drifted into the dining room, drinking coffee to wake themselves up for a courtly night's work, and to mask any whiskey odor that still clung to their breath.

Louise stood in the kitchen, stirring soup and dying of love for the mysterious Justin, whose involvement with another woman had driven Louise into joint-aching fits of jealousy for weeks now. She had lost much sleep, and her eyes had formed the dark circles meant for much older women—those who have already won a man's heart, had his children and disappeared from his thoughts.

Today Justin had put on a clean shirt and left for the afternoon.

"Where are you going?" Louise had asked.

"Someone invited me to Sunday lunch."

"Who?"

"Someone."

He'd returned at dusk with the look of a man enraged.

"Hello, Justin," she'd said brightly from the pruned edge of a rosebush. He had not replied, but had stomped in the house tracking mud across her porch. His muddy footprints had presented a dilemma for her: they were full of the germs of the uncontrollable world, and yet they were Justin's. The need for cleanliness won, because this urge had saved her lately. The footprints had come up, one by one, while the hot cloth dirtied itself.

Now Louise stirred the soup. "Get me the nutmeg," she told Daniel, who was helping her cook. She sniffed and stirred while Daniel darted to the cupboard. He handed her the nutmeg and bestowed a tiny kiss, soothing Louise's face but leaving her heart still sore. To allow Daniel a few more kisses would mean to feel better, as the invisible balm spread from regret to injury to sadness to longing, but a soothed woman is a woman slow on her feet. To win Justin would require the lightning-quick instincts of a constant agony.

Louise had lived on little pieces of Justin these past weeks. A smile here and there, a few words, aftershave escaped from its bottle and spicy on a sheet. His leaving for the afternoon had panicked her, even though he hadn't seemed to enjoy the outside world at all, judging from the way he'd stomped to his room. But what if the world gradually pricked him less and less, until it no longer drew blood? What if one day he left the house and did not return? Would she have to wrap his things in brown paper and send them to him? His aftershave lotion and his socks and his black comb and the hateful lamb that rested on his night table? Every part of him until there was no more Justin, just as her mother's shoes and liniments and perfume and tea gown had disappeared with her, until nothing was left of her as well?

Justin was not a man in love, Louise was sure. She could see it on his face. Instead he seemed a man addicted to whatever was making his demons leave him slowly and with great regret, as an old woman leaves a flower garden. What did Charlotte know that Louise didn't? To know Justin's secrets would be to know his heart. The clues in Justin's room told her nothing. The real clues were downstairs, written in her father's educated prose and then locked away.

That very afternoon, with Justin gone and the men sleepy in their Creole chairs, and her father in town buying kerosene oil and pig wire, Louise had stolen downstairs to the cellar. Very carefully, with the dull edge of a butter knife, she had tried to open the safe by force. Failing that, she had once again swirled the numbered dial around, trying to luck upon the correct combination. She had already tried every possible set of numbers she knew. The birthdays of the entire family. Her father's wedding day. The day her mother left him. Her mother's dress and shoe sizes, arranged this way and that. The word "Janey" assigned numbers letter by letter, with the number for *J*

repeated at the end. And all possibilities that meant nothing but sounded promising:

22–34–36.

18–28–10.

06–30–17.

The number of choices was as dizzying as trying to
find just the right path through the maze that leads to
heaven, or one particular leaf in a live oak tree whose
branches are endlessly spread. It maddened her. Possibilities
screamed at her in her sleep, and when she was not
crouching in front of Justin's room with her ear to the
door, she was lurking down the cellar steps with the bad
posture of a sneaky girl.

Her father was not a random man. She knew that any
combination he had picked would have to mean something deep, for her father loved to brood and if numbers
could increase his melancholy for a few seconds a day,
then all the better. She imagined him kneeling before the
safe, the numbers speaking to him, reminding him, chastis-
ing him, causing him regret. His fingers twirling. And
then the safe opening with a mysterious creak. The secret
suddenly available, and the clandestine cellar light just right
for reading Justin's heart.

Louise had given up spinning the dial and used the
butter knife once again, so madly that it left marks in the
metal. But the door to the safe had not budged. The truth
about Justin was once again denied her.

"Get the salt," Louise now told Daniel. "Thank you. And the pepper."

She tasted the soup before it was ready to receive her tongue, and was burned for her trouble.

"Are you hurt?" Daniel asked anxiously, and Louise looked down at him.

"No, lamb," she said, stroking his light hair. He seemed sad lately. Perhaps he was feeling Louise's grief, as angels do, or perhaps he was pining for the world Louise had denied him, afraid that he would be seen, for rumor caught in full light is eventually owned by everyone. Louise could not bear this. Daniel was hers. Found and captured among the unbathed trees, borne home close to her chest, her prize and her reward.

Daniel helped her pour the soup into the clay-fired bowls and bring them into the dining room to the men. Louise scanned the room for a glimpse of Justin, then moved with a sadder heart among the men, placing the soup bowls on the straw mats and mumbling her greetings.

Mr. Olen drifted in and Louise served him too. He patted her waist with one hand as he took a spoonful of soup with the other and blew on a single sliced carrot turning in the captured broth.

"How are you, Louise?" he asked. She didn't answer, angry at him, somehow, for prying all those secrets from Justin and then hoarding them for himself. Storing the secret away like money in a mattress, where it couldn't grow into anything.

Louise and Daniel finished serving the men, dished up their own plates and took a seat on either side of Louise's father. Daniel blew softly on his spoonful of soup, his lips pursed as if just returned from a healing kiss. He stopped blowing when Benjamin entered the room. The other men noticed him too, for he had walked in slowly and quietly. No insults for the men or for his sister. Very strange for this boy who loved to swagger and shout and spill his milk deliberately.

He had been sulking out in his sweet potato barn, going over the day's events again and again. What had begun so well—the sight of Belinda in broad daylight, confirmation that the woman was real and so was his love—had ended so poorly. *You are just a stinking boy.* Why, Benjamin wondered, did Belinda love this man who, according to rumors and to Benjamin's own eyes, radiated so purely a man's violence? And if she did love him, why had she come to a house that offered the kind of love that had never carried a gun or slapped a hand-cuffed prisoner or run over a dog just because it didn't have a collar? Benjamin had wanted to stay in Belinda's yard and gather clues to her urges and intentions. The color of the chosen flowers. The arrangement of the passion vine, empty of blooms, which curled along the wrought-iron fence. The temperature of the water in the fountain. Fingerprints on the mailbox. The pattern of the flagstones. Anything. Benjamin had to understand this woman, why she stayed with this man.

Benjamin did not take a seat at the table, but cleared his throat instead. The son had finally inherited the haunted look of the father.

Mr. Olen noticed the darkness in his son's eyes. "What's wrong, Benjamin?"

Benjamin pulled a hank of hair away from his face and tucked it behind his ear. He felt around in the pocket of his shirt for a cigarette, found one.

"Benjamin, you know there's no smoking in this house. Burn down the sweet potato barn if you want to. What's *wrong*, son?"

"Nothing." Benjamin looked around at the faces of the men. Their soup had stopped steaming, save for a bare tendril that wound up from the centers of the bowls and danced toward the ceiling fan. Outside, sunlight was gone. Dogs jumped in the empty Creole chairs. Geese flew overhead, winter's high-pitched warning.

"I want to ask you all a question," said Benjamin. He lowered his head. "I mean, I want to learn something."

"Learn what?" asked Mr. Olen.

"I want to learn what a woman wants!" Benjamin blurted out.

The men exploded in laughter. Rocking on their chairs and stirring up the catarrh deep in their throats, slapping each other on the back, hot tears falling from the most shameless of them.

"If that don't beat all!"

"But we thought you knew everything!"

"Look at his face! A woman's got him!"

"You sure you want the sissy kind of schooling?"

Mr. Olen crossed his arms. "Now, now, everyone," he said, but the men would not be tamed. A delegated and paid-for sensitivity to women had made them only more brutal with their own kind.

"How to treat a woman!"

"Who is this special lady?"

"Try not hopping on every one of them you see!"

Louise picked up her bowl and then slammed it down hard. The soup jumped out, spreading down the center of the butcher-block table and spilling through the cracks to the floor. The startled men fell silent.

"There's nothing funny," said Louise, "about suffering over someone."

Benjamin looked at Louise gratefully, and she returned to him a sad, knowing smile.

Louise said, "Either help him or leave him alone."

"All right, all right, we'll help him," said Willy. "Listen, boy. The first thing you need to know about women is that they're delicate. They have got female parts that men don't understand. Very complicated. Even doctors don't really know what's what. They've got what are called *ovaries*. Six of 'em. They're arranged different each month."

"Why are you scaring the boy talking about female

parts?" Willy's friend Ray asked. "What the hell does that have to do with anything?"

"Where would you start, Ray?" Willy demanded crossly.

"Not there, dimwit."

"You think you know more than me? I got twice as many tips as you did last week."

"Bullhockey! You got mercy money from that old lady with the dead son!"

"Stop it, stop it!" said Mr. Olen. "You know it's against the rules to discuss tip money or clientele. Now, if you want to teach Benjamin anything, you can wait until after dinner." He looked at his son. "Welcome to the horrible world, boy. No one understands a woman. God should have taken all our ribs to make her. Because that's what a woman really wants. A boneless man."

Benjamin looked at the floor as the other men laughed.

"Hold on," said the old doctor, who had appeared in the doorway. "You're not giving women the awe that they deserve. True, they are complicated. But the love of a woman ennobles a man. Like drinking milk instead of scotch. A man without a woman would never understand love at all. It would remain an urge to us, its glory covered by the crotch of our pants."

The room went silent as the men considered this.

Finally Willy shouted: "Lay off the nervine, old man!" and the room filled with laughter again.

Benjamin looked mystified.

★   ★   ★

Two floors above this fractious discussion of women, Justin paced. His toes kept finding the limit of the room and then kicking it, as his dirty shoes left the natural litter of the woods on the ridiculously scrubbed floor. A bit of moss, a brush of sand, a smear of something green that looked like the pulp of a plant. The laces of his shoes were crusted with vomit. He had been devastated that afternoon, by Charlotte and her story and the look on her face and the white sand that had stretched to where the dry river bent and then disappeared into the brambles. He had listened without wanting to listen, and felt all his good work leave him in a rush.

Night after night he'd lain with her, pressed to her prone body once again, but this time with no hands over the eyes, no knees pressing on the shoulders. No one holding the pale ankles. Kiss by kiss, he'd covered over the crime, filled in the imprint of the twisting body, found every evidence and erased it. Brought back the voice that had died trying to call for help. Strengthened the color in the eyes. Revalued the smile.

Fallen in love. Or had he?

For if love is just some sort of a sparkling peace, where was his peace now? Charlotte's story in the woods had reminded him that his strongest demon remained in his blood. The demon that kept his senses dull, his kisses penitent and sexless, the one who said *There is no truth to what you do. You are piecing back together what you yourself destroyed and it is all a lie. She loves you who pressed her down until her voice leaped into your body, you who crushed her spirit like tattooed numbers crushed the spirits of those who had to wear them, like dogs crushed the spirits of prisoners, like the thought of hell crushes the spirits of those who pine for a loving God, and if your nursing is so profound and real then so must be the wound you made.*

He owed her the truth and this he could not give.

A knock on the door.

"Who is it?"

"It's me," said Mr. Olen. "Can I come in?"

"If you want."

Mr. Olen's expression was still grave from the dinner conversation and the sight of his sad, sad son. "Why didn't you come down and eat?" he asked. "We're having soup."

Justin sat down on the cot, so heavily that it slid a little. He picked up the cypress lamb and turned it in his hands. "I don't want to eat," he said.

"Something happen today?" Mr. Olen closed the door.

"She took me to the river."

"What river?"

The river which had dried up like a smothered voice. "You know."

"I do?"

"The one full of white sand. The one where the thing happened."

"The thing? You'd feel better if you called it what it was."

"I can't."

"What did Charlotte say?"

"She just talked about it. And I listened. I'm a priest these days, Mr. Olen."

"I'm sorry. That must have been hard for you."

"When Charlotte comes here tonight, tell her I can't see her. Tell her I'm not feeling well."

"It's a lie."

"It's the truth. I threw up in the woods."

"Wouldn't it be better to just face her? To get it out in the open?"

Justin shook his head. His fingertips soothed themselves on the cotton back of the cypress lamb.

"When are you going to tell her what happened, Justin?"

"I don't know. I need time." He turned his head so that Mr. Olen saw his full face, that haunted presentation of eyes, nose, mouth. "I thought I was feeling pretty good. You said the kisses would help me."

"You can't buy all things back with kisses, son," said Mr. Olen. "How I wish that it were true. How I wish."

"Tell Charlotte I can't see her. Please."

Mr. Olen sighed. "All right. I'll take care of it. But you have to tell her the truth soon. It's the only way to help yourself."

"Can I ask you something?"

"What?"

"Does the truth always set you free?"

The question made Mr. Olen remember standing behind the door in a triangle of neglected dust, holding a blue sock in his hands. A sock not his own.

"Not always," he said.

22

Lovesick Benjamin lost his boyhood bravely. On the first day he learned not to squash bugs; on the second, not to spit in his hand; on the third, not to unzip his pants and water the white blooms of the pampas grass that grew parallel to the clothesline. Overhead, more geese were flying south, shrieking at the warm place in the distant sky that would be their destination.

Willy sat himself down in a chair. "All right, Benjamin," he said. "Stroke my face."

Benjamin hesitated. "Where do I start?"

"The brow line will do."

Benjamin nervously jabbed his fingers in the direction of Willy's bushy eyebrows.

"Ahhh!" said Willy. "Got me in the eye!"

"He's new at this," Matthew said.

But Willy was rubbing his eye and regarding Benjamin balefully. "No tip for you, you little bastard," he mumbled.

Louise gave him his new haircut, though the old doctor lingered in the vicinity, holding his old stainless-steel
shears and looking hurt.

"Stay still," she told Benjamin, but gently.

The men showed him how to shave using cream from
an impressive-looking black tube rather than shaving soap.
"Makes the face softer," they said. "Shave close, now.
That's it."

Willy's friend Ray brandished his bottle of Aqua Velva.
"An essential," he said. "A good, strong scent gives a
woman something to remember."

Benjamin sniffed at it. "Really?" he said. Ray poured
the Aqua Velva on his palm, rubbed his hands together
and slapped Benjamin on each cheek. "This makes the
women melt," he assured Benjamin.

Willy pressed a bottle of vanilla extract into Benjamin's hand.

"What's this for?"

"My secret trick," said Willy in a low voice. "Rub a
drop of it into each shoulder. Women are scent hounds."

All that week the men worked on him. They gave
him clean socks for his feet. A washcloth for his ears. A
clipper for his nails. Baking soda for his teeth. They made
Benjamin take off his jeans and put on a pair of wool
pants that fit him rather well. Then a button-down shirt
and a soft cardigan. Dark blue, a color that has never
known violence.

"Women like talcum powder," Benjamin was told.

"Rub it on your hands so they can smell it when you stroke their faces."

"When do you stroke their faces?" Benjamin demanded. "Before the kiss, or after the kiss?"

"Before, for God's sake."

The men argued briefly over what to use to dress Benjamin's hair. Some wanted bay rum. Others thought Brylcreem would be best. Finally they agreed on Wildroot Creme-Oil.

"There are reasons for its popularity," Ray assured Benjamin, slicking down Benjamin's hair until it showed a part.

"Why do I have to wear this if my hair is clean?" asked Benjamin.

"It makes a man look tame . . . damn it, Benjamin, you just squashed a bug."

"It was crawling on my shirt."

"You must learn tolerance. A woman's going to vex you a million times more than a stupid bug."

Benjamin was taught how to stand, sit, walk, eat, drink, take off his shoes, wipe perspiration (not sweat) from his face, hold a rose, kiss a hand, whisper, blot off excess Aqua Velva, and waltz, should it ever come up. A short man named Jimmy used an extension cord to set up a portable radio in the backyard, and soon the music of Glenn Miller was blasting through the trees and up into the sky. The other men watched and shouted directions as Benjamin put one hand on Ray's waist and took Ray's hand with the other, then swooped to the dreamy music through the low grass, stepping on colored leaves and whirling until their clasped hands swung out and knocked the last Confederate rose bloom off the bush.

"That ain't an omen," said Ray, looking down at the bloom.

But it was the doctor who took Benjamin aside, laid his shaky old hand on Benjamin's shoulder and said, "Son, women get the short end of the deal on this earth. They love men, and men ain't worth loving, really. They're never told to know theirselves. They don't even understand they have breasts until some man has his hands on 'em, or some baby has his mouth on 'em. All women really want is someone who'll listen to them. They hurt to tell their story. It's usually sad and it's usually about some other man who's done them wrong or hit them or left them at the altar, or told them they looked fat in a sundress. Just listen to them, Ben."

Occasionally when Benjamin was busy practicing his steps or going over his sweet repertoire out loud ("You look so pretty. You feel so soft. You smell so nice"), he would run into his sister, Louise. The two would stop and exchange a look of understanding and guarded friendliness, like two soldiers who meet in a field and realize that there is not enough daylight left for continued bloodshed. Another day, perhaps.

"How's the training going, Benjamin?"

"I feel stupid."

"You look handsome."

"Thank you." Benjamin lowered his voice. "How's Justin?"

"Better. I mean, not better because he's eating or sleeping. Better because he's not seeing that woman with the long black hair."

"How do you know?"

"I heard Daddy last night, turning her away at the side door again. Maybe he's tired of her. Maybe he's just resting for the next one. Someone younger this time."

"You're cleaner than her for sure," said Benjamin encouragingly. "I mean, you'd have to be. No one's cleaner than you."

Louise smiled again. Benjamin did look handsome, and perhaps through his dedication he would win the woman who had stolen his heart. Perhaps love was mappable and definable. Curl the hair just perfect with the iron held down in the chimney of the kerosene lamp, scent the neck just so, whiten the teeth through repeated brushings. Move with the grace of a cat, stare openly like a hoot owl.

Win.

Meanwhile, the object of Louise's affection paced his room like something wild. He did not bathe and he did not shave. He turned and counter-turned, his own pungent odor mixing with that of the kerosene lamp when night fell. His shadow clearly defined on the wall, though twice as big as his suffering body and interrupted by the looming shadow of the lamb, plus the shadows of other things whose source was not specific.

It was always fifteen paces from wall to wall. The sheet was always too short for the cot. His hair always tickled his left ear. He was always the same man.

He missed Charlotte, but was not sure exactly why. Perhaps he just missed the cautiously peaceful feeling of holding her in his arms and kissing her neck, her face. Was this love? He didn't know. He had not seen her since the day she had taken him into the woods, although one night he had wandered to the window at the end of the hall and watched her leave. Her long black hair unmistakable in moonlight. Her head bowed.

He imagined the moment of truth, over and over. And yet he could not imagine it. The confession seemed more obscene than the act, because the act was shared and the confession was entirely his. He paced the room. During the daylight hours he did not open the window, but occasionally glimpsed out of it to see Benjamin going through his paces, responding to the shouted orders.

Learning how to treat a woman.

Mr. Olen sat outside on the front porch in his socks and his gray winter coat. His shoes off to the side, soles up. He balanced a pad on his lap. When he wrote he felt the pressure of the pen against his crotch, and found this sadly sensual.

"Dear Jane, I do not know where to begin. On the

day I first met you? On our wedding day? Or on the day that I moved into this house in the hope you might come back to me? You see, Janey, you made me believe in magic and I didn't even know it. Perhaps I should begin with the day I realized this was true . . ."

The pages filled up, the earnest ink representing the love talk never offered, the compliments he meant to give her but somehow did not. The soldier upstairs and the newly tormented Benjamin had put him in a thoughtful mood. When does the peace come? At the moment of confession? Forgiveness? Reconciliation? Is peace as fleeting as love?

". . . and for the times I did not kiss you, Janey, let me tell you that I wish your lips were once again just a foot and a half below my chin, like a lovely fountain that would be mine but for the bended knee. My knee will bend for you, Janey, if you give me one more chance . . ."

The head of the pen grew warm to the touch. The fading sun encouraged the deer hunters who sat in their blinds with their shotguns across their knees. Still Mr. Olen wrote, as he had for eight years now.

23

Charlotte stood by the front door for a long time, breathing in fall air that tasted faintly of ammonia and wondering if the house had been wiped clean of every trace of her. A house that clean never gets to be familiar. All the linking scents are murdered before the next visit. And yet Charlotte had felt she belonged here.

She was trying the front door in the hope it would change her luck, for she had been turned away from the side door these past seven nights by the haunted-looking giant, Mr. Olen, who said Justin wasn't feeling well, but with such sorrow in his voice that Charlotte knew it went beyond a virus or a cold, this thing that was wrong with Justin.

"Why doesn't he call?" asked Charlotte. "Or send down a note?"

"I don't know," said Mr. Olen. "Please, try again tomorrow."

By the second day Charlotte's heart began to sink. She

should never have told Justin the story of that day when the meadow was bright and the woods were dark.

The story of her mother's death had been safe to relate. That particular tragedy left her neither dirty nor clean. A man could stand to hear about that. But no, Charlotte had to press on, to cover the second Event in the hope that, very soon, she could relate the third (the lonely swelling) and then the fourth (the baby's arms, waving from the stump by a well-traveled path). Because Charlotte really wanted to remember this last thing, and to find this child who would now be six years old.

She wished she had left her baby in the riverbank sand so that she could have followed the footprints of whoever found him back to some unfamiliar house. She would have knocked upon the door and found the words to say, "He's mine. Give him back to me."

Who knew how Justin would have received this confession? Because after the story she told on the dry riverbank he had thrown up between his shoes and hadn't spoken to her all the way back to her house. Then seven days of a silence so complete that it panicked her soul. The silence of lost men. Lost mothers. Lost babies. Deep and wild.

Milo had paced around Lake Swane, mumbling to himself as Charlotte fished. "It's not fair it's not fair it's not fair," he said.

"People leave each other," Charlotte told him. "It's the way of the world."

Milo had stopped pacing and was leaning down to her, listening intently to her every word as though afraid that her language would die with her faith.

"He should call you," Milo said. "Even if it's bad news. I'm going to go talk to that man."

Milo was halfway up the bank before Charlotte stopped him. "No, Milo. Let him do what he wants."

Milo turned around. "I don't understand what happened."

What Charlotte didn't say was that Justin had taken the news of her violation better than Milo would have. She could imagine his reaction: the red face, the punched trees, the old shotgun taken up and loaded. Since Charlotte had not seen the faces of the soldiers and could not point a finger at the guilty ones, Milo would declare war on all men, in the fury of his tantrum, and kill someone innocent. The first man he saw, no doubt.

"Don't worry," she told her brother. "Everything will be all right. Justin will call me."

"He will?"

"Of course."

When Justin did finally call, his voice was a hoarse whisper: "I need to talk to you."

Well, I need to talk to you too, Charlotte thought as she stood on the Olens' porch with the night newly damp behind her. *I need to tell you about the butterflies. Once when I was a child my family drove to Oklahoma to visit my mother's sister, and I went alone for a walk in the woods and was caught*

*in a migration of monarch butterflies. They filled that part of the
woods. Fanning themselves in bushes and in the branches of trees,
waving from deep in the high grass. They lined my sleeves and
clung to my hair and whirled around me like a cloud. My voice
was perfect in me then, but I kept it quiet in my throat because
I did not want to disturb the perfect silence of the butterflies.
They covered my chest as if my sweater's color were some secret
they had to lick and I stood there without voice or movement.
The way God loves a person, Justin! When they flew away they
left tiny specks of colored dust on my clothes. And the dust was
my secret. And so, you see, my body has known peace and war.
I am seized by soldiers and by butterflies. I have more to share
than bad news, Justin.*

Someone cleared his throat behind her. Charlotte
whirled around. A boy stood on the porch, dressed like a
man, fidgeting with the buttons on his cardigan sweater.

"Hello, ma'am," he said. "How are you?"

Charlotte did not answer.

"Don't be alarmed, I am just practicing."

"Practicing what?"

"Uh . . . you look real pretty tonight, ma'am."

The boy took a step or two. The earnestness on his
face was unsettling. "Tell me . . . tell me your sorrows.
I am a good listener."

"Go away."

The boy's face fell. "Really?" He searched his pockets
and pulled out a piece of paper as Charlotte turned away
from him. Just before she closed the door gently behind

her, she heard the boy mutter to himself, "Damn! I was supposed to say that part last."

Charlotte darted through the dark foyer, noticing that the air was warm from the discreet presence of the women who lined the railroad benches. She looked neither right nor left, but took the set of stairs just beyond the hall tree, gripping a banister that was slippery with oil soap. On the second-floor landing she ran into Milo's friend Louise, who looked so absolutely stricken to see her that Charlotte looked down to see if there was mud on her shoes. No mud. She stepped over Louise's scrub bucket and continued on, glancing quickly behind her to see the girl set down her brush and bury her head in her hands. Charlotte's stomach knotted as she crept down the third-floor hallway, past rooms in which the ministrations had already begun: kiss, touch, dance, flatter, listen. No matter what, she decided, she would keep her new voice, that one solitary part of herself that she'd thrown away and then managed to retrieve.

Justin paced the room, his eyes wide, his breath short, his carelessly flung shadow moving down the wall. Louise hadn't come in to clean for seven days, and yet the room wasn't dirty enough. He wanted to kick little pieces of trash, worry little stains with the toe of his shoe. The sterility of his environment only made him turn inward. And there he found no relief. He heard her footsteps in the hallway, and his mouth went dry. The approach of mortar shells as he crouched in the hedgerows of France had not been as dreadful as this. Smoothing his hair and making sure his shirt was buttoned, as if that would make a difference, he walked across the room and opened the door.

Downstairs, Louise lay on her bed crying. What she had just witnessed had killed her seven days of hope, and now she went over, again and again, the sight of Charlotte in a new calico dress and the inevitability of her quiet ascension to the room on the third floor. She stared at the ceiling and thought of everyone she hated: Charlotte, of course; Milo, too crazy to love for more than just one summer; her father, who had driven off her mother, dragged her to this silly house and finally denied her access to the safe and therefore access to any organized plan of seduction; her brother, Benjamin, whose transformation tortured her by proving that some men still loved some women; and Justin himself, who had lived in her house for over three months but was still as aloof as a stranger.

And now he was back with the black-haired woman who tracked in dirt and removed hope. How she hated that woman. Her flowing dress and her long black hair, but also the look in her eyes as she'd passed Louise on the stairs. The look of a woman starving for attention.

She recognized that look. She had seen it years ago, on a woman whose hair was red and whose laughter was a distracting thing that bothered the neighbors. A woman who flouted tradition by wearing blue jeans to the dry-goods store. A woman who warned her daughter in soft whispers of the difficulty of keeping a man's focus.

"Here's a hint, dear," she'd said. "Sometimes just before he comes home, I drop dinner on the floor. He stops, he looks down at the mess, I go in for the kiss."

Kisses were her mother's obsession, and prying them from her husband was her greatest victory. "I wait until he's asleep. Then it's kiss, kiss, kiss. I'm careful to avoid the ears because that wakes him up. Another good time is just after he's finished a crossword puzzle. He's sitting down and in a good mood. But don't try to kiss a man while he's shaving, or especially when he's writing out a check for the electric bill. Men hate to be kissed when they're thinking about numbers."

Louise's mother had been her best friend, sweet and dazed and the confessor of kissing lore. So why, after her mother left forever, did Louise suddenly begin cleaning the halls and the doorjambs, the ceilings, the curtains, the tile, until no trace remained of that endearing woman?

Lying on the bed with tears dropping on the blue sheet beneath her with distinct little pops, like acorns falling in a pond, Louise realized that she hated her mother the most. She was still sighing from this revelation when she heard a distinct crash, far above her head. She bolted up in bed.

★　　★　　★

On the third floor, the sound of the crash was more distinct, as were the high screams that followed it.

"YOU! YOU! YOU!"

In the other rooms, women ceased whispering their own tales of woe long enough to listen to this brand-new one. And a doozy it was, from the sound of the crash and from the screaming voice. Mr. Olen, who was guiding an old lady down the third-floor hall, stopped in his tracks. The old lady dropped a blueberry pie she had baked for her pretend son.

"Excuse me," Mr. Olen said hurriedly, and rushed down the hallway. When he opened Justin's door, the light from the hallway leaped into the dark room. Justin was leaning back in the chair, his arms covering his face, and Charlotte was lashing at him with her fingers curved like claws.

"YOU! YOU! YOU!"

Mr. Olen seized Charlotte around the waist and pulled her away from Justin. Glass crunched under Mr. Olen's feet and Charlotte struggled wildly in his arms.

"Now, Charlotte," said Mr. Olen. "Just calm down. Please."

The old doctor rushed in, Louise right behind him. Some of the other men had left their women and had crowded around the doorway to listen to this much more interesting tale.

The doctor seized both of Charlotte's hands and held

them together, as if he were forcing her to pray for her own sedation. "Please," he said. "Take deep breaths."

"Justin," Louise called. "Are you all right?" Justin did not speak or move from his position. Louise wanted to rush to his side, but when she took a step she felt the broken shards of glass. "Ohh," she said, and hopped backward.

Charlotte struggled out of Mr. Olen's grip and dashed from the room.

"Wait!" Mr. Olen cried. "Don't leave! Come back and talk to me!" He ran to the doorway and looked down the hall. In the retreating figure of Charlotte he saw his own fleeing wife. "Please!" he called desperately after her. "Give me—give him a chance to explain!"

Charlotte paid him no heed. She nearly bowled over the old lady as she darted past her, stepping into the ruined blueberries of the pie on the floor and pressing down purple footsteps all the way down the stairs and out the back door. She stumbled off the porch, fell knees-first into the cold grass, recovered herself and plunged into the woods.

Back in Justin's room, two lanterns had finally been brought and now Mr. Olen and the old doctor could see the damage to the room. A broken window, the sheets torn off the cot, the lantern shattered on the floor. The doctor pulled Justin's hands away from his face.

"Justin!" shrieked Louise. Blood was streaming from many wounds.

"Uh-oh," said the doctor. "Got you with the lamp, did she? Are you burned?"

Justin didn't answer.

"Go back to your rooms," Mr. Olen told the men. "Everything's fine here. Louise, honey, get some towels."

He wanted to go and find Charlotte. But, after all, he wasn't good at bringing women back.

24

Daniel crouched in the darkness of the oaks and pines and sycamores. He had felt increasingly lonely lately, for Benjamin no longer mussed his hair or played with him but instead stared at him with all the seriousness of a grown-up man. And since Benjamin had forced upon himself this premature manhood and this new sensitivity, no more heartbroken women had curled up in the woods begging for comfort. The absence of the crying women had made Daniel lonely as well, for along with their tears they brought little stories from the outside world, where husbands and wives lived together, and children shared clothes and played softball. Even as he soothed them with the ministration of his hands and kissed away their spent and clinging tears, he wondered what it was like to be part of a real family, with a real mother and a traceable history.

Once, he'd asked Louise about it.

She had stopped sewing a button on a blouse and

looked down at him. "Who was your mother? What brought that up?"

Daniel looked at his feet.

"You're not old enough to know yet, Daniel."

"But when?"

"I don't know. I'll tell you someday. I promise."

And so he'd begun to study the women he met in the dark woods. After the healing kisses, a long deep stare. Words of comfort and then a quick sniff below the chin. Searching for the scent forgotten and yet kept near.

"Please," the women would say. "Could you please just talk to Benjamin for me? Could you tell him I love him? Could you tell him my children are almost grown?"

My children. Daniel moved his lips over their skin as the women healed in his arms. Their necks smelling of lavender and citrus, their hands of bleach or soap or turpentine. He sniffed at the necks of the single women too, who were clumsy from their lack of intimacy, and who cried the hardest over Benjamin. He did not quite know what he was hoping to find. Still he had searched, night after night, his nose down among the gauzy material, the thick hair and the sad stories, every sense alert for the possibility that his mother had come back for him.

And so Daniel now sat in the woods, scanning the high branches for panthers as he knit his small fingers together and waited with an otherworldly patience to be needed again. A few minutes before, he had heard a crashing sound and felt his heart beat wildly until he realized it was the distant shattering of a window. He had looked away from the sound, uninterested by the antics going on in the house. It was Benjamin's antics he was waiting for.

The night was growing cold, and he had just decided to admit defeat and return to the house when he heard sudden footsteps coming from the direction of the yard. A movement in the brush—like an animal turning around and around—then a heavy sigh that fluttered into a sob and continued. His heart jumped. Perhaps Benjamin had been up to his old tricks again. Daniel moved toward the sound, crouching low, his feet easy on the ground. A briar caught his leg and he winced, reached down and peeled it off his skin.

He moved around the mulberry bush and saw her. A black-haired woman weeping, in a little clearing that was so bright in moonlight that the pine needles around her could be counted. As he stepped closer, he could feel that her grief was not from Benjamin. It was a different kind of grief, so primal and so deep that it shook him. He came to within a few feet of her and knelt down. His hands stretched out for her and stopped. They were trembling. He hesitated and then reached his hands out again, but returned them to his own face and covered his eyes as, to his consternation, he began to weep himself. Because he was afraid of panthers, and snakes, and pirates. Because his leg was punctured by briars. Because his only playmate, Benjamin, had abandoned him. Because he had comforted a hundred women and none of them had ever returned the kindness.

Charlotte had not cried since the day Belinda had given her the four dollars, and now as she crouched on a bed made of twigs and straw and the brittle remains of summer honeysuckle, the stored-up tears came rushing out. Disbelieving tears. Angry tears that jumped down her face with the animation of living things. The sound that poured from her along with the tears had been stored up as well. A woman in love weeping for loss. A woman made victim weeping for justice. A woman forced into motherhood weeping for her baby.

She had been prepared for Justin to tell her he was leaving her, for the story she had told had come too early for him to understand. She had jumped the gun and shaken him to the core—like a woman who talks of marriage and children too early, or who tries to change her man's habits before his love can grow and make these alterations tolerable—and now Justin was going to tell her, very kindly, that things had changed between them.

She had been devastatingly unprepared for what he had actually said.

He had already known the story of the riverbank, because he had been there, a third of that horrible offense. Part of the weight that made her sink into the bank. One of the murmuring voices. And yet being part of it made him all of it.

She had simply stared at him for a few long moments before she went wild, crazy, kicking—the way she'd always wished she'd acted the first time she'd met him, back in the white sand. She hit Justin, clawed at his eyes and his mouth, seized the kerosene lamp and smashed it across his face so that the room went dark around his moaning. Somehow the window broke. She remembered the pane shattering, but the sounds that might have trickled through the shattered glass were lost to her, since she was screaming, "You! You! You!" Justin had covered his face but had not struggled. Mr. Olen had burst in and grabbed her around the waist, and somehow his arms had been soft as a mother's. And she had fled, trailing blueberry pie down the stairs and across the porch.

Justin had taken her voice and then returned it, like a thief who had stolen her last piece of bread and then, years later, given it back to her, the bread magically still soft and sweet, while she herself had withered in its absence. He had vomited after her Sunday confession because he was her confession. Her worst memory. He was the bath that took four hours. He was all the years of her silence. He was the stump roiling with dried sap upon which her baby lay.

And now it was all set out before her, set up by the God she'd thought she had silenced with her own insult. To have Justin now would require forgiving him, and this she would not do, for that would take away all things save the baby on the stump.

To forgive Justin would make her the solitary criminal. And so she must hate him, forever.

She did not hear the small footsteps or the sound of a small knee touching the ground in front of her, but a small sighing sound made her look up, and she was astonished to see a blond-haired boy kneeling in front of her, weeping, his hands over his face. She rubbed her wet eyes and looked again. He was still kneeling there and she was seized with a wild hope, one that she desperately tried to contain in herself.

She crawled toward the boy, very slowly so as not to startle him. When she touched his shoulder he jerked slightly but did not move away.

"What's the matter?" Charlotte murmured, but the boy did not respond. She put her hand on his head, her fingers finding tangles and a solitary burr, which she worked out and then tossed aside. "It's so cold out here," she said. "And your shirt's so thin."

She touched one of the pale hands that covered his face and found it chilly.

"Little boy," she said. She had already sensed the miracle and she was afraid, but she had to know. Very gently she took hold of the pale wrists, which, unlike his wrestling thumbs, yielded easily to sudden force. His hands slid off his eyes and she saw a color that had stayed with her since that June afternoon of 1942.

For a long time she looked at him and could not speak. Finally she put her fingers to his wet face and whispered the words that came naturally: "What's the matter?" As she spoke she felt her sorrow over Justin leave her suddenly. Not because of the magic of Daniel, but because all mothers forget their own grief when they see their children suffer.

25

Louise applied a cotton ball soaked in witch hazel to Justin's face. He winced but did not speak. He had not spoken at all since the night before, when Charlotte had fled from the house. Louise dipped and rubbed, dipped and rubbed, softening dried blood, as the bowl of witch hazel took on the pink tint of summer water. After his entire face had been doctored, she started all over again.

"It's not right for a woman to hurt you this bad," Louise said. "She's got some nerve, attacking you in this peaceful house."

He shrugged.

"Why did she hurt you?"

Having a conversation like this wasn't bad, Louise decided, even if he wouldn't answer her. Something about it felt intimate.

"I got hurt last night too," said Louise. "I stepped on some glass." Her father had swept up the shattered glass, nailed three pine boards over the broken window and set the unharmed cypress lamb back on the nightstand.

Louise put down the cotton ball, dipped her wet fingertips in the witch hazel and ran them over his face. "That feels better, doesn't it? You'll heal up in no time."

Neither Louise nor Justin responded to the knock on the door.

Mr. Olen walked in. "Louise," he said. "Go downstairs. I need to talk to Justin."

"Good luck," said Louise. "He's not very talkative." She left the room and walked down the hall, following the blueberry footprints that had defied all attempts to scrub them up. Louise didn't mind, as long as Charlotte's footprints led out of the house, not in.

The black-haired woman was gone again, and maybe for good this time. But Louise was taking no chances. This was war, and all wars call for crimes in one way or another.

Mr. Olen took a seat. "How's everything, Justin?" he asked.

Justin folded his arms.

"Don't pull that with me, son," said Mr. Olen.

"Leave me alone."

"Why are you angry at me?"

"Because you told me to tell her. You said everything would be fine if the truth came out."

"Don't you feel better?"

"Do I look better?"

Mr. Olen stood up and paced the room. Inspected the boarded-up window as if trying to look out of it. Sat back down again. "The important thing is that you're free now. You've said you're sorry, right?"

Justin nodded.

"And you begged her forgiveness?"

"Yes."

"Then you've done what you could do."

"I wish Charlotte had found me the night I hanged myself. Not your daughter."

"Why?"

"Then she could have seen how sorry I was. But you know what? It still wouldn't matter. I thought my apology would at least have some value. Now I realize how little it counts."

"It does count."

"She didn't seem to think so."

"Give her time."

"Mr. Olen?"

"Yes?"

"Did you tell your wife you're sorry?"

"Yes."

"And did you beg her forgiveness?"

"Yes."

"Do you think that wherever she is, she's forgiven you?"

★　　★　　★

When her father had burst into Justin's room, Louise could tell from the look on his face that he would be in there for a while. She left her bedroom and glanced down the hallway. All the men were out playing cards, and the old doctor was out on the front porch, teaching Daniel his multiplication tables.

She wasn't really doing anything wrong, was she? After all, hadn't her own father looked through her mother's drawers, and through the pockets in her clothes? Hadn't he sniffed her towels and shone a flashlight under her bed?

All's fair in love and war.

She crept into her father's room and slowly closed the door behind her. She opened his drawers and looked through them carefully, went through his clothes, checked the windowsill. She felt sneaky and sly and she loved the feeling. And if it was her father's snooping that had chased off her mother, he really had no right to insist on such privacy under his new roof. If he only understood how much Louise loved Justin, he would have told her himself about the secret hidden in the safe. She was looking for something, anything, that connected to numbers. She checked his music box, the top of his closet, his shaving mug, even his father's old collar box. Then she went through some papers on his dresser. Mostly bills, a few old letters from relatives in Georgia. Nothing she could use to discover a combination.

She was walking to his night table when her foot hit his wastebasket. It tipped over, spilling its contents. Balls and balls of crumpled paper. Hadn't she just emptied that basket a few days before? Why so much paper? She picked up one of the balls and smoothed it out on the floor.

Dear Janey:
God I'm so

The letter ended there and so she tried others:

Dear Janey:
I was a stupid man to deny you your kisses. I was a hundred percent wrong and I am so sorry. Sorrow is a weak thing that only makes some women angrier, and I know that this is a case of too little, too late . . .

Dear Janey:
As I sit here I meditate upon ways to reach you. Nothing else matters to me but the hope of finding you. Isn't it funny that you have caused me to put down my crossword puzzle? I would burn every crossword puzzle in the world for you, Janey.

Dear Janey:
I do not know where to begin. On the day I first met you? On our wedding day? Or on the day that I moved in this house in the hope you might come back to me? You see, Janey, you made me believe in magic and I didn't even know it . . .

Louise read the last letter over again and then sat back, thinking. She didn't know the day her father first met her mother, and she had already tried the numbers of their wedding day: 09-01-28. But that day he had moved her and Benjamin into this house and baked up his scheme of turning it into a sanctuary . . . that day she had never tried.

She tried to think back. It was in the late spring of 1940. Yes, in May. Three days after her ninth birthday.

05-04-40.

26

Charlotte wanted to go to her brother and whisper the story into his ear, then watch him turn crazy. In her imagination she tried several beginnings:

"Milo, you know what Justin did to me?"

"Milo, I have something to tell you."

"Milo, I found the man who took my voice."

It would all be so simple, and so right. Justin deserved it. He had opened his stupid mouth and taken himself away from her with his story that was also hers. She had finally found a man to love, but just as fervently, all these years, she had searched for a man to hate, a face to put with a voice, and now she had this too. Only it was the same man.

When Milo had asked her again what was wrong with Justin, she had simply told him that he had been sick.

"Really?" said Milo. "Should I go see him?"

"No. Don't go see him."

Her little boy, magically restored to her, accounted for

her mercy. She'd thrown him at God so long ago, and now God had handed him back to her, blond and angelic and needful of her touch. When night fell, Charlotte would set off for The House of Gentle Men. But when she reached the front yard she would go around to the back and meet Daniel secretly in the woods. There they would lie together, the mother and the son, once again hidden from the world, and she would tell him stories her mother had told her, when Charlotte had been a little girl. Most of them were stories of God's wrath that had made her tremble, but when she recounted these to Daniel she cut out the hellfire and brimstone.

She told him other stories:

There was once a magic horse, Daniel. And this horse could fly above the trees . . .

And the prince saw the princess disguised as a peasant girl . . .

The grasshopper said to the ant, I don't need to spend my time working . . .

Charlotte never told him, *Daniel, I am your mother, I left you on a stump and now I have found you again,* because she was afraid that would break some magic spell. And besides, Daniel seemed to know.

Three soldiers had taken her that day in the woods. She wondered which one of them had been Daniel's father. But if the act makes for fatherhood as much as the substance, then all three were his father.

The air was colder now, although the wild snapdragons

were still showing their colors. Charlotte held Daniel close to her.

Sweet boy of three fathers.

Miles away from the dark woods, Belinda was laying her own son down on his bed. She tucked the sheet up under his chin.

"I want a story!" said Ralph.

"No, baby," said Belinda. "Mommy's tired."

"I want a story! I want a story!"

Too exhausted to argue, Belinda read him the tale of Joseph and his coat of many colors. Ralph was asleep before Belinda got to the part where Joseph's brothers betray him. She kissed his forehead and went into the living room, sinking down on the green couch.

As she leaned her head back, a fresh bruise was clearly visible on the side of her face. "You wouldn't believe what happened!" she had told her women friends that day at lunch. "I was coming in from the backyard, thinking about my husband, and I just ran right into the bird feeder!"

"Really?" her friend Lucy had said. "I try not to think about my husband until he comes back home."

"It's an all-day thing for me," said Belinda.

"How is Richard, anyway?"

"Oh, it's hard to keep up with him. Someone's always calling him about silly things. A cow loose in the cane, a drunk causing trouble or a fight between husband and wife."

"Really?" Lucy whispered. "Like a fight with fists?"

"Sometimes," Belinda had said solemnly, "Richard has to pull men off their wives. He comes home very upset over it."

"Really?" said Belinda's other friend, Mary. "He cries?"

"I wish my husband cried," Lucy said. "I guess if we really wanted sensitive men, we could go to The House of Gentle Men!" She'd lowered her voice when she'd said it, and all three of them had giggled.

"I don't need to go there," Belinda said, thinking of the dark hallways, Charlotte's face, the cool grass and the silly boy who had brought her purse back. "My husband is everything I need."

"Well, the perfect man doesn't just fly over everyone's head and drop them a note," said Lucy with a trace of bitterness. "Some of us girls had to settle."

The perfect man. Belinda closed her eyes as she considered those three words, touching her bruise very gently. Seven years had passed since she had waved at his passing plane. Sometimes she remembered the old propaganda films they'd watched during the war, before the Lance LaRue movies. German soldiers versus American ones. Killing each other. She always thought Richard above it all, as if killing on the ground meant something base, while murder from the sky was glorious and true. And in fact, not even murder. Just raining discipline down on evil people.

Someone knocked at the door and she panicked, wanting time to dab more makeup on her face to cover up the bruise. She looked through the peephole and could not believe what she saw. The silly boy again, cleaned up and in a pair of serge pants. A nice tie and black oxfords. His hair slicked down and his face shining.

"Hello," he said when she opened the door. "How are you? I don't know if you remember me. My name's Benjamin."

Belinda grabbed his hand, pulled him inside and slammed the door.

"Did anybody see you?" she demanded.

"No," he said. "I don't think so."

Belinda rushed to the window, pulling aside a gathered drape. She saw only the empty street and what must be the boy's bicycle leaning against the ligustrum tree.

"What are you looking for?" asked Benjamin.

"Nothing," she said, turning. "What are you doing here again? Go away right now. My husband will be home any minute . . ."

"No, he won't," said Benjamin. "There's been a shooting at the Gaines Bar. Two men are dead. Cajuns, I think. The news traveled all the way to our house."

"News carried by lonely women, I suppose," Belinda snapped.

"No offense, ma'am, but you've been there too."

"Who asked you? Get out."

"Please. I'd like to stay for a little while."

She looked at his determinedly formal posture and his

pleading eyes. "Are you sure he's not coming any time soon?"

"I'm sure."

"All right, then. Sit down. I'll get you some sugar cookies."

"No, please don't," he said. "Sugar cookies are for boys. I'm a man now."

"How old are you?"

"Very close to sixteen."

"All right, then. No cookies. Would you like an Orange Crush?"

He considered this for a moment. "Yes," he said carefully.

She went into the kitchen, got the drink out of the refrigerator and poured it in a glass that said: "Hires Root Beer. 5¢." She smiled. The silly boy. So obviously smitten. Like Richard on their wedding day, when they had waltzed around and around among the guests. What a day that had been.

She brought the orange drink to the boy and sat down on the couch.

"So what can I do for you?"

He drank slowly. When he finished he had an orange stain on his lip. "I just wanted to see you again," he said.

"Do you know that I'm a married woman, with a child?"

"Yes."

"And does that matter to you?"

"I know it should, but it doesn't." He straightened up on the couch and turned to her. A short hank of well-oiled hair fell down on his face. "I'm new to the study of women, and I wanted to ask you something."

"What?"

"Why did you pick him?"

The question took her by surprise. "My husband?"

He nodded and she thought for a long moment before she spoke. "Well, in a sense, he picked me . . ." She started to tell the story of the plane and how she'd bested her enemy, Charlotte, and how this had led to a storybook romance and a storybook wedding, but somehow the tale suddenly bored her. She'd told it all these years until it was a worn-out, ragged thing, still shiny to the listeners but dull to her mouth. She stopped talking and simply stared at the wall. Their wedding picture, and Richard in his pilot's uniform, posing with his plane. Then some framed flowers—an amaryllis and some peonies—which, unlike the other pictures, radiated exactly what they were.

"Ma'am?" said Benjamin.

"I picked him because he was handsome and brave," Belinda said abruptly. "He went off to fight the Germans and he came back a hero. He's got a drawer full of medals that Ralph's always getting into."

"And that's why?"

"Why do you want to know?"

"Because I've heard that he's mean," said Benjamin. "I heard that he likes to punch drunk people until their teeth fall out. And that he ripped out a chunk of a woman's hair when he caught her stealing a dress. And that he beat up a man who ran a moonshine still and held his head under the water until he—"

"All lies," Belinda interrupted. "My man spent his savagery on the Germans. He is wonderful and gentle."

"But why did you come to the house, then?" he insisted. "Did you just get tired of him?"

She sighed. Her ribs ached and so did her back and her hand, where a tiny bone had broken.

"I don't want to talk about this anymore."

"All right."

"You'll understand when you're older."

"I hope so."

She looked at his clothes and his hair. "You look different than you did before," she said.

"I'm learning about how to be a man. And about, you know, the things women want."

"Really?" Belinda laughed bitterly. "Who's teaching you?"

"The men at the house."

"And what do they say women want?"

"It's hard to explain," said Benjamin. "It's a step-by-step kind of thing."

Belinda was surprised to find her laugh girlish. She got up, looked out the window and sat back down. "Show me," she said, stunned by her own words.

"Really?"

"You sure about the dead Cajuns?"

"Yes."

"Then go ahead."

Benjamin hesitated. "All right." He moved over close to her. "Smell my collarbone."

"What?"

He pointed. "Here and here."

Belinda moved her nose from right to left. "Vanilla," she said.

"Now sniff my neck."

"Aqua Velva," said Belinda.

"Willy says women are scent hounds."

Belinda laughed. "True. Keep going."

"May I take your hand?"

Belinda nodded.

Benjamin took her hand and kissed the back of it, finding a bruise. Kissed the bruise twice.

"How did you hurt your hand?" he asked.

"In the kitchen."

"No woman should ever have a bruise, or even a cut finger."

"Who told you that?"

"Ray."

"Hmmm."

"You look very pretty tonight."

"Thank you. Now what?"

"You use the fingertips," said Benjamin. "And you watch out for the eyes." He slowly brushed her face, moving his fingers down the smooth cheek and onto the purple spot at the line of the jaw.

"My son kicked me there," she said.

Benjamin nodded. His fingers continued down her neck, then lightly stroked her shoulder. Belinda felt a rush of blinking peace. She knew that being seen doing this with a boy would get her thrown out of even a reasonable man's household, and yet something about it seemed oddly natural.

Still stroking her shoulder, he leaned forward and kissed her above her brow, twice. He stopped and looked at her. "Jimmy says that you should stop and look at a woman sometimes. Like you've just thought of something and it's all about her."

Belinda suddenly stood up. The spell slid off her. "I can't do this anymore, Benjamin. You have to leave."

He looked sad. "All right," he said. "But I didn't get a chance to get to the listening part."

"The listening part?"

"That's when a man tells a woman he wants to hear all her sorrows."

"Yes? Go on."

"Jimmy says that this is the most important part. Do you want to whisper in my ear, ma'am?"

She walked over to the window and checked it again. "Whisper what?" she said.

"Anything you want."

"Anything?" She laughed suddenly. A tear ran from her eye. "How about the alphabet?"

"That'll do, I guess," said Benjamin.

"This is what they do at the house?"

"Yes. Except it's not the alphabet. It's real sorrows."

"What do the women around here know about real sorrows?" Belinda said with a sudden bitterness.

Benjamin shrugged. "Plenty, to hear the men tell it."

"Well, I'm just going to say the alphabet."

"All right."

She sank down next to him on the couch and put her mouth to his ear. And, in a sudden exhilarating rush of freedom she hadn't felt since she was a teenager running after the smoky trail of a plane, she told him not the alphabet but the truth.

As Belinda was whispering into Benjamin's ear, Louise was whispering into the mirror. "Justin," she said. "How are you? Are you well tonight?" She pulled a tortoiseshell comb through her hair. Like her brother, she had dressed up for the evening. A blue wool dress and a lovely crepe scarf to fill in the neckline. She had held the curling iron down the chimney of a kerosene lamp until it was hot, then had created tendrils in her hair with it.

Lipstick. Pond's cold cream. Nylon hose. Evening in Paris cologne. A bath in orange slices and dried rose petals.

She had spent the afternoon reading Justin's file, going over each word carefully, even the words in the margins, as his demon glided out of the shadows and revealed itself in full light. A secret that thrilled her with its detailed edges. The feel of the sand. The fiery itch of chiggers. The color and length of the girl's hair. The mole above the eyebrow.

Charlotte Gravin.

Suddenly Louise had understood Charlotte's hold on Justin.

He'd felt guilty. That was why he'd stayed with her. But something had gone wrong, and Charlotte had smashed the kerosene lamp over his head and fled into the woods. Now Louise had to move quickly before Charlotte came back.

Louise waited until night had fallen, and the moon had risen, and the women had all been led upstairs and were now murmuring into compliant ears, and her father, Mr. Olen, had completed the night's work and was attending to his own memories. Then she went up the stairs to knock on Justin's door.

He did not answer, so she opened it for him. She felt mature and womanish, very aware of the heaviness of her breasts beneath the fabric of her dress, and the weight of her hair, the throbbing of a finger where it had burned itself on the curling iron. She and Justin had just shared a deep, shameful intimacy that he did not know about; she had seen his terrible secret and now she was quite prepared to use it against him.

Justin looked up from the cot. "I don't want dinner tonight."

She closed the door behind her. "I'm not bringing you dinner." She looked at his face. Two cuts—one near the eye and another on the chin—would leave a scar. She felt proud to see those scars as fresh wounds. It was like knowing a man from the beginning.

"What do you want, then?"

"I want to talk to you."

He sighed. "You and your father."

"I love you, Justin."

"What?"

"I love you."

He looked taken aback. "You don't even know me."

Oh yes I do. "I know enough to know that Charlotte doesn't make you happy."

"She brings me—she brought me peace."

"You can do better than that." She moved over to him and touched his face. No witch hazel on her fingers. Seduction was new to her and yet she was thrilled by its basic steps.

"Please, just go away. I'll tell your father."

"I'm new," Louise said. "I'm just a girl. I'm not like the other women who come to this place. I haven't been hurt by a man. You can just kiss me. You don't have to make things better first."

She touched his face again and this time he did not pull away.

"I just want love from you," Louise continued. "Nothing else." Her fingertips lightly ran over his face, stroking the clear patches of skin and swerving around the cuts.

"I don't know how to give love."

"Sure you do."

"I've done bad things."

"I don't care. Believe it or not, some women don't spend their lives judging."

"I don't know, Louise."

"Come on. The people here make things so complicated."

Louise kissed him, full on the mouth. In the stink of the kerosene lamp. In the odor of his unbathed body—like the odor of chrysanthemums, or yarrow.

Justin kissed her back, put his arms around her waist, drew her body to his.

Louise did not need the elaborate gentleness going on in the rooms around her. She had never been hurt by a man, save the stupidity of her father. Had never been hit. Had never been pushed or slapped. Had never been raped. Had never been called a bitch or a whore. Had never married a man who drank too much. Had never lost a husband to a young girl in a seedy bar while she sat at home with the children.

She had no history to soothe, no forgiveness to bestow, no sad story to tell of her own, and so Justin kissed her, hard.

27

Cold air slid through the boarded-up window in Justin's room, and a new secret lived in the house. After the chores were done and the women were settled, Louise would creep up to the third floor to meet Justin for the night.

Love, this time, did not begin with an apology. It was pure enough to make dirty. Justin's hand moved down her body and her breasts that were bare in the darkness. He did not ask. Didn't have to ask. This unbroken girl who begged for breaking.

Louise slept late and ignored her duties. Stains grew on the porch, and in the dining room, and down the dark hallways. The first motes of dust landed on the sideboards and the windowsills. A small brown spider found a quiet place in a corner and began a web. The smell of ammonia faded from the curtains. Tobacco juice hardened in cans. Milk spilled on the floor and dried in the shape of a pear.

The women in the other rooms smelled the musky

odor of the house and murmured. They grabbed their men and kissed them harder. Soft love like soft ice cream had made them all feel like children, and in the absence of the strict ammonia smell that once reminded them of propriety, they roamed wild. In room after room, passion replaced confession, clothes were thrown off, sad stories crumbled between gleefully frantic rhythms.

Mr. Olen spat in a can. The new odor of the house had made the vision of his absent wife stronger. Her kisses sweeter. Her breath more pungent with forgiveness. He sat in his quiet office, his house trembling around him with the breaking of rules. His eyes watered. *Janey, men are made of second chances. Adam was thrown from the garden but invited into heaven. The cock crowed more than once. The Romans killed Jesus and he came back again. Lazarus rose, Janey.*

Upstairs, Mr. Olen's daughter moved her hand through Justin's hair, then touched his healing face. The shallow wound under his eye shed its scab on the sheet.

Charlotte and Daniel curled in the woods. The secret mother and the secret son.

As the crickets muted their song, as the periwinkle died in a sparkle of frost, Louise's legs began to open. The war on germs was forgotten in the pleasures of Justin's unbathed hand. She had grown impatient with her innocence. Her teeth pressed on his skin.

Benjamin stared at the ceiling of his shack. His hair, slick with Wildroot Creme-Oil, collected lint from his pillow. Belinda had told him never to come back, had presented the tale of her husband in the same way that history books would later present the Nazis. A stark, bewildered rendition of the crimes.

Charlotte's words were slightly smoky as she whispered into Daniel's ear the tale of Justin, the soldier she had loved and lost. She left out the parts that must be kept from a boy, even an angelic boy who can hear all things without judgment. "I want to hate him and I want to love him," she told her boy. *And you, Daniel,* she thought to herself, *I wanted to hate you and love you too. You had the eyes of God but a body made by soldiers. I left you on the stump so someone could love you without remembering. Now I love you and I remember and the two can live together. We can live together. My son.*

The chimney of the kerosene lamp in Justin's room darkened with fresh soot. A spiral of smoke rose to the beams. Louise murmured something. The shadow of her bent knees trembled on the wall. On this same wall, the shadow of his dangling feet once horrified and thrilled her.

"Ouch," Louise said.

"What?"

"Nothing."

His heaviness was necessary. Louise gritted her teeth. The motions of her body taunted her absent mother.

The air had turned warm again, a trick this climate played when least expected. One night Justin sat on the porch, staring out into the woods. Louise had gone back to bed, and he was alone again with this nagging ache. He had enjoyed the new girl and the new odor in the house, an earthy and forgiving kind of scent that permeated the rooms, and yet he could not rid himself of this enduring pain, right between the ribs. An itch, perhaps, that reminded him in a silly way of the chiggers that used to plague him. The thought of Charlotte had come to his mind again and again, and he had pushed it away. During their time together she had made him tired because she was really two people: the woman in his arms, the girl on the riverbank. Keeping the two of them still and quiet had exhausted him.

Mr. Olen had told him that he was free, but if this was freedom it itched like fire. Justin idly scratched at his face, finding the brittle end of a long, thin scab and pulling on it until the scab unpeeled from his skin, leaving a bloody trail. Hurting what had slowly been healing. As he'd done to Charlotte.

Justin heard a disturbance in the brush and looked up. The little boy was walking through the yard. He saw Justin and looked furtive.

"Come here," Justin called. He had seen this boy at the breakfast table a few times, but had never asked about him or learned his name. At times he had glanced out his window—before Charlotte broke it—and noticed the boy playing in the backyard, swinging from a branch of the camphor tree or stroking the long back of a sleepy hound.

Just a quick glance, nothing more, because Justin could not shake the feeling that the boy knew something—knew, in fact, everything.

"Come here," Justin called again.

The boy walked up to him. His blue eyes shone.

"What is your name, little boy?"

"Daniel."

"Do you know my name?"

"Justin."

"Why were you out in the woods tonight?"

Daniel lowered his eyes. "A secret."

"Tell me."

"I can't."

"Why?"

Daniel's eyes leaped back to him. "Because you are part of the secret." He brushed past Justin and faded into the house.

Justin barely had time to wonder what that meant before the itch made itself known again, but this time the itch was deepening into an ache, then a searing pain that seemed to spread across his chest into an area already pioneered by guilt.

This was more than guilt. The sight of the little boy, so defined in the moonlight, so close as to leave a scent, had made him wolfishly hurt for the love of Charlotte.

The unseasonably warm weather had brought out a desire for fishing. Charlotte sat on the bank on a patchwork quilt, her line in the water and an empty Coke bottle turned down in a bowl of water. She watched her cork grimly, even though she had seen his approaching shoes out of the corner of her eye.

"Charlotte, I need to talk to you."

The cork moved a little.

"Please look at me," he said.

"Why now?" she murmured. "I couldn't look at you before. My eyes were covered."

She heard his breath catch as she said the words. Then a brief silence.

"Please," he said. She turned to him and saw his face. Half a dozen wounds healing and one with the scab stripped away. "You shouldn't pick at your face," she said, before silently shushing the nurse in herself.

Justin knelt down next to her. A leaf whirled out of nowhere and fell into her lap. Water moved up the neck of the Coke bottle.

I am haunted by the antics of a stupid boy, Charlotte. A boy who thought the heat and the torment of chiggers made him God's martyr to the cause of freedom. A boy who scratched his itch on a nameless girl, in the deep woods removed from judgment. I couldn't slap him and so I healed you. And then I tore your wound open like I've wanted to tear the woods open, take out the part that hurt you, pull out the history with it, burn it until nothing's left. The trouble is, Charlotte, in the process of undoing I have been undone. Separate and equal to the force of the crime, I have been undone by you. The way one person should be undone by another. Not through violence but through love. You haunt me, Charlotte, in a new and different way. You haunt me clean and glorious.

Charlotte watched the bobber move and felt his eyes on her, smelled his tears like a change in the weather, waited for him to speak. The bobber moved again, but she could not tell whether it was a fish or simply the hooked minnow. When at last he spoke, it was simple.

"I love you, Charlotte."

She fought the feeling inside her body. Sweet forgiveness, anger so bitter it ruined her blood. The bobber moved again and she jerked it back, impatient from the false signals.

"Go away," she said.

That night, the house sighed as women forgot to cry and men remembered their buried instincts. Cardinal rules were broken in three-quarters of the rooms.

The old doctor slept fitfully. The odors around him, the strange new sounds, made him remember he was once the center of his own house, with his own wife and children. Now his children were grown and his wife was dead.

Manly with knowledge, Benjamin stared at the ceiling of his shack. The new warm weather had brought the odor of sweet potatoes. It came seeping out of the rotten wood like termites stirred by the heat. He blinked, and made a man's decision.

Mr. Olen put his feet on his desk. He noticed his fingernails were long. He sighed, irritated at the new chore. Fingernails were meant to grow on women, not men.

Charlotte and Daniel curled in the woods. The best-kept secret. The mother and the child.

Across town, Belinda slipped out of bed and paced the living room. Her nightgown flowed behind her.

Justin sat on the cot and stared at the boarded-up window.

Louise knocked on his door. She heard no answer.

"Justin?" she whispered. She knocked again, louder. She had given up so much to him and he owed her the unlocking of that door.

28

Daniel slid under the bed, his belly and his face collecting the first fine grains of the dust that had gathered in the wake of Louise's new affair. Louise had already gone up to Justin's room for the fourth time that night, and Daniel had been given the precious few moments to accomplish his mission. He groped around blindly and found the rope still knotted in its heartbreaking noose. He pulled himself out from under the bed and returned to his room.

He'd comforted enough crying women to know that they were always looking for an excuse to forgive a man, even at the height of their sorrow and anger, for deep down, all men were their sons. Daniel held the rope up to the light and tested its griminess with a thumb and forefinger.

He slipped outside to meet his mother, past the sweet potato barn where Benjamin was gathering his courage.

"What is this?" whispered Charlotte when Daniel put

the rope in her hands. The warmth had faded from the woods, and the two of them were huddled together.

"What Justin used," Daniel answered.

"On what?"

"On Justin." Daniel's words mixed solemnly with the thin mist of his breath.

"On himself?"

"Yes."

"When?"

"The first night."

"When he came to stay at the house?"

"Yes."

Charlotte turned the rope wonderingly in her hands, feeling a motherly concern fill her on behalf of Justin's fragile neck. She had thought of him constantly since he met her at the lake. Now she was stunned by the violence he had wreaked upon himself. Proof, in a strange way, of his gentleness.

"Tell me what happened, Daniel," she said, and Daniel put his mouth to her ear and began to tell his own story, for once, about the soldier with the haunted eyes. On and on he spoke, as Charlotte listened intently.

Years before, she had scorned God for the things He let happen, or perhaps engineered. She hated His silence, which had covered Auschwitz, Buchenwald, Dachau and the dark part of the Louisiana woods. And so she had left her blue-eyed baby waving at her from the stump. Now, with Daniel's breath in her ear, she looked back and, instead of her little boy, she saw God waving. God, who has no words but only gestures. God, who is perfect. God, who removed from sight can grow bigger and return, not as an enemy but as a loved one.

And Daniel whispered: "His neck was hurt all the way around."

Benjamin did not hear the whispering as he pedaled his bicycle out of the backyard, around the side of the house and onto the road. He had spent the evening smoking in his barn and gathering his courage, and thinking about Belinda. Blowing rings in the air and watching them disappear. Breathing in the odor of long-forgotten sweet potatoes. A rich, fragrant odor like love old and realized. Earthy, like the sex used to be and, later, the solitude. Before he set out on his mission, a little of his boyhood had tickled at him, and he wrote this note to his sister:

Dear Louise,
If you're reading this I am dead. Don't let them bury
me smelling like a girl.

Now he pedaled slowly down the dirt road that led to the more civilized streets of the town, the night lit by stars he'd never seen before, and oak leaves wrestling with the spokes of his wheels. He wondered, as he steered around dark clumps in the path and dodged the swirl of dead leaves, if fate had a way of punishing the sins of former boys. All those innocent bugs he'd crushed. He had been a bully like the sheriff. Stomping on things that could not stomp back. Would he pay for that tonight? Would the stomped-upon bugs cry for justice?

The trees on his left side blew leaves at the trees on his right side, which retaliated. And the stars above so bright. The bicycle so fast and the cooling air so fresh. A good time to be a boy. Too late.

The sheriff set his beer down and licked his lips. The beer had made his laughter loud, but certain things irritated him on the edges of his consciousness. The way that people opened the door too long and let in the changing air. The too-bright red of the dress on the waitress. The amount of beer foam he had to blow on so gently before he could take a drink. The too-loud bar.

"So I finally learned the secret," he told John Dewly and Charlie Fifer, two friends from the Maneuvers who had come back to pull their sweethearts from the woods and marry them. They had all settled down within ten streets of one another. The war never had to end.

"What secret?" asked John.

"About why that old Burgess man hates the Pentecostals. He's the one that tried to burn down their church, I'll bet."

"I thought that crazy boy Milo did that."

"Who knows? But anyway, you know old man Burgess used to live down the road from a Pentecostal church, right? Well . . ." The sheriff leaned forward so far that his chin brushed the foam. "You know he had a son?"

"No," said Charlie. "Really? I thought he didn't have any children."

"Well, he did, once," said the sheriff. He turned around and called to the waitress. "Honey? Can we please get some peanuts over here?"

"Finish the story," said Charlie.

"Hold on. Just hold on. Wait until I get my peanuts." This was the sheriff's favorite trick. Get them hanging on a story and then stop and let them suffer for a while. Sometimes he never bothered to finish a story, feeling the pleasure of denying others that cleansing resolution.

The waitress brought over the peanuts and the sheriff held one to his ear and rattled it. "All right," he said. "So this son was a sweet little boy, and old man Burgess thought the world of him. Anyway, one Sunday Burgess goes off to tend his sheep, the son's out in the woods and he gets bit by a big old timber rattler, high up in the arm. No phone in the house, of course, so Mrs. Burgess runs into the front yard, screaming for Burgess. He's out in the field across the way, right?"

The sheriff stopped.

"So?" asked Charlie.

"So there was so much screamin' and hollerin' coming from that Pentecostal church, Burgess couldn't hear his wife. By the time she went and fetched him, it was too late. The boy died."

"Whew!" said Charlie. "I bet he was the one that burned down that church."

"Well," said the sheriff, "you got to remember that behind every crime there's a grudge of some kind. Or at least a reason." Out of the corner of his eye the sheriff caught another glimpse of the waitress's red dress. That bright color in this dark bar disturbed him. It didn't fit. She demanded too much from the eye.

"You like that waitress?" asked Charlie.

"Hell, no. She looks like a cheap whore. I got better than that at home."

"Your wife sold any of those pillows lately?"

"Hell, no. Not for profit. She sells them to her women friends and then she buys their damn quilts. We got a closet full of quilts."

He took a drink of beer and was annoyed to find it warm. He felt bored by his friends. Always, it seemed, he was the one to provide the entertainment.

He didn't notice the boy at first, so quietly did he stand by the table. Finally the stiff and motionless body attracted his attention. Something wasn't quite right about a boy standing so still. Like a woman in a red dress, it stuck out and he didn't like it.

"What are you doing here, boy?" asked the sheriff. "This bar is for men."

"I'm here to talk to you, Sheriff."

"Oh, yeah?" The sheriff peered at him. "Aren't you

the one that came by my house a couple weeks ago? Talking to my wife?"

"Uh-oh," said Charlie, and he and John laughed.

The boy shifted on his feet. "I'm the one, I guess."

"You guess? Well, how many boys you think come around talking to my wife?"

"No smart ones!" said Charlie.

"What's your name?" asked the sheriff.

"Benjamin Olen."

"Olen? There aren't any Olens in this town. Where do you live?"

Benjamin took a deep breath. "I live," he said, "at The House of Gentle Men."

The bar went quiet.

The sheriff looked around. "This ain't none of your business, folks," he said loudly. "Go on and drink your beer." He pulled Benjamin down into a chair. "Are you crazy, boy?" he asked. "You aren't supposed to mention the Sissy House out loud."

"Does it really exist?" John whispered.

"Shut up, John," said the sheriff. "Of course it exists. I'm the sheriff. I know all about the sissies that live at the end of that old dirt road."

The boy stiffened. His tongue moved over his upper lip, wiping away the sweat. He used his index finger to rub dry the spit his tongue left. He wore too much hair dressing, and a certain sweet odor drifted out from his clothes.

"They aren't sissies," he said. "They're gentle men."

"Gentle men? Men with no balls, that's what they are. Must mean you ain't got no balls. I hear they keep 'em in jars in a pie safe."

"Hey," whispered Charlie. "Maybe the boy was over at your house tryin' to give your wife a pamphlet."

The sheriff turned his head. "Shut up, Charlie. And you, boy. Tell me. Do you have balls, or are they in the pie safe with the others?"

"I have balls," said Benjamin. "But around women, you're supposed to call them testicles."

"Is that so?" asked the sheriff. He called over to the waitress. "Honey, come here a second."

The waitress came over slowly. She stood a few feet away from the sheriff's outstretched hand. "What is it?" she asked.

"You ever been over to The House of Sissy Men?"

"No," she said. She looked at Benjamin long and hard. He'd grown up some. She wanted to smooth his hair.

"You like sissies or real men?"

"Real men," she said, looking at Benjamin, hoping he heard the insult. It had taken so long to get over him.

"Thank you, honey. Run along." The sheriff took another gulp of his beer. It was definitely warm. Warm beer reminded him of the Maneuvers, when he was just a fresh-faced kid getting shit on by the officers. "You know what I think, boy?" he asked.

"What?" asked Charlie, leaning forward.

"I think those men at the Sissy House do it to each other."

Benjamin looked over at the slot machines. "No," he said. "It's all men with women. That's how my daddy set it up."

"Well, thank you for the lesson. Now get out of here."

"I can't."

"You can't? You telling me no?"

"I want to talk to you about your wife," said Benjamin. The other men fell silent. They looked at Benjamin almost tenderly, thinking about their own boys and hoping this one would turn around and run, very fast. They had seen their friend the sheriff in war and in peace, and had noticed no difference in him from one to the other.

"My wife?" said the sheriff. "What about my wife?" His beer was annoyingly warm, the foam annoyingly foamy, the waitress annoyingly red, the boy's hair annoyingly greasy, the world annoyingly peaceful, the Nazis annoyingly vanquished, his plane annoyingly grounded, and so the sheriff poured his beer on the boy's foot.

Benjamin jumped out of his chair, away from the splash, breaking the hearts of the other two men—that this boy would worry about getting his socks wet when his bones were so close to snapping.

"Can you come outside with me?" Benjamin asked the sheriff.

★　　★　　★

Back at the house, women set free from misery and grudge moved close to their men and licked their ears playfully. The men responded with the eagerness of boys. They whispered and wrestled, stroked and kissed and scuffled and barely heard the shushing sound of the demons outside, who hung from the camphor tree, caught the dangerous scent of freedom and waited for a foothold back in. The ammonia smell had vanished from the house and left only the aroma of humanity: slick skin, crushed grass, cedar and vinegar, old bicycle seats, rain, roses, bread, catfish heads, chicken feathers, sweat, tears, blood. And Aqua Velva poured over it all.

As she climbed the stairs with the noose in her hand, Charlotte felt dizzy with joy. Forgiveness, she realized, had the same scent whether given or received. She had always thought it would smell clean and delicate, like newly washed hosiery. Instead she found it to smell like a human body under moderate sunlight.

Charlotte, forgiven by her son as God forgives—without words but with an agreeable silence—now could forgive Justin. The simplicity of it stunned her, and in this she saw the simplicity of heaven. A bright, simple blue, a primary blue parented by no other colors. A beginning blue from which to start again.

Charlotte knocked on Justin's door.

★　　★　　★

Benjamin followed the sheriff outside, around the back of the building to a clear gravel area where the trucks pulled up to unload their beer. Overhead the stars pulsed, sending their dying chill down to the planet, to the animals that crept in the forest, to the ground underneath the feet of the boy and the man.

Benjamin's shirt had begun to untuck from his serge pants, and now it billowed a little around his waist. The wind chose a new part for his hair. He put his hands in his pockets and paced around in a little circle while the sheriff watched him.

My enemies used to be men, thought the sheriff. Perfect men. Blond hair and blue eyes and tanks and guns. Now my enemies have shrunk into boys. And not even perfect ones. This one's face is a little too round. His teeth a little crooked. "Getting colder, isn't it?" he asked.

Benjamin shrugged.

"But I don't really think you care, do you?" asked the sheriff. "When I was a boy like you, growing up in Ohio, the cold weather wouldn't stop me from doing anything. One time, me and my brother went looking for a wild horse in the middle of a snowstorm. When we got back, my mother tanned us good. I almost lost two fingers to frostbite. These two." He held them out to Benjamin. "Good thing I didn't. Would have kept me from flying."

"What happened to your hand?" asked Benjamin.

"I picked up a flaming oxygen bottle to save my crew." He read Benjamin's expression. "I guess you're thinking you haven't heard anything good about me. Just bad things."

"I wasn't thinking that."

"Good. Because I try real hard to be a fair sheriff and a fair husband. And if there's something bothering my wife, I need to know about it. I love that woman more than life itself. I stayed alive in Buchenwald for her. Came back to these god-awful backwater woods of hers because she didn't want to leave her mama. And if anything's wrong, I'm here to make it better. Isn't that a man's job, making things better?"

"It's supposed to be."

"Then tell me what you want to say."

Benjamin dug his hands deeper into his pockets, pulling the waist of his pants down past another button on his shirt. The wind played havoc with his hair, despite the Wildroot Creme-Oil. "I just don't think you should hit her."

"What?"

"You know, how you give her bruises. You see . . ." Benjamin took a cautious step in the direction of the sheriff's boots. "I used to treat women bad myself. Not hitting, but hurting in other ways. That's before I learned that real men treat women like queens."

"And what makes you think I don't treat Belinda like a queen?"

"She told me."

"She did, did she?" The sheriff laughed. "Oh, son.

Let me tell you about my wife. She's bored. That's why she stuffs those damn pillows and stinks up the house. That's why she dresses Ralph up like a damn girl, two or three different outfits a day. She has nothing to do, and so she likes to tell stories."

"I don't think they're stories."

"Oh, they are, son. I'm embarrassed that you had to hear them. And I really appreciate you bringing me out here alone to tell me about it." The sheriff took his hat off, smoothed his blond hair, put the hat back on again. "But there's one thing that's bothering me a little. When did you see my wife?"

Justin heard the knocking again. Why couldn't Louise just give up? He felt trapped in here with the boards nailed across the window. And since it seemed that she was going to knock all night, he wearily rose to his feet.

Opening the door let in the rush of warm roiling air from the rest of the house, and the woodsy scent of Charlotte, who stood with a noose in her hands. Astonishing, this vision. Not just Charlotte's location—here in the doorway of his room—but the look on her face. A far cry from the look she'd had the night she caused his wounds. Whose scabs he now fingered nervously.

"Come in," he said, taking Charlotte's noose from her hand as if it were a coat and laying it carefully across the foot of the cot.

She sat down on the bentwood chair as Justin closed the door.

She did not speak for several moments and he allowed her the silence as he walked around the room, straightening things and tending to the wick, which was set too high and sending smoke out the top of the chimney toward the beams whose acquaintance he had made that very first night.

"When you told me about what happened, I wanted to kill you," said Charlotte. "Or I wanted to tell Milo, who would have killed you. You were the one who pretended you didn't want to. You were the one the others were goading into it. You were the one I hated the most. My ears and my hair were full of sand, it was all over me, and the three of you were standing there talking about chiggers and Germans. And I couldn't forgive you for that. That's what I wanted to say to you, all of you, only my throat wouldn't work."

Justin nodded. Something new was in the room. Her words were horrible in shape but soft and smooth in presentation. Holy.

"And I hated you so much that I didn't talk for seven years. I wanted to save my voice for you, because there weren't enough words to scream at you when the time came. I had a little boy, Justin. No one saw, because everyone's eyes were covered. I gave birth in the woods and I nursed that boy for two days and then I left him on a stump. I know it sounds terrible, what I did, but try to remember that the sight of that boy was my first glimpse of my attackers. And that boy was perfect. Beautiful like an angel.

"I left him there because I needed to be enemies with God. It helped harden my heart. Now I've found my boy and I'm forgiven. I see the angel in him and so I have to see the angel in you. All three of you. I forgive you. Because God forgives you. And when I held that noose in my hands, I realized that the two of us—me and God—forgive you more than you do, Justin."

She finished talking and then let the silence push the last echoes of her words through the cracks in the window boards, underneath the door. A perfect stillness in a corner of a house roiling with whispers, huffing with groans. Tears ran down Justin's face in rapid succession. Charlotte winced at the sight of salt water running into his open wound.

"You had a child, Charlotte? And you found him?"

"Yes," she said, and realized, deeply and fully, what she'd known all along. That Justin, whose kisses also healed, whose voice also soothed, whose eyes also had a curious light, had a son.

Daniel, sweet boy of one father.

Benjamin lay on the ground. Blood ran from his mouth. "Get up," said the sheriff.

★　　★　　★

Justin blew the flame out in the kerosene lamp. He turned in the darkness and found Charlotte's body. Kissed her soft and sweet. Kissed her new as a baby. Kissed her quiet as an ambush by migratory butterflies. Kissed her cool as the glass on a shadow box.

The sheriff picked Benjamin up by the hair.

Justin's hands moved down Charlotte's back.

The sheriff punched Benjamin in the mouth again.

Charlotte touched Justin's face and felt the edges of his wounds in the dark.

The sheriff threw Benjamin on the ground.

The window was boarded up and starlight could not get in. The lovers held each other. And the riverbank of sand was white, lovely white, so clean so pure so soft you could swaddle a baby in it.

Benjamin spat blood on the gravel.

Charlotte and Justin lay back on the cot.

29

Dogs noticed the frost on the ground and walked gingerly. The frost sparkled with light but the air stayed dull. Inside the house, men came downstairs to breakfast exhausted, slumping at the table and mumbling to each other. They looked away nervously from the eyes of Mr. Olen. Upstairs, the sheets were rumpled, and the first notches had been discreetly carved into the bedposts, for even though each man was shamed by his unsanctioned acts of love, he was also secretly proud. By the oaken hall tree just inside the foyer, the syrup can was stuffed so tightly with tips that, later, Mr. Olen had to use a pair of tongs to extract the dollar bills.

Louise served them breakfast. Haunted by her unanswered knocks on Justin's door, she had spent the night staring at the ceiling, crying intermittently and going over her short history with him again and again. Had she said something wrong? Curled her hair in a way that wasn't pleasing? Worn too much cologne, or the wrong color of Bakelite jewelry?

Or had the change in weather affected Justin's heart? If all of Louise's womanly preparations had been undone by Mother Nature, then that conniving old woman was her enemy too.

She moved around the table slowly, setting bowls of oatmeal down. The oatmeal was lumpy and unstirred and the men who stared at it bleakly were too nervous to grumble. This was it, the first punishment handed down for their new sins. Lumpy oatmeal. What was next? Locusts, boils, high winds? Fire from an angry sky?

"What's the matter with everyone?" asked Mr. Olen. "Louise, you look dead on your feet. And I never thought I'd say this to you, but the floor needs mopping."

Louise sat down heavily next to Daniel, who looked at her mildly and touched her arm.

A strand of her hair fluttered into her bowl. She stared into her oatmeal, noticed the hair and didn't bother to remove it. The men around her fell abruptly silent and she looked up to see Justin entering the room, leading Charlotte by the hand.

Justin helped Charlotte with her chair and then sat down himself.

Louise dropped her spoon.

The men looked at the couple and elbowed each other, made grateful by this open-air, early-morning, full-light, blatant breaking of the rules that pulled attention away from the ones broken under cover of the night.

Mr. Olen let loose a newly cooled spoon of oatmeal

back into his bowl and tried to hide his joy. He could smell forgiveness in the room, for it had physical properties that could be inhaled like the new dust that coated the tables and the arms of chairs. That a woman could forgive such a crime gave Mr. Olen hope for other women, other crimes. He stirred his oatmeal thoughtfully for a few moments, picked up his coffee, blew on it and sipped with outstretched lips. All those nights without her. He felt like crying and he was a man who'd earned the right to a few tears, but he knew that the others were expecting a reaction from him.

He set the coffee down. "What's going on here, Justin?" he asked.

"What do you mean?"

"You know you're not supposed to bring a woman to the table. All women are supposed to be gone by first light." Out of the corner of his eye Mr. Olen noticed the look on his daughter's face. Pure steaming hatred. He hadn't seen that look since the day her mother had left.

"I know about the rules," said Justin, "but this might be an exception."

"Why?"

"Because Charlotte and I are getting married."

Louise pushed her chair back and fled from the room.

"Louise," Mr. Olen called after her.

The couple seemed not to notice, so intensely were they looking at Daniel.

The men suddenly erupted in congratulations and

slapped Justin good-naturedly on the back. "When did you decide?" asked one.

"Last night."

Willy slapped his hand down on the table. "Just remember, Justin," he said. "Marriage is a noose no one can cut you down from."

"Willy," said Mr. Olen.

Louise lay on the bed in the position of a corpse, her arms crossed and her feet pointed. The turn of events was too astonishing to elicit tears. Daniel came in and tried to kiss her, but she pushed him away, scorning peace.

She couldn't believe what she had given away for nothing. Like scrubbing a floor just to see it dirty again. Like hanging sheets with her mother just to find her mother's best dress gone, and all her shoes.

Tracing Justin's demon back to its sandy source had only made Louise love him more. She didn't know or care about Justin the boy. And if the boy had to sin for the man to have such haunted eyes, such a somber presence, then so be it. The utter depravity of the act, safe in the past and covered over with sand, had given Louise a slight tingle. Nothing could have culled Justin from this sleepy group more than this shameful thing released from the safe in the cellar.

But the Mute had won. She had drawn Justin in with silence and then captured him with a web of sudden words. Played the victim and then the stalker. The hunted and then the hunter. And now they were to be married. Past and present, crime and forgiveness, silence and words, sin and redemption, had joined hands to exclude Louise. She had nothing to do but go back and scrub the floors. Wipe Justin's final footprints off the porch. Wash his final scent off the sheets. Wash the walls he'd once leaned his head against. Pour out the witch hazel that had dressed his wounds.

Her father came in about four o'clock. His footsteps were light and when he spoke his voice was boyish. "Louise, it's a beautiful day. Cold but sunny. You ought to be outside."

"I don't want to be outside."

"What's wrong? Don't you feel well?"

"No, I don't."

"Are you sick?"

She did not answer. She heard her father's footsteps around the room, pictured him standing by the window and squinting his eyes at the sun. "Amazing, isn't it, that Justin and Charlotte are getting married?"

"What's so amazing?" Louise said dully.

"Well . . . there are things you don't know."

"What a surprise."

"Now, Louise. You know this house runs on secrets. Privacy is sacred."

"Is that why you went through Mama's drawers?"

When he walked over to her bed his steps were heavier. The clomp-clomp-clomp of a depressed circus bear returning to the cage. His face loomed into her view of the ceiling. "Am I to pay for that forever?" he whispered. Before Louise could answer, he left the room.

A room's capacity to dull the senses is legendary. Sight, smell, hearing, touch, taste. Sadness. Respect. Joy. Anger. Louise felt as though she were in a trance, where any decision made was as lifeless and as harmless as the dull brain that made it. Yes, it felt good not to feel. Nothing. Like the Germans felt. It was all about the plan. A perfect plan. Ridding oneself of something unpleasant or unsettling. A race of people. Or a sudden marriage.

In the pleasantness of this new dull brain she had, a soaking gray sponge or a dead gray squid, Louise shifted on the bed. Beneath her back, beneath the mattress, the file on Justin shifted too.

Milo looked a little skinnier than when she'd seen him last. His hands down in the pockets of his pea jacket. His boots worn. His lip curled against a sudden breeze. By way of greeting, he picked up a rock and threw it in the lake. It tore three blue holes in the black water.

"I'm out of practice," said Milo.

"Looks like it."

"What did you want to see me about? Gonna give me my kiss?"

"No."

"Why not? We got something to celebrate now. You hear?"

"About Charlotte and Justin getting married? Yes, I've heard."

Milo twirled around and went up on his toes like a ballet dancer. "Ain't it great? I've never seen Charlotte so happy. That boy took a while to come around, but shit, he came around. We're going to be brother-in-laws! I've never had a brother."

"I don't think he's right for Charlotte."

Milo picked up another rock. The sun was very low now, and the rock skipped into bad lighting conditions. Maybe three skips. Maybe five. The number lost forever. "What do you mean, not right? He's a gentleman."

"How do you know?"

Milo shrugged. "He's got good manners and a soft voice."

Louise had willed her brain into sluggishness, which accounted for her monotone. Now she followed the plan like a path in the woods, not noticing the shadows or flowers or the cries of wild things. "I thought you wanted someone who was safe."

Milo narrowed his eyes. "What are you talking about?"

"I know something you don't know. About Justin."

"Don't tell me. I don't care. As long as he's good to Charlotte."

"But it's about Charlotte."

"It is?"

The low flat sun was throwing out its light on the lake.

"Yes," said Louise. "I'm going to give you something and then I'm going to walk away." She handed the file to Milo.

"What's this?"

"A secret."

"I can't read this. It's almost dark."

"Squint."

Milo started to open it.

"Wait," said Louise. "I don't want you to look at it before I'm gone. I don't want to get punched. I'm not a tree, Milo."

As the sun set, Leon Olen went down to the cellar to find Justin's file. It was time to make notes much more hopeful than the ones in the margins. *Imagine that,* he thought. *Not just a grudging forgiveness but a joyous marriage. What magic.*

As he turned the dial on the safe he noticed the scratches around the door. Someone had tried to break in. Louise, probably. He shook his head and shuffled through the files. Justin's was missing.

There must be some mistake, Mr. Olen thought, going through them again. Willy, Ray, Jimmy, Sam, Henry, Matthew, Roger, Rufus. Nothing more.

Mr. Olen let the files fall to the floor and put his head in his hands. Louise had discovered the combination. His daughter, whom he had taught to look for clues.

30

Louise lay shivering. On her bed she'd found a note from her father—*Louise, I need to talk to you*—which she had crumpled and thrown into a corner before crawling under the covers. The thing she'd done had left her body paralyzed, her legs weak, her arms heavy, her fingers too stiff to worry the fringe on the bedspread. In darkness she listened to the sounds of the house. Whispers, music, footsteps on the wooden floors. And next to her—in her father's office—murmurings that could only mean another woman was here to make her claim on some man she was sure would bring her peace.

Two hours had passed since Louise had left Milo the file on Justin, and she figured that he had probably waited until he got back to his house in the woods before he opened it. She remembered that Milo took forever to read anything, and imagined him now with his eyes struggling down the page. His face turning red. His hands shaking. His breath coming fast. The confessions of Justin turning

Milo into the monster everyone thought he was. Uncontrollable, deadly.

Louise had wanted to hurt Justin, push her finger into the soft place the secret made on his body. Now she had her own demon, debased enough to lock in the cellar safe. Now she needed her own tip can. She was as guilty as any man in the house had ever been. For she knew Milo's outrageous temper, and though she didn't know what exactly was going to happen, she was certain something big and bad was coming.

She gathered the covers around her, but the shivering grew worse.

Maybe I can go to Milo and reason with him. Help him to make out the big words and to calm down about them. But then she remembered the trees, and imagined Milo punching them one by one while dirt flew off their bark and his knuckles turned to blood. The vision suddenly exhausted her, and she slept.

In the rooms above her head, women and men rolled on the beds, pushing aside the covers. The beds creaked. Pillows shifted. Bodies moved together. Clothes lay on the floor in a tangled heap. Branches heavy with demons scratched at the windows.

An unfamiliar car turned down the dirt road.

In one room in the house, an old woman—a familiar guest—placed herself in a Windsor chair. She took off her pillbox hat, placed it on the floor by her feet and then folded her hands.

"You're looking well, my son," she said.

The young man looked at her, absently stroking a bedpost that did not contain a single notch. He walked up to her and placed his hands on her shoulders. Bent down until her lavender scent was a caught flower. Kissed her on the cheek and felt the powder she'd dabbed on her face. He heard the bed squeak in the next room, then loud, raucous laughter. *Damn it,* he thought. *This is not fair.*

The car stopped and pulled over to the side, near a bank of trees. The driver's door opened.

Up in Room 21, the man and the woman talked quietly in the glow of the lantern as they lay on the cot, shielding each other from the cold air coming from the outside, between the boards that were nailed over the window.

"He likes to climb trees," Justin said. "I know that. And I know he likes to thumb-wrestle."

He kissed Charlotte, and when his mouth left hers, she said: "He's afraid of big dogs and pirates and panthers. He hates wearing shoes. He likes stories about Indians. And when he's worried he shakes his head. Like this."

Justin watched Charlotte. "I do that too."

Her fingers slid down his face, starting at the forehead, closing his eyes on the way down to his cheekbone, widening to miss the scars and then coming back together at the line of his jaw. She said: "I know you do."

The dogs outside saw, heard, smelled it first. They sniffed at the odor of gasoline, then bucked away from the growing flames. They barked in excited high yips like coyotes as the flames followed the gasoline and then ate past it, spreading around the periphery of the front of the house, first turning black the edges of the porch and then moving inward. The dogs raised their noses to the stars and began to howl.

The men and women heard the muffled howling of the dogs and were not warned. Instead the howling—loud and mournful and lonely and savage—reminded them of their deepest selves. The instincts they could not banish with candlelight and waltzes. Their windows were shut and the smoke rose unseen outside in the dark. Down on the first floor, the flames had darted inside—furtively, like the lonely women who had brought their dollars and their best gowns.

The fire moved through the foyer, raging and murmuring as it tore through the longleaf pine, rare pine known for its beauty and the way it surrenders to this murderous light. The oak hall tree burned, and the pine dining table. The railroad bench that women used to sit on with their eyes straight ahead. Bakelite ran off the radio, leaving bare metal and glass. The swirls in the curly pine baseboards blackened. The kitchen table fell. The flames tumbled down the stairs, broke the cellar door and wrestled with the safe as endangered confessions trembled.

The door to Mr. Olen's office disintegrated, and fire swept through the office, sweeping pictures off the walls, finding a shoelace and an empty tobacco pouch in the trash can and papers in the drawers of the old oaken desk. As it finished blackening the carpet, the flames closest to the door moved back into the hallway, upstairs and into the rooms.

So many things consumed in an instant. Velveteen curtains went up, and flannel sheets, linen towels, house slippers and hosiery, chenille and chambray, a handkerchief in the pocket of a camel's hair jacket. Socks, silk ties, nightshirts. Beds and closets. Shoes and diaries. Hair and grosgrain ribbons. An old Effanbee doll. A gravity clock. One by one, they flashed, melted, exploded, curled, crumbled.

The fire broke the rules. It put its feet on desks. It left its fingerprints on glass. It was not discreet, nor sorry. It did not listen without judgment. It did not keep secrets. It did not love and it was not kind. From a distance it seemed romantic, beautiful, like a pilot in the sky. Up close it simply burned.

Mr. Olen woke up to find his bedroom suddenly made wavy and pliable by the orange and yellow walls. The heat, too intense to be painful, shimmered over his possessions, his nylon brush, his ancient slippers, his father's old collar box. The enormous flames like a vision of heaven—preparing the body with their weight and heft until the body could believe, and in this belief were peace and even joy.

Among the flames his wife Janey stood, in a red dress that he had so long ignored and then so long remembered. She was the darkest part of the flames around her. Her eyes remembered too, as forgiveness hushed off her body and made the fire sigh and move.

"Janey," said Mr. Olen. "Have you come for a tall and meddlesome man?"

He held her close, her body so real he could feel the sweat and heat. The scent once again moving into his nostrils, so powerful it banished smoke. He held her. Kissed her. Ran his hands over her dress as he spoke to her.

Tell me your sorrows, Janey. Tell me about a man you could not capture. Tell me a story so lonely I will sink to my knees.

Upstairs, the fire gained in intensity, fed by unsent letters, pulled threads, fingernails, the wax of secret candles. It melted buttons. Broiled Panama hats on searing brass hooks. Turned the notches black on bedposts. Broke cologne bottles and tormented the scent within them.

Some of the men had been moving inside the women when the smoke began to slide beneath their doors. But the sex was so new, the threat of fire so dreamy, that they went back to work as the smoke filled their room, and stopped only when they began to cough with every other sigh.

Now windows burst as the lovers threw themselves through them, into the smoky air, down to the ground. Burning by moonlight, rolling in the yellow grass. Hugging the ground with the fervor of new converts. The flames running down their backs. Some of them made it to the wading pond and threw themselves into the image of the burning house carried by the surface of the water. Willy wiped his red eyes and died at the edge of the pond.

Thirty yards away, in the sweet potato barn, the sound of shattering glass interrupted Benjamin's sleep. An orange light came through the cracks of the barn and nursed his bruised face. Smoke followed the light. Benjamin coughed and shook the woman who slept with her head on his chest.

"Belinda," he whispered. "Something's on fire."

Daniel woke up to a roomful of smoke and the sounds of screaming instead of the usual murmurs of love. He ran into the hallway, into the dirty smoke and clean flames, coughing and sputtering. He turned toward the back door but then remembered something, changed his mind and darted up the stairs with the fire not only behind him but on either side and above.

In Room 13, a young man coughed and rushed for the door. He tried to turn the handle but found it white-hot. He jerked his hand away and moved back toward the window. The old woman who sat in the Windsor chair raised her head and saw her long-dead son open the door, his tin helmet under his arm.

Is that you, my son? You've come back from the war?

Yes.

I have to tell you something. Come and kneel beside me.

Like this?

Yes. Like that.

I'm listening.

The old doctor rolled on the grass with the others, his black legs martyrs to his unblemished torso. He felt no pain, only surprise at the uninvited drama that had suddenly seized and shaken his quiet old life. Inside, the fire had moved into his tiny office and was consuming everything in its path: crepe bandages, bottles of iodine, sulfa, penicillin, Novocain, suture thread, rubber gloves, tongue depressors, terpin hydrate syrup with codeine. Everything he'd employed to convince people he was really a doctor when he was not. He was just an old pharmacist with a half-dead mind who loved the feel of a stethoscope.

Louise sat under a camphor tree which had been made fragrant by the heat. She had no idea how she'd come to leave the house and find this place outside in the backyard. She watched the chaos around her, amazed and in horror, helpless. After a few moments she put her hands up to her face and covered her eyes. Her father had told her that a secret let go can be deadly as a virus, and yet she hadn't listened. Had thought all secrets were like the secret of her mother's affair, and didn't matter, and could neither cause grief nor prevent any.

Milo had done this, out of revenge. The boy who loved fire, crazy enough to burn up his own mother, crazy enough now to burn up his own sister in his rage to destroy the man who had held her down in the riverbank.

Louise raised her head and watched the fire brigade—made up of half-burned men and a few distant neighbors who had seen the blaze—begin its grim and impossible task. She opened her mouth, but no sound came out. There were a few names that she wanted to scream, but she could not. Someone shook her shoulder and she turned and looked into her brother's face, bruised from where the sheriff had kicked him.

"Where is Daddy?" Benjamin said urgently. "Where is Daniel?"

31

Milo's hands were so bloody from the trees he'd punched that the steering wheel of his old Chevrolet slid around in his grip as he screeched toward The House of Gentle Men. This time of year most trees were useless, stripped of leaves and unable to cool such a fury. He had punched a dogwood so hard that a marlin, a guest of winter, had flown off the very top branches to search for more peaceful wood. A pump shotgun lay on the seat next to him—the same shotgun that God had jammed twice after Milo found his wife in bed with another man.

He pressed on the accelerator. He was crazy, crazy. Rumors that he'd always denied about himself he now took in gulps down his throat. Yes, he was Milo the bad man, the monster destined to kill someone on purpose.

Milo didn't care if he spent the rest of his life in prison. His future—that schoolmarm that cautions men to stay gentle—had been ruthlessly silenced. He didn't belong to his future anyway, but to his sister's past. Out of that past had come an enemy that went unrecognized. Now the enemy was finally clear. Not a pilot but a soldier. Like the ones he'd admired as they trained in the woods. The war was starting again, and this time Milo was old enough to fight.

He turned down the long dirt road. He had come here once as a boy through the woods, alone, just to see for himself if the legend was true. Now legend no longer concerned him, but fact. Details written down on a page.

Suddenly Milo slammed on the brakes. His mouth fell open. His eyes stung but did not blink.

The house was shuddering in flames. A fire huge and beautiful enough to put a shotgun to shame, even a shotgun with a history of attempted violence.

Milo jumped out of the car without putting it in park. The car rolled down into a gully, came back up again and slammed into a stand of loblolly pine.

On the far side of town, windows were dark and pets were sleeping.

The sheriff pulled into the driveway and got out of the car with his son in his arms. He opened the front door and shut it behind him, set Ralph down and turned the switch that lit up the swag lamp. Ralph blinked.

"We're home now, boy," the sheriff said. "You like going out with Daddy? You like riding in the car?"

"Why did you leave me there? I was cold."

"Come on, Ralph. It was just for a few minutes. You're all right, aren't you?" He tousled his son's hair.

"I want to go to the bathroom."

"Go, then." The sheriff sank down on the sofa, crossed his legs, went to light a cigarette and thought better of it.

He heard the toilet flush and Ralph's little footsteps fading into his room. He glanced over at the wall of framed flowers, snorted at the goldenrod. Only Belinda would look at a weed and see art. After a few moments he rose wearily, went into the kitchen and scrubbed his hands with soap until the gasoline was gone. He dried off with a tea towel and went to stand in Ralph's doorway. His boy had fallen asleep on the bed, fully dressed in his blue jumpsuit and his tiny lace-up shoes. His deep breathing made the tiny feet tremble so that the laces moved like butterflies.

The sheriff lit a cigarette, kept his thumb on the lighter and watched the flame, thinking of all the fire he'd rained down on Germany, on their precise little railroad yards, their factories, their munitions plants. He used to look down through the bomb-bay doors and watch the yellow light, for Germany left unburned would have ruled the world. At Buchenwald they had taken his Zippo lighter at the gate, stripped him of his fire, for the Germans understood the lessons of flame.

Sid Havens, owner of the miraculous ribbon cane, had needed those lessons. So had the man who sat in the fourth pew of the First Pentecostal Church. So had many other people in this foreign little state.

So had Belinda.

He had followed her, past her mother's house where her car should have turned, down the main street of town, through a maze of smaller streets, then dark country lanes, then left on the dirt road that led to that house and the boy who lived there. He had sat in his car, amazed. The House of Gentle Men. The House of Gentle Men. The name had pounded in his ears. The legend suddenly real.

Now the sheriff exhaled, and smoke poured out of his nose and mouth. He ground out his cigarette, crossed the room and sat on his little boy's bed, unlacing the shoelaces of his tiny boots, removing his socks and rubbing feet still tender from their newness to the world.

"Son," he said.

The Nazis scoured the Poles looking to steal boys like this. Blond, blue-eyed. Beautiful boys for the beautiful race. The sheriff leaned over and kissed Ralph's cheek.

32

The fire brigade had arranged itself in a long line from the well to the edge of the searing heat, and buckets were passed down man to man. One of the neighbor men had the bucket poised in his hands when he looked down at a strange light at his feet. He squinted.

"Evelyn?" he said. His wife was rolling on the ground in a nightgown he'd never seen before.

Burning.

The man stepped back, stunned. He'd been pulled out of bed by someone else's tragedy and found his own. Here at his feet. "Evelyn, I thought you were sleeping in the baby's room tonight."

She didn't answer, and so he did the only thing he could do. He tipped the bucket and drowned her flames in well water.

Daniel had shaken his parents awake and now the three of them sat huddled together near the far corner of Justin's room as the heat came up through the floorboards. Justin had closed the door on the smoke and stuffed a sheet under the crack, but more smoke came in between the pine boards that had been nailed over the broken window. And since every tool had long ago been taken from the room, Justin had tried and failed to pull off the boards with his bare hands.

Charlotte held Daniel close to her, stroking his head. She coughed.

Justin whirled around and faced the door. "I'm going out there," he said.

"Don't go," said Charlotte. "Stay here with us."

"I have to." Justin wrapped a pillowcase around his hand and pulled on the doorknob with all his might. The door creaked but did not open. The heat of the fire had swelled the wood. He jerked on the knob again and again, and when he failed he kicked the door and threw his body against it and punched it until his hands were bloody.

"It's no use, Justin," Charlotte called. "Come here."

Justin ran to the window and pressed his lips to the narrow cracks between the boards. "Help!" he shouted. "Help! Help!"

"They can't hear you. Come over here."

He rejoined his family, and they sat with their arms around each other. Outside, they could hear screams and the orders of whatever man had appointed himself the leader of the fire brigade. The sticky roar of the fire. The shattering of glass. The falling of beams. And the small, sad sound of a bucket of water hitting the side of the flaming house. Two gallons of cure against an ocean of flame. The heat coming up through the floorboards had begun to feel intolerable on their legs, and they moved to a slightly cooler place, nearer to the corner. More smoke came into the room and Charlotte began to feel sleepy. How strange and peaceful this seemed. She remembered looking out her window as a teenage girl and seeing the toolshed on fire. How angry the fire had seemed then. How full of judgment. Now its roar lulled like the sea.

Daniel coughed. "Are we going to die?" he asked.

"No."

"I'm afraid."

Outside, the shouts had grown louder, and she felt the house move.

"What was that?" Daniel asked.

"Nothing." She pulled her son closer, and smoothed his hair. "Do you want to hear a story?"

"Yes."

"All right . . . There once was a boy who had a frog, and the frog was magical, and every time the little boy rubbed the frog's back it would grant him a wish . . ."

Outside, the inferno continued. A tree was now aflame, and a row of bushes. The dogs had run into the woods. Benjamin and a group of men were fighting the fire at the foyer, making little progress. Two men were holding their arms out to a woman on the second floor who hesitated at the window. "Jump," one of the men begged her. "Please, it's not that far down."

Charlotte was feeling so tired she could barely go on with the story. "And the frog said, 'You have two more wishes,' and the boy took a few minutes to think about what he wanted . . ."

Justin was quiet, his arms around her. Charlotte kept talking but was thinking to herself: *Please, God, we are such a new family.*

33

Milo had abandoned his car to the loblolly pines and, red-faced and sweating, had run the rest of the way down the old dirt road to the burning house, the heat sloshing down upon him before he'd reached the front gate. Men were trying to fight the fire at the front porch and were being driven back, for the fire was roaring out the windows and the doorway as the house shook and rocked and disintegrated in a skyward direction. One of the men turned around and shouted something at Milo, but he did not slow his pace as he ran through the smoke and the flying debris around to the backyard, where the scene was terrible. Like the war he'd missed. Like his nightmares after the fire in the toolshed, all those years ago. People whispered and wept and howled and rolled and pleaded, crawled on their hands and knees in the red mist of steam and smoke and ashes or sat cross-legged and patient and quiet, sitting in the sitz bath of fragrant ether that only the dying enjoy.

"Charlotte! Charlotte!" Milo screamed. "Where are you?"

A woman lay facedown in the grass, her body naked and burned. He turned her over and saw that she was dead, that her pale face was unblistered and that she was not his sister but some other woman—single, widowed, lonely, divorced, married. Needful of something. With relief he turned away from her.

He caught sight of Louise underneath the camphor tree, rushed up to her and seized her by the shoulders, shaking her until her shocked eyes met his. She looked confused and wild with grief.

"What's the number?" Milo demanded.

She blinked. "Of the safe?"

"No! Of Justin's room!"

Louise closed her eyes and Milo shook her again.

"Tell me, Louise! Tell me now!"

"Twenty-one," she murmured. "Third floor."

Milo released her and stood up, stepping back and gazing up at the burning house as he tried to think of what to do. In that moment of uncertainty and panic and desperate love he stood, as behind him the dogs howled from the woods and the people screamed and his pigeon roasted and his mother twirled in flames and his father drank and the sheriff kicked him and his ex-wife moved against her lover and his sister struggled against the hands that pinned her to the sand.

He ran back to the front of the house, back to the

black, smoking patch of burning cinder where a porch had once stood spotless. Benjamin and the others were still battling the blaze with buckets. Milo elbowed past Benjamin and tried to rush into the foyer, but was driven back as a flaming board fell close to his ear. He worked his way back around the house, looking for a way in. The side door was black and hot as a furnace, but the knob on the door that led up the back stairs was cool enough to seize and turn. The back stairway was filled with smoke, but the fire was only just reaching that part of the house. He stopped on the second-story landing, coughing, then recovered himself and pushed himself into motion. Around him he could feel the heat coming through the walls and hear the crackling of wood. His eyes spilled tears but he did not stop.

When he reached the third-floor landing he ran down the hall toward Room 21, his shirt pulled up and held over his mouth, his eyes squinting through the smoke. He moved his shirt away from his face so that he could shout: "I'm here, Charlotte! I'm coming for you!"

He found the door and reached for the knob. It burned him but he held on, turning it. The door would not budge and he began kicking it, inhaling more smoke as he did so. He coughed violently and kicked the door again.

"Charlotte!" he shouted again, and this time there were returning voices. Three of them, soft and muffled and full of desperation.

Milo summoned all his strength and rage and began kicking and beating on the door as he had beaten on trees, only this door was his true enemy and this anger was righteous, this anger made him feel alive, for he was not a boy but a man, not a fire starter but a firefighter, not a monster but a savior, he was smart enough to outwit a burning house, he was not helpless, his sister was calling to him, she needed him as a boy trapped in a burning shed needs his mother, and he had the blood and the spirit and the love of such a mother, and he faced the door and beat on it and kicked it, roaring, his mother was behind him and around him and above him, she had hold of his shirt, she forgave him, she had never blamed him, she had realized like all Southern women that stupid things happen and stupidity can be forgiven in an instant, and Milo kicked and punched and screamed as his hands began to bleed again but he couldn't feel the pain or the smoke in his lungs, he felt alive he felt alive and he kicked the door one more time and it flew open and he entered that room a hero.

Another bad man saved.

What peculiar grace.